James Patterson is one of the best-known and biggest-selling writers of all time. He is the [...] popular series of the past decad[...] the Alex Cross novels and Maxi[...] many other number one bestsellers including romance novels and stand-alone thrillers. He has won an Edgar Award, the mystery world's highest honour. He lives in Florida with his wife and son.

Praise for James Patterson:

'The man is a master of this genre. We fans will have one wish for him: write even faster' *USA Today*

'Unputdownable. It will sell millions' *The Times*

'A novel which makes for sleepless nights' *Daily Express*

'Reads like a dream' *Kirkus Reviews*

'A fast-paced, electric story that is utterly believable' *Booklist*

'Ticks like a time bomb – full of threat and terror'
Los Angeles Times

'Absolutely terrific' *Bookseller*

'Patterson's action-packed story keeps the pages flicking by'
The Sunday Times

'A fine writer with a good ear for dialogue and pacing. His books are always page-turners' *Washington Times*

'Patterson is a phenomenon' *Observer*

'Keeps the adrenaline level high' *Publishing News*

'Murder mystery at its best' *Mirror*

'Rattles along like a refurbished caboose, shaking out corpses as it goes' *Daily Mail*

By James Patterson and available from Headline

When the Wind Blows
Cradle and All
Miracle on the 17th Green *(and Peter de Jonge)*
Suzanne's Diary for Nicholas
The Beach House *(and Peter de Jonge)*
The Jester *(and Andrew Gross)*
The Lake House
Sam's Letters to Jennifer
SantaKid
Honeymoon *(and Howard Roughan)*
Lifeguard *(and Andrew Gross)*
Beach Road *(and Peter de Jonge)*
Step on a Crack *(and Michael Ledwidge)*
The Quickie *(and Michael Ledwidge)*
You've Been Warned *(and Howard Roughan)*

Alex Cross novels
Cat and Mouse
Pop Goes the Weasel
Roses are Red
Violets are Blue
Four Blind Mice
The Big Bad Wolf
London Bridges
Mary, Mary
Cross
Double Cross

The Women's Murder Club series
1st to Die
2nd Chance *(and Andrew Gross)*
3rd Degree *(and Andrew Gross)*
4th of July *(and Maxine Paetro)*
The 5th Horseman *(and Maxine Paetro)*
The 6th Target *(and Maxine Paetro)*

Maximum Ride series
Maximum Ride: The Angel Experiment
Maximum Ride: School's Out Forever
Maximum Ride: Saving the World and Other Extreme Sports

JAMES PATTERSON

FOUR BLIND MICE

headline

First published in Great Britain in 2002
by HEADLINE BOOK PUBLISHING

This edition published in 2014
by HEADLINE PUBLISHING GROUP

9

Cataloguing in Publication Data is available from the British Library

ISBN 978 0 7553 4936 4

Typeset in Palatino Light by Palimpsest Book Production Limited,
Falkirk, Stirlingshire

Printed and bound in Great Britain by
Clays Ltd, St Ives plc

Headline's policy is to use papers that are natural, renewable
and recyclable products and made from wood grown in
sustainable forests. The logging and manufacturing processes
are expected to conform to the environmental regulations of
the country of origin.

HEADLINE PUBLISHING GROUP
An Hachette UK Company
338 Euston Road
London NW1 3BH

www.headline.co.uk
www.hachette.co.uk

FOUR BLIND MICE

Here's to Manhattan College on her Sesquicentennial Anniversary. Go Jaspers!

This one is also for Mary Jordan, who holds everything together, and I mean everything.

Did you ever see
such a sight in your life . . .

THE 'BLUELADY MURDERS'

Chapter One

Marc Sherman, the district attorney for Cumberland County, North Carolina, pushed the old wood captain's chair away from the prosecution table. It made a harsh scraping *eeek* in the nearly silent courtroom.

Then Sherman rose and slowly approached the jury box, where nine women and three men, six white, six African-American, waited with anticipation to hear what he had to say. They liked Sherman. He knew that, even expected it. He also knew that he had already won this dramatic murder case, even without the stirring summation he was about to give.

But he was going to give this closing anyway. He felt the need to see Sergeant Ellis Cooper held accountable for his crimes. The soldier had committed the most heinous and cowardly murders in the history of Cumberland County. The so-called 'Bluelady Murders'. The people in this county expected Sherman to punish Ellis Cooper, who happened to be a black man, and he wouldn't disappoint them.

The district attorney began, 'I have been doing this for a while, seventeen years to be exact. In all that time, I have never encountered murders such as those committed in December last by the defendant, Sergeant Ellis Cooper. What began as a jealous rage aimed at one victim, Tanya Jackson, spilled over into the shameless massacre of three women. All were wives, all were mothers. Together these women had eleven children, and of course, three grieving husbands, and countless other family members, neighbors and dear friends.

'The fateful night was a Friday, "ladies' night" for Tanya Jackson, Barbara Green and Maureen Bruno. While their husbands enjoyed their usual card night at Fort Bragg, the wives got together for personal talk, some laughter and the treasured companionship of one another. Tanya, Barbara and Maureen were great friends, you understand. This Friday night get-together took place at the home of the Jacksons, where Tanya and Abraham were raising their four children.

'Around ten o'clock, after consuming at least half a dozen shots of alcohol at the base, Sergeant Cooper went to the Jackson house. As you have heard in sworn testimony, he was seen outside the front door by two neighbors. He was yelling for Mrs Jackson to come out.

'Then Sergeant Cooper barged inside the house. Using an RTAK survival knife, a lightweight weapon favored by United States Army Special Forces, he attacked the woman who had spurned his advances. He killed Tanya Jackson instantly with a single knife thrust.

'Sergeant Ellis Cooper then turned the knife on

thirty-one-year-old Barbara Green. And finally, on Maureen Bruno, who nearly made it out of the slaughter-house, but was caught by Cooper at the front door. All three women were killed with thrusts delivered by a powerful male, who was familiar with hand-to-hand fighting techniques taught at the John F. Kennedy Special Warfare Center, headquarters for the Army's Special Forces.

'The survival knife has been identified as Sergeant Cooper's personal property, a deadly weapon he has kept since the early 1970s, when he left Vietnam. Sergeant Cooper's fingerprints were all over the knife.

'His prints were also found on the clothing of Mrs Jackson and Mrs Green. DNA from particles of skin found under the nails of Mrs Jackson were matched to Sergeant Cooper. Strands of his hair were found at the murder scene. The murder weapon itself was discovered hidden in the attic of Cooper's house. So were pathetic "love letters" he had written to Tanya Jackson – returned *unopened*.

'You have seen unspeakable photographs of what Sergeant Cooper did to the three women. Once they were dead, he "painted" their faces with ghoulish-looking blue paint. He "painted" their chests and stomachs. It is gruesome and twisted. As I said, the worst murders I have ever encountered. You know that there can only be one verdict. That verdict is guilty. Put this monster down!'

Suddenly, Sergeant Ellis Cooper rose from his seat at the defendant's table. The courtroom audience gasped. He was six feet four and powerfully built. At age fifty-five, his waist was still thirty-two inches, just as it had been when he had enlisted in the Army at eighteen. He was wearing his dress greens and the medals on his chest included a Purple Heart, a Distinguished Service Cross and a Silver Star. He looked impressive, even under the circumstances of the murder trial, and then he spoke in a clear, booming voice.

'I didn't kill Tanya Jackson, or any of those poor women. I never went inside the house that night. I didn't paint any bodies blue. I've never killed anyone, except for my country. I didn't kill those women. I'm innocent! I'm a war-hero, for God's sake!'

Without warning, Sergeant Cooper hurdled the wooden gate at the front of the courtroom. He was on Marc Sherman in seconds, knocking him to the floor, punching him in the face and chest.

'You liar, liar!' Cooper shouted. 'Why are you trying to kill me?'

When the courtroom marshals finally pulled Cooper away, the prosecutor's shirt and jacket were torn, his face bloodied.

Marc Sherman struggled to his feet and then he turned back to the jury. 'Need I say more? The verdict is guilty. Put this monster down.'

Chapter Two

The *real* killers had taken a small risk and attended the final day of the trial in North Carolina. They wanted to see the end of this; couldn't miss it.

Thomas Starkey was the team leader, and the former Army Ranger colonel still looked the part, walked the walk and talked the talk.

Brownley Harris was his number two, and he remained deferential to Colonel Starkey, just like it had been in Vietnam, and just like it would always be until the day one or both of them died.

Warren Griffin was still 'the kid', which seemed marginally funny, since he was forty-nine years old now.

The jury had come in with a verdict of guilty less than two and a half hours after they were sent out to deliberate. Sergeant Ellis Cooper was going to be executed for murder by the state of North Carolina.

The district attorney had done a brilliant job – of convicting the wrong man.

The three killers piled into a dark blue Suburban parked

on one of the narrow side streets near the courthouse.

Thomas Starkey started up the big car. 'Anybody hungry?' he asked.

'Thirsty,' said Harris.

'Horny,' said Griffin, and snorted out one of his goofy laughs.

'Let's get something to eat and drink – then maybe we'll get into some trouble with the ladies. What do you say? To celebrate our great victory today. *To us!*' shouted Colonel Starkey as he drove down the street away from the courthouse. '*To the Three Blind Mice.*'

PART ONE

THE LAST CASE

Chapter Three

I came down to breakfast around seven that morning and joined Nana and the kids around the kitchen table. With little Alex starting to walk, things were back in 'lock-down' mode. Plastic safety locks, latches and outlet caps were everywhere. The sounds of kid chatter, spoons clattering in cereal bowls, Damon coaching his baby brother in the art of blowing raspberries, made the kitchen almost as noisy as a precinct house on a Saturday night.

The kids were eating some kind of puffed-up chocolate-flavored Oreo's cereal *and* Hershey's chocolate milk. Just the thought of all that sugar at seven in the morning made me shiver. Nana and I had eggs over-easy and twelve-grain toast.

'Now isn't this nice,' I said as I sat down to my coffee and eggs. 'I'm not even going to spoil it by commenting on the chocoholic breakfast two of my precious children are eating for their morning's nourishment.'

'You just did comment,' said Jannie, my daughter, never at a loss.

I winked at her. She couldn't spoil my mood today. The killer known as the Mastermind had been captured and was now spending his days at a maximum-security prison in Colorado. My twelve-year-old, Damon, continued to blossom – as a student, as well as a singer with the Washington Boys' Choir. Jannie had taken up oil painting, and she was keeping a journal, which contained some pretty good scribbling and cartoons for a girl her age. Little Alex's personality was emerging – he was a sweet boy, just starting to walk.

I had met a woman detective recently, Jamilla Hughes, and I wanted to spend more time with her. The problem was that she lived in California and I lived in DC. Not insurmountable, I figured.

I would have some time to find out about Jamilla and I. Today was the day I planned to meet with Chief of Detectives George Pittman and resign from the DC police. After I resigned, I planned to take a couple of months off. Then I might go into private practice as a psychologist, or possibly hook up with the FBI. The Bureau had made me an offer that was flattering as well as intriguing.

There was a loud rap at the kitchen door. Then it opened. John Sampson was standing there. He knew what I was planning to do today, and I figured he'd come by to show me some support.

Sometimes I am so gullible it makes me a little sick.

Chapter Four

'Hello, Uncle John,' Damon and Jannie chorused, and then grinned like the little fools they can be when in the presence of 'greatness', which is how they feel about John Sampson.

He went to the refrigerator and examined Jannie's latest artwork. She was trying to copy characters from a new cartoonist, Aaron McGurder, formerly from the University of Maryland and now syndicated. Huey and Riley Feeman, Caeser, Jazmine DuBois were all taped on the fridge.

'You want some eggs, John? I can make some scrambled with cheddar, way you like them,' Nana said, and she was already up out of her place. She would do anything for Sampson – it had been that way since he was ten and we first became friends. Sampson is like a son to her. His mum was in jail much of the time he was growing up, and Nana raised him as much as anybody.

'Oh no, no,' he said, and quickly motioned for her to sit back down, but when she moved to the stove, he said,

'Yeah, scrambled, Nana. Rye toast be nice. I'm starved away to nothing, and nobody does breakfast like you do.'

'You know that's the truth,' she cackled, and turned up the burners. 'You're lucky I'm an *old*-school lady. You're all lucky.'

'We know it, Nana,' Sampson smiled. He turned to the kids. 'I need to talk to your father.'

'He's retiring today,' Jannie said.

'So I've heard,' said Sampson. 'It's all over the streets, front page of the *Post*, probably on the *Today Show* this morning.'

'You heard your Uncle John,' I told the kids. 'Now scoot. I love you. Scat!'

Jannie and Damon rolled their eyes and gave us looks, but they got up from the table, gathered their books into backpacks and started out the door to the Sojourner Truth School, which is about a five-block walk from our house on Fifth Street.

'Don't even think about going out that door like that. *Kisses*,' I said.

They came over and dutifully kissed Nana and me. Then they kissed Sampson. I really don't care what goes on in this cool, unsentimental post-modern world, but that's how we do it in our house. Bin Laden probably never got kissed enough when he was a kid.

'I have a problem,' Sampson said as soon as the kids left.

'Am I supposed to hear this?' Nana asked from the stove.

'Of course you are,' John said to her. 'Nana, Alex, I've

told you both about a good friend of mine from my Army days. His name is Ellis Cooper and he's still in the Army after all these years. At least he was. He was found guilty of murdering three women off post. I had no idea about any of it until friends started to call. He'd been embarrassed to tell me himself. Didn't want me to know. He only has about three weeks to the execution, Alex.'

I stared into Sampson's eyes. I could see sadness and distress there, even more than usual. 'What do you want, John?'

'Come down to North Carolina with me. Talk to Cooper. He's not a murderer. I know this man almost as well as I know you. Ellis Cooper didn't kill anybody.'

'You know you have to go down there with John,' Nana said. 'Make this your last case. You have to promise me that.'

I promised.

Chapter Five

Sampson and I were on I-95 by eleven o'clock that morning, our car wedged between caravans of speeding, gear-grinding, smoke-spewing tractor-trailers. The ride was a good excuse for us to catch up, though. We'd both been busy for a month or so, but we always got back together for long talks. It had been that way since we were kids growing up in DC. Actually, the only time we'd been separated was when Sampson served two tours in Southeast Asia and I was at Georgetown, then Johns Hopkins.

'Tell me about this Army friend of yours,' I said. I was driving and Sampson had the passenger seat as far back as it would go. His knees were up, touching the dash. He almost looked comfortable somehow.

'Cooper was already a sergeant back when I met him, and I think he knew he always would be. He was all right with it, liked the Army. He and I were both at Bragg together. Cooper was a drill sergeant at the time. Once he kept me on post for four straight weekends.'

I snorted out a laugh. 'Is that when the two of you got close? Weekends together in the barracks?'

'I hated his guts back then. Thought he was picking on me. You know, singling me out because of my size. Then we hooked up again in 'Nam.'

'He loosened up some? Once you met him again in 'Nam?'

'No, Cooper is Cooper. He's no bullshit, a real straight arrow, but if you follow the rules, he's fair. That's what he liked about the Army. It was mostly orderly, consistent, and if you did the right thing then you usually did all right. Maybe not as well as you thought you should, but not too bad. He told me it's smart for a black man to find a meritocracy like the Army.'

'Or the police department,' I said.

'Up to a point,' Sampson nodded. 'I remember a time,' he continued, 'Vietnam. We had replaced a unit that killed maybe two hundred people in a five-month period. These weren't exactly soldiers that got killed, Alex, though they were supposed to be VC.'

I listened as I drove. Sampson's voice became far away and distant.

'This kind of military operation was called "mopping up". This one time, we came into a small village, but another unit was already there. An infantry officer was "interrogating" a prisoner in front of these women and children. He was cutting skin off the man's stomach.

'Sergeant Cooper went up to the officer and pressed his gun to the man's skull. He said if the officer didn't stop what he was doing, he was a dead man. He meant it, too. Cooper didn't care about the consequences. He *didn't* kill those women in North Carolina, Alex. Ellis Cooper is no killer.'

Chapter Six

I loved being with Sampson. Always had, always will. As we rode through Virginia and into North Carolina, the talk eventually turned to other, more hopeful and promising subjects. I had already told him everything there was to tell about Jamilla Hughes, but he wanted to hear more scoop. Sometimes he's a bigger gossip than Nana Mama.

'I don't have any more to tell you, big man. You know I met her on that big murder case in San Francisco. We were together a lot for a couple of weeks. I don't know her that well. I like her, though. She doesn't take any crap from anybody.'

'And you'd *like* to know her more. I can tell that much.' Sampson laughed and clapped his big hands together.

I started to laugh too. 'Yes, I would, matter of fact. Jamilla plays it close to her chest. I think she was knocked about somewhere along the line. Maybe the first husband. She doesn't want to talk about it yet.'

'I think she has your number, man.'

'Maybe she does. You'll like her. Everybody does.'

John started to laugh again. 'You do find nice ladies. I'll give you that much.' He switched subjects. 'Nana Mama is some kind of piece of work, isn't she?'

'Yeah, she is. Eighty-two. You'd never know it. I came home the other day. She was shimmying a *refrigerator* down the back stairs of the house on an oil cloth. Wouldn't wait for me to get home to help her.'

'You remember that time we got caught lifting records at Spector's Vinyl?'

'Yeah, I remember. She loves to tell that story.'

John continued to laugh. 'I can still see the two of us sitting in that store manager's crummy little office. He's threatening us with everything but the death penalty for stealing his crummy forty-five records, but we are so cool. We're almost laughing in his face.

'Nana shows up at the record store, and she starts *hitting* both of us. She hit me in the face, bloodied my lip. She was like some kind of mad woman on a rampage, a mission from God.'

'She had this warning: "*Don't cross me. Don't ever, ever cross me, ever.*" I can still hear the way she would say it,' I said.

'Then she let that police officer haul our asses down to the station. She wouldn't even bring us home. I said, "They were only records, Nana." I thought she was going to kill me. "I'm already bleeding!" I said. "You're gonna bleed more!" she yelled in my face.'

I found myself smiling at the distant memory. Interesting how some things that weren't real funny at the time suddenly get that way. 'Maybe that's why we became big, bad cops. That afternoon in the record store. Nana's vengeful wrath.'

Sampson turned serious and said, 'No, that's not what straightened me out. The Army did it. I sure didn't get what I needed in my own house. Nana helped, but it was the Army that set me straight. I owe the Army. And I owe Ellis Cooper. *Hoorah! Hoorah! Hoorah!'*

Chapter Seven

We drove onto the sobering and foreboding high-walled grounds of Central Prison in Raleigh, North Carolina.

The security housing unit there was like a prison within a prison. It was surrounded by razor-sharp wire fences and a deadly electronic barrier; armed guards were in all the watchtowers. Central Prison was the only one in North Carolina with a death row. Currently, there were over a thousand inmates, with an astounding two hundred twenty on the row.

'Scary place,' Sampson said as we got out of the car. I had never seen him look so unsettled and unhappy. I didn't much like being at Central Prison either.

Once we were inside the main building it was as quiet as a monastery, and the extremely high level of security continued. Sampson and I were asked to wait between two sets of steel-bar doors. We were subjected to a metal detector, then had to present photo IDs along with our badges. The security guard who checked us informed us that many of North Carolina's 'First In Flight' license plates were made here at the prison. Good to know, I suppose.

There were hundreds of controlled steel gates in the high-security prison. Inmates couldn't move outside their cells without handcuffs, leg irons and security guards. Finally, we were allowed to enter death row itself, and taken to Sergeant Cooper. In this section of the prison each block consisted of sixteen cells, eight on the bottom, eight on top, with a common dayroom. Everything was painted the official color, known as 'lark'.

'John Sampson, you came after all,' Ellis Cooper said as he saw us standing in a narrow corridor outside a special hearing room. The door was opened and we were let in by a pair of armed guards.

I sucked in a breath, but tried not to show it. Cooper's wrists and ankles were shackled with chains. He looked like a big, powerful slave.

Sampson went and hugged Cooper. He patted his friend's back and they looked like a couple of large, socialized bears. Cooper had on the orange-red jumpsuit that all of the death row inmates wore. He kept repeating, 'So good to see you.'

When the two men finally pulled apart, Cooper's eyes were red and his cheeks wet. Sampson remained dry-eyed. I had never, ever seen John cry.

'This is the best thing that's happened to me in a long, long while,' Cooper said. 'I didn't think anybody would come after the trial. I'm already dead to most of them.'

'I brought along somebody. This is Detective Alex

Cross,' Sampson said, and turned my way. 'He's the best I know at homicide investigations.'

'That's what I need,' said Cooper as he took my hand, 'the best.'

'So tell us about all this awful craziness. *Everything*,' Sampson said. 'Tell us from start to the finish. Your version, Coop.'

Sergeant Cooper nodded. 'I want to. It will be good to tell it to somebody who isn't already convinced that I murdered those three women.'

'That's why we're here,' Sampson said. 'Because you *didn't* murder the women.'

'That Friday was a payday,' Cooper began. 'I should have gone straight home to my girlfriend, Marcia, but I had a few drinks at the club. I called Marcia around eight, I guess. She'd apparently gone out. She was probably ticked off at me. So I had another drink. Met up with a couple of buddies. I called my place again – it was probably close to nine. Marcia was still out.

'I had another couple highballs at the club. Then I decided to walk home. Why walk? Because I knew I was three sheets to the wind. It was only a little over a mile home anyway. When I got to my house, it was past ten. Marcia still wasn't there. I turned on a North Carolina Duke basketball game. Love to root against the Dukies and Coach K. Around eleven o'clock I heard the front door open. I yelled out to Marcia, asked her where she had been.

'Only it wasn't her coming home after all. It was about a half-dozen MPs and a CID investigator named Jacobs.

Soon after that, supposedly, they found the RTAK survival knife in the attic of my house. And traces of blue paint used on those ladies. They arrested me for murder.'

Ellis Cooper looked at Sampson first, then he stared hard into my eyes. He paused before he spoke again. 'I didn't kill those women,' he said. 'And what I still can't believe, somebody obviously *framed* me for the murders. Why would somebody set me up? It doesn't make sense. I don't have an enemy in the world. Least I didn't think so.'

Chapter Eight

Thomas Starkey, Brownley Harris and Warren Griffin had been best friends for more than thirty years, ever since they served together in Vietnam. Every couple of months, under Thomas Starkey's command, they went to a simple, post-and-beam log cabin in the Kennesaw Mountains of Georgia and spent a long weekend together. It was a ritual of machismo and would continue, Starkey insisted, until the last of them was gone.

They did all the things they couldn't do at home: played music from the Sixties – the Doors, Cream, Hendrix, Blind Faith, the Airplane – *loud*. They drank way too much beer and bourbon; they grilled thick Porterhouse steaks that they ate with fresh corn, Vidalia onions, tomatoes, and baked potatoes slathered with butter and sour cream. They smoked expensive Cuban cigars. They had a hell of a lot of fun in what they did.

'What was the line in that old beer commercial? You know the one I'm talking about?' Harris asked as they sat out on the front porch after dinner.

'It doesn't get any better than this,' Starkey said as he flicked the thick ash from his cigar onto the wide-planed floor. 'I think it was a shit beer, though. Can't even remember the name. 'Course, I'm a little drunk and a lot stoned.' Neither of the others believed that. Thomas Starkey was never completely out of control, and especially not when he committed murder, or ordered it done.

'We've paid our dues, gentlemen. We've earned this,' Starkey said, and extended his mug to clink with his friends. 'What's happening now is well deserved.'

'Bet your ass we earned it. Couple of three foreign wars. Our other exploits over the past few years,' said Harris. 'Families. Eleven kids between us. Plus we did pretty good out in the big, bad civilian world, too. I sure never figured I'd be knocking down a hundred and a half a year.'

They clinked the heavy beer glasses again. 'We did good, boys. And believe it or not, it can only get better,' said Starkey.

As they always did, they re-told old war stories – Grenada, Mogadishu, the Gulf War, but mostly Vietnam.

Starkey recounted the time they had made a Vietnamese woman 'ride the submarine'. The woman, a VC sympathizer of course, had been stripped naked then tied to a wooden plank, face upward. Harris had tied a towel around her face. Water from a barrel was slowly sprinkled onto the towel. As the towel eventually became flooded, the woman was forced to inhale water to breathe. Her lungs and stomach soon swelled with the water. Then Harris pounded on her chest to expel the water. The woman talked, but of course she didn't tell them anything they didn't already know. So they dragged her out to a kaki tree which produced a sweet fruit and was always covered with large yellow ants. They tied the mamasan to the tree, lit up marijuana cigars and watched as her body swelled beyond recognition. When it was close to busting they 'wired' her with a field telephone and electrocuted her. Starkey always said that was about the most creative kill ever. 'And the VC terrorist bitch deserved it.'

Brownley Harris started to talk about 'mad minutes' in Vietnam. If there were answering shots from a village, even one, they would have a 'mad minute'. All hell would break loose because the answering shots *proved* the whole village was VC. After the 'mad minute', the village, or what remained of it, would be burned to the ground.

'Let's go into the den, boys,' Starkey said. 'I'm in the mood for a movie. And I know just the one.'

'Any good?' Brownley Harris asked, and grinned.

'Scary as hell, I'll tell you that. Makes *Hannibal* look like a popcorn fart. Scary as any movie you ever saw.'

Chapter Nine

The three of them headed for the den, their favorite place in the cabin. A long time ago in Vietnam, the trio had been given the code name *Three Blind Mice*. They had been élite military assassins – did what they were told, never asked embarrassing questions, executed their orders. It was still pretty much that way. And they were the best at what they did.

Starkey was the leader, just as it had been in Vietnam. He was the smartest and the toughest. He hadn't changed much physically over the years. He was six feet one, had a thirty-three-inch waist, a tan, weathered face, appropriate for his fifty-five years. His blond hair was now peppered with gray. He didn't laugh easily, but when he did, everybody usually laughed with him.

Brownley Harris was a stocky five feet eight, but with a surprisingly well-toned body at age fifty-one, considering all the beer he drank. He had hooded brown eyes with thick bushy eyebrows, almost a unibrow. His hair was still black, though flecked with gray now, and he wore it in a military-style buzz cut, though not a 'high and tight'.

Warren 'the Kid' Griffin was the youngest of the group, and still the most impulsive. He looked up to both of the other men, but especially Starkey. Griffin was six feet two, lanky, and reminded people, especially older women, of the folk-rock singer James Taylor. His strawberry blond hair was long on the sides but thinning on top.

'I kind of like old Hannibal the Cannibal,' Griffin said as they entered the den. 'Especially now that Hollywood decided he's the good guy. Only kills people who don't have nice manners, or taste in fine art. Hey, what's wrong with that?'

'Works for me,' said Harris.

Starkey locked the door into the den, then slid a plain, black-box videotape into the machine. He loved the den, with its leather seating arrangement, thirty-six-inch Philips TV, and armoire filled with tapes that were categorized chronologically. 'Showtime,' said Starkey. 'Dim the house lights.'

The first image was shaky, as someone approached a small, ordinary-looking redbrick house. Then a second man came into view. A third person, the camera operator, moved closer and closer until the shot was through a grimy, bug-specked picture window into the living room. There were three women in the room, laughing and chatting up a storm, totally unaware that they were being watched by three strangers, and also being filmed.

'Take note that the opening scene is one long camera move without a cut,' said Harris. 'Cinematographer is a genius, if I don't say so myself.'

'Yeah, you're an artist all right,' said Griffin. 'Probably some latent fagola in you.'

The women, who looked to be in their mid-thirties, were now clearly visible through the window. They were drinking white wine, laughing it up on their 'ladies' night'. They wore shorts and had good legs that deserved to be shown off. Barbara Green stretched out a leg and touched her toes, almost as if she were preening for the movie.

The shaky camera shot continued around the brick house to the back door at the kitchen. There was sound with the picture now. One of the three intruders began to bang on the aluminum screen door.

Then a voice came from inside. 'Coming! Who is it? Oohh, I hope it's Russell Crowe. I just saw *A Beautiful Mind*. Now that man is beautiful.'

'It's not Russell Crowe, lady,' said Brownley Harris, who was obviously the camera operator.

Tanya Jackson opened the kitchen door and looked terribly confused for a split second, before Thomas Starkey cut her throat with the survival knife. The woman moaned, dropped to her knees, then fell onto her face. Tanya was dead before she hit the black and olive-green checkerboard linoleum of the kitchen floor.

'Somebody's *very good* with a survival knife. You haven't lost your touch over the years,' Harris said to Starkey as he drank beer and watched the movie.

The hand-held camera shot continued, moving quickly through the kitchen. Right over the bleeding, twitching body of Tanya Jackson. Then into the living room of the house. A jumpy song by Destiny's Child was playing on the radio and now became part of the movie soundtrack.

'What's going on?' Barbara Green screamed from the couch, and curled herself into a protective ball. 'Who are you? Where's Tanya?'

Starkey was on her in an instant with the knife. He even mugged for the camera, leered eerily. Then he chased Maureen Bruno into the kitchen, where he drove the RTAK into the center of her back. She threw both arms into the air as if she was surrendering.

The camera reversed angles to show Warren Griffin. He was bringing up the rear. It was Griffin who had brought the blue paint, and who would actually paint the faces and torsos of the three murder victims.

Sitting in the den of their cabin, the buddies watched the film twice more. When the third showing was over, Thomas Starkey removed the videocassette. 'Hear, hear!' said Starkey, and they all raised their beer mugs. 'We're not getting older, we're getting better and better.'

Chapter Ten

Hoorah!

In the morning, Sampson and I arrived at Fort Bragg, North Carolina, to begin our investigation into the Bluelady Murders. C-130s and 141s were constantly flying overhead. I drove along something called the All American Freeway, which I then took to Reilly Road. Surprisingly, there had been no security cordon around the Army base, no fence around the post, no main gate until September 11. The Army had allowed local motorists to use base roads as transit from one side of Bragg to the other.

The base itself measured twenty-five miles east–west, ten miles north–south. It was home for combat troops ready to be sent anywhere in the world within eighteen hours. And it had all the amenities: movie theaters, riding stables, a museum, two golf courses, even an ice skating rink.

There were a couple of signs as we entered at one of the new security posts. One read: *Welcome to Fort Bragg, North Carolina, Home of America's Airborne and Special Operations*

Forces. The second was common to just about every US base around the world: *You are entering a military installation and are now subject to search without a warrant.*

The grounds were dusty, and it was still hot in the early fall. Everywhere I looked I saw sweaty soldiers running PT. And humvees. Lots of humvees. Several of the units were 'singing cadence'.

'Hoorah!' I said to Sampson.

'Nothing like it,' he grinned. 'Almost makes me want to re-up.'

Sampson and I spent the rest of the day talking to men dressed in camouflage with spit-shined jump boots. My FBI connections helped open doors that might have stayed closed to us. Ellis Cooper had a lot of friends and most had originally been shocked to hear about the murders. Even now, not many of them believed that he was capable of the mayhem and cruelty involved.

The exceptions were a couple of non-coms who had gone through the Special Warfare School under his command. They told us that Cooper had physically bullied them. A PFC named Steve Hall was the most outspoken. 'The sergeant had a real mean streak. It was common knowledge. Couple of times, he got me alone. He'd elbow me, knee me. I knew he was hoping I'd fight back, but I didn't. I'm not that surprised he killed somebody.'

'Just chicken-shit stuff,' Sampson said about the training-school stories. 'Coop has a temper and he can be a prick, if provoked. That doesn't mean he killed three women and painted them blue.'

I could feel Sampson's tremendous affection and

respect for Ellis Cooper. It was a side he didn't let show often. Sampson had grown up with a mother who was an addict and a dealer, and a father who'd run out on him when he was a baby. He had never been much of a sentimentalist, except when it came to Nana and the kids, and maybe me.

'How do you feel about this mess so far?' he finally asked.

I hesitated before giving an answer. 'It's too early to tell, John. I know that's a hell of a thing to say when your friend has less than three weeks to live. I don't think we'll be welcome around Fort Bragg much longer either. The Army likes to solve its problems in its own way. It'll be hard to get the kind of information we need to really help Cooper. As for Cooper, I guess my instinct is to believe him. But who would go to all this bother to set him up? None of it makes sense.'

Chapter Eleven

I was starting to get used to the C-130s and 141s that were constantly flying overhead. Not to mention the artillery booming on the shooting range near Fort Bragg. I'd begun to think of the artillery as death knells for Ellis Cooper.

After a quick lunch out on Bragg Boulevard, Sampson and I had an appointment with a captain named Jacobs. Donald Jacobs was with CID, the Army's Criminal Investigation Division. He had been assigned to the murder case from the beginning and had been a key, damaging witness at the trial.

I kept noticing that the roads inside Fort Bragg were well trafficked by civilian vehicles. *Even now, anyone could get in here and not be noticed.* I drove to the section of the base where the main administration buildings were located. CID was in a redbrick building that was more modern and sterile-looking than the attractive structures from the Twenties and Thirties.

Captain Jacobs met us in his office. He wore a red plaid

sport shirt and khakis rather than a uniform. He seemed relaxed and cordial, a large, physically fit man in his late forties. 'How can I help?' he asked. 'I know that Ellis Cooper has people who believe in him. He helped a lot of guys when he was a DI. I also know that the two of you have good reputations as homicide detectives up in Washington. So where do we go from there?'

'Just tell us what you know about the murders,' Sampson said. We hadn't talked about it, but I sensed he needed to be the lead detective here on the base.

Captain Jacobs nodded. 'All right. I'm going to tape our talk if you don't mind. I'm afraid I think that he did it, Detectives. I believe that Sergeant Cooper murdered those three women. I don't pretend to understand why. I especially don't understand the blue paint that was used on the bodies. Maybe you can figure that one out, Dr Cross. I also know that most people at Bragg haven't gotten over the brutality and senselessness of these murders.'

'So we're causing some problems being here,' Sampson said. 'I apologize, Captain.'

'No need,' said Jacobs. 'Like I said, Sergeant Cooper has his admirers. In the beginning, even I had a tendency to believe him. The story he told about his whereabouts tracked pretty well. His service record was outstanding.'

'So what changed your mind?' Sampson asked.

'Oh hell, a lot of things, Detective. DNA testing, evidence found at the murder scene and elsewhere. The fact that he was seen at the Jackson house, although he swore he wasn't there. The survival knife found in his attic, which turned out to be the murder weapon. A few other things.'

'Could you be more specific?' Sampson asked. 'What kind of other things?'

Captain Jacobs sighed, got up, and walked over to an olive-green file cabinet. He unlocked the top drawer, took out a folder and brought it over to us.

'Take a look at these. They might change your mind, too.' He spread out half a dozen pages of copies of photographs from the murder scene. I had looked at a lot of photos like these, but it didn't make it any easier.

'That's how the three women were actually found. It was kept out of the trial so as not to hurt the families any more than we had to. The DA knew he had more than enough to convict Sergeant Cooper without using these brutal pictures.'

The photographs were right up there with the most grisly and graphic evidence I'd seen. Apparently, the women had all been found in the living room, not where each of them had been killed. The killer had carefully arranged the bodies on a large, flowered sofa. He had art-directed the corpses, and that was an element that definitely caught my attention. Tanya Jackson's face was resting in Barbara Green's crotch; Mrs Green's face was in Maureen Bruno's crotch. Not just the faces but the crotches were painted blue.

'Apparently, Cooper thought the three women were lovers. That may have even been the case. At any rate, that's why he thought Tanya rejected his advances. I guess it drove him to this.'

Finally I spoke up. 'These crime scene photos, however graphic and obscene, still don't prove that Ellis Cooper is your murderer.'

Captain Jacobs shook his head. 'You don't seem to understand. These aren't copies of the crime scene photos taken by the police. These are copies of Polaroids that Cooper took himself. We found them at his place along with the knife.'

Donald Jacobs looked at me, then at Sampson. 'Your friend murdered those women. Now you ought to go home and let the people around here begin to heal.'

Chapter Twelve

In spite of Captain Jacob's advice, we didn't leave North Carolina. In fact, we kept talking to anybody who would talk to us. One first sergeant told me something interesting, though not about our case. He said that the recent wave of patriotism that had swept the country since September 11 was barely noticeable at Fort Bragg. 'We have always been that way!' he said. I could see that, and I must admit, I was impressed with a lot that I saw on the Army post.

I woke early the next morning, around five, with no place to go. At least I had some time to think about the fact that this could be my last case. And what kind of case was it, really? A man convicted of three gruesome murders claiming to be innocent. What murderer didn't?

And then I thought of Ellis Cooper on death row in Raleigh, and I got to work.

Once I was up, I got on-line and did as much preliminary research as I could. One of the areas I looked at was the blue paint on the victims. I checked into VICAP and got three other cases of murder victims being painted, but none of them seemed a likely connection.

I then ran down a whole lot of information on the color blue. One thing that mildly interested me was the Blue Man Group – performance artists who had started a show called *Tubes* in New York City, then branched out to Boston, Chicago and Las Vegas. The show contained elements of music, theater, performance art, even vaudeville. The performers always worked in blue, from head to toe. Maybe it was something, maybe nothing – too early to tell.

I met Sampson for breakfast at the Holiday Inn where we were staying – the Holiday Inn Bordeaux, to be more precise. We ate quickly, then drove over to the off-base military housing community where the three murders had taken place. The houses were ordinary ranches, each with a small strip of lawn out front. Quite a few of the yards had plastic wading pools. Tricycles and 'cozy coupés' were parked up and down the street.

We spent the better part of the morning and early afternoon canvassing the close-knit community where Tanya Jackson had lived. It was a working-class, military neighborhood, and at more than half the stops nobody was home.

I was on the front porch of a brick-and-clapboard house, talking to a woman in her late thirties or early forties, when I saw Sampson come jogging our way. Something was up.

'Alex, come with me!' he called out. 'C'mon. I need you right now.'

Chapter Thirteen

I caught up with Sampson. 'What's up? What did you find out?'

'Something weird. Maybe a break,' he said. I followed him to another small ranch house. He knocked on the door and a woman appeared almost immediately. She was only a little over five feet, but easily weighed two hundred pounds, maybe two-fifty.

'This is my partner, Detective Cross. I told you about him. This is Mrs Hodge,' he said.

'I'm Anita Hodge,' the woman said as she shook my hand. 'Glad to meet you.' She looked at Sampson and grinned. 'I agree. Ali when he was younger.'

Mrs Hodge walked us through a family room where two young boys were watching *Nickelodeon* and playing video games at the same time. She then led us down a narrow hallway and into a bedroom.

A boy of about ten was in the room. He was seated in a wheelchair that was pulled up to a Gateway computer. Behind him on the wall were glossy pictures of more than two dozen Major League baseball players.

He looked annoyed at the intrusion. 'What *now*?' he asked. 'That's short for *get out of here and leave me alone. I'm working.*'

'This is Ronald Hodge,' Sampson said. 'Ronald, this is Detective Cross. I told you about him when we spoke before.'

The boy nodded but didn't say anything, just stared angrily my way.

'Ronald, will you tell us your story again?' Sampson asked. 'We need to hear it.'

The boy rolled his eyes. 'I already told the other policemen. I'm sick and tired of it, y'know. Nobody cares what I think anyway.'

'Ronald,' said his mother. 'That's not true and you know it.'

'Please tell me,' I said to the boy. 'What you have to say could be important. I want to hear it in your words.'

The boy frowned and continued to shake his head, but his eyes held mine. 'The other policemen didn't think it was important. Fuckheads.'

'Ronald,' said the boy's mother. 'Don't be rude. You know I don't like that attitude. Or that kind of language.'

'Okay, okay,' he said. 'I'll tell it again.' Then he began to talk about the night Tanya Jackson was murdered, and what he'd seen.

'I was up late. Wasn't s'posed to be. I was playing on the computer.' He stopped and looked at his mother.

She nodded. 'You're forgiven. We've been over this

before. Now please tell your story. You're starting to get me a little crazy.'

The boy finally cracked a smile, then went on with his story. Maybe he had just wanted to set up his audience a little.

'I can see the Jacksons' yard from my room. It's just past the corner of the Harts' house. I saw somebody out in the yard. It was kind of dark, but I could see him moving. He had like a movie camera or something. I couldn't tell what he was taking pictures of, so it made me curious.

'I went up close to this window to watch. And then I saw there were three men out there. I saw 'em in Mrs Jackson's yard. That's what I told the police. Three men. I saw 'em just like I see two of you in my room. *And they were making a movie.*'

Chapter Fourteen

I asked young Ronald Hodge to repeat his story, and he did.

Exactly, almost word for word. He stared me right in the eye as he spoke, and he didn't hesitate or waver. It was obvious that the boy was troubled by what he had witnessed, and that he was still scared. After learning that murders had been committed in the house, he'd been living in fear of what he'd seen that night.

Afterward, Sampson and I talked to Anita Hodge in the kitchen. She gave us iced tea, which was unsweetened, with big chunks of lemon in it, and was delicious. She told us that Ronald had been born with spina bifida, an outcropping of the spinal cord that had caused paralysis from the waist down.

'Mrs Hodge,' I asked, 'what do you think about the story Ronald told us in there?'

'Oh, I believe him. At least I believe he thinks he saw what he said. Maybe it was shadows or something, but Ronald definitely believes he saw three men. And one of them with a movie camera of some kind. He's been consistent on that from the first. Spooky. Like that old Hitchcock movie.'

'*Rear Window*,' I said. 'James Stewart thinks he sees a murder outside his window. He's laid up with a broken leg at the time.' I looked over at Sampson. I wanted to make sure he was comfortable with me asking the questions this time. He nodded that it was okay.

'What happened after the Fayetteville detectives talked to Ronald? Did they come back? Did any other policemen come? Anyone from Fort Bragg? Mrs Hodge, why wasn't Ronald's testimony part of the trial?'

She shook her head. 'Same questions I had – my ex-husband and I both. A captain from CID did come a few days later. Captain Jacobs. He talked to Ronald some. That was the end of it, though. No one ever came about any trial.'

After we finished our iced teas, we decided to call it a night. It was past eight and we thought we'd made some progress. Back at the Holiday Inn Bordeaux, I called Nana and the kids. Everything was fine and dandy on the home front. They had taken up the cry that I was on 'Daddy's last case', and they liked the sound of that. Maybe I did, too. Sampson and I had dinner and a couple of beers at Bowties inside the hotel, then we turned in for the night.

I tried Jamilla in California. It was around seven her time, so I called her work number first.

'Inspector Hughes,' she answered curtly. 'Homicide.'

'I want to report a missing person,' I said.

'Hey, Alex,' she said. I could feel her smile over the

phone. 'You caught me at work again. Busted. *You're* the missing person. Where are you? You don't write, you don't call. Not even a crummy e-mail in the last few days.'

I apologized, then I told Jam about Sergeant Cooper and what had happened so far. I described what Ronald Hodge had seen from his bedroom window. Then I broached the subject that had prompted my call. 'I miss you, Jam. I'd like to see you,' I said. 'Any place, any time. Why don't you come East for a change? Or I could go out there if you'd rather. You tell me.'

Jamilla hesitated, and I found that I was holding my breath. Maybe she didn't want to see me. Then she said, 'I can get off work for a few days. I'd love to see you. Sure, I'll come to Washington. I've never been there. Always wanted to when I was a kid.'

'Not so long ago,' I said.

'That's good. Cute,' she laughed.

My heart fluttered a little as the two of us made a date. *Sure, I'll come to Washington.* I played that line of Jamilla's over and over in my head for the rest of the night. It had just rolled off her tongue, almost like she couldn't wait to say it.

Chapter Fifteen

E arly the next morning I got a call from a friend of mine at Quantico. I had asked Abby DiGarbo to check on rental-car companies in the area and to look for any irregularities that took place during the week of the murders. I'd told her it was urgent. Abby had already found one.

It seemed that Hertz had been stiffed on the rental of a Ford Explorer. Abby had dug deeper and discovered an interesting paper trail. She told me that scamming a rental-car company wasn't all that easy, which was good news for us. The scam required a fake credit card and a driver's license on which everything matched, including the description of the driver renting the car.

Someone had hacked into SEC files that are maintained as a public record. The fake identity used on the card was obtained and the information submitted to a company in Brampton, Ontario, where the card was made. A fake driver's license to match was then obtained from a web-site, Photoidcards.com. A photograph had been submitted, and I was staring at a copy of it right now.

White, male, nothing memorable about the face, which possibly had been changed with makeup and costume props anyway.

The FBI was still checking to see what else they could find. It was a start, though. Somebody had gone to some trouble to rent a car in Fayetteville. We had *somebody's* picture, thanks to Abby DiGarbo.

On the way over to Sergeant Cooper's house I told Sampson about the rent-a-car scam. Sampson was drinking steaming hot coffee and eating an éclair from Dunkin' Donuts, but I could tell he was appreciative in his own way. 'That's why I asked you in on this,' he said.

Cooper lived in a small, two-bedroom apartment in Spring Lake, north of Fort Bragg. He had one side of a redbrick duplex. I saw a sign: *Caution, Attack Cat!*

'He has a sense of humor,' Sampson said. 'At least he did.'

We had been given a key to open the front door. Sampson and I stepped inside. The house still smelled like cat after all this time.

'It's good not having anybody in the way for a change,' I said to John. 'No other police, no FBI.'

'Killer's been caught,' Sampson said. 'Case is closed. Nobody cares but us now. And Cooper sitting there on death row. The clock's ticking.'

Apparently, nobody had figured out what to do about the apartment yet. Ellis Cooper had felt secure enough in his posting that he'd bought the place a few years back.

When he retired, he'd planned to stay in Spring Lake.

The table in the front hallway contained photos of Cooper posing with friends in several locations: what looked like Hawaii, the south of France, maybe the Caribbean. There was also a more recent photo of Cooper hugging a woman who was probably his girl-friend, Marcia. The furniture in the apartment was comfortable-looking, not expensive, and appeared to have been bought at stores like Target and Pier One.

Sampson called me over to one of the windows. 'It's been shimmied. The place was broken into. Could be how somebody got Cooper's knife, then returned it. If that's what happened. Coop said he left it in the closet of his bedroom. The police say the knife was in the attic.'

We went into the bedroom next. The walls were covered with more photographs, mostly from places where Cooper had been posted: Vietnam, Panama, Bosnia. A Yukon Mighty Weightlifting Bench was lined up near one wall. Near the closet was an ironing board. We searched through the closet. The clothes were mostly military but there were civilian threads, too.

'What do you make of this stuff?' I asked Sampson. I pointed to a table with a grouping of odd knickknacks that looked like they came from Southeast Asia.

I picked up a straw doll that looked strangely menacing, even evil. Then a small crossbow with what looked like a claw for its trigger. A silver amulet in the shape of a watchful, lidless eye. What was this?

Sampson took a careful look at the creepy straw doll, then the eye. 'I've seen the evil eye before. Maybe in

Cambodia or Saigon. Don't remember exactly. I've seen the straw dolls, too. Think they have something to do with avenging evil spirits. I've seen the dolls at Viet funerals.'

The creepy artifacts notwithstanding, the sense I got from the apartment was that Ellis Cooper had been a lonely man without much of a life besides the Army. I didn't see a single photograph of what might be called family.

We were still in Cooper's bedroom when we heard a door open inside the apartment. Then came the sound of heavy footsteps approaching.

The bedroom door was thrown open and banged hard against the wall. Soldiers with drawn pistols stood in the doorway.

'Put your hands up! Military Police. *Hands up now!*' one of them yelled.

Sampson and I slowly raised our arms.

'We're homicide detectives. We have permission to be here,' Sampson told them. 'Check with Captain Jacobs at CID.'

'Just keep those hands up. High!' the MP in charge barked.

Sampson spoke calmly to the leader of the three MPs who now crowded into the bedroom with their guns leveled at us.

'I'm a friend of Sergeant Cooper's,' Sampson told them.

'He's a convicted murderer,' snarled one MP out of the side of his mouth. 'Lives on death row these days. But not for much longer.'

Sampson kept his hands high, but told them there was

a note from Cooper in his shirt pocket and the house key we'd been given. The head MP took the note and read:

To whom it may concern, John Sampson is a friend, and the only person I know who's working on my behalf. He and Detective Cross are welcome in my house, but the rest of you bastards aren't. Get the hell out. You're trespassing!

Sergeant Ellis Cooper.

Chapter Sixteen

I woke the next morning with the phrase 'dead man walking' repeating itself in my head. I couldn't get back to sleep. I kept seeing Ellis Cooper in the bright orange death row jumpsuit.

Early in the morning, before it got too hot, Sampson and I took a run around Bragg. We entered the base on Bragg Boulevard, then turned onto a narrower street called Honeycutt. Then came a maze of similar side streets, and finally Longstreet Road. Bragg was immaculate. Not a speck of trash anywhere. A lot of soldiers were already up running PT.

As we jogged side by side, we planned out our day. We had a lot to do in a relatively short time. Then we needed to get back to Washington.

'Tell you what's bothering me the most so far,' Sampson said as we toured the military base on foot.

'Same thing that's bothering me, probably,' I huffed. 'We found out about Ronald Hodge and the Hertz car in about a day. What's wrong with the local police

and the Army investigations?'

'You starting to believe Ellis Cooper is innocent?'

I didn't answer Sampson, but our murder investigation was definitely disturbing in an unusual way: it was going too well. We were learning things that the Fayetteville police didn't seem to know. And why hadn't Army CID done a better job with the case? Cooper was one of their own, wasn't he?

When I got back to my room after the run, the phone was ringing. I wondered who'd be calling this early. Had to be Nana and the kids. It was just past seven. I answered in the slightly goofy Damon Wayans voice I sometimes use around the kids.'Yeah-lo. *Who's* calling me so early in the morning? Who's waking me up? You have some nerve.'

Then I heard a woman's voice. Unfamiliar, with a heavy Southern accent. 'Is this Detective Cross?'

I quickly changed my tone and hoped she didn't hang up.'Yes it is. Who's this?'

'I'd rather not say. Just listen, please. This is hard for me to tell you, or anyone else.'

'I'm listening. Go ahead.'

I heard a deep sigh before she spoke again.

'I was with Ellis Cooper on the night of the three terrible murders. We were together when the murders took place. We were intimate. That's all I can say for now.'

I could tell the caller was frightened, maybe close to panic. I had to keep her on the line if I could. 'Wait a minute. Please. You could have helped Sergeant Cooper at the trial. You can still help him. You could prevent his execution!'

'No. I can't say any more than I already have. I'm married to someone on the base. I won't destroy my family. I just can't. I'm sorry.'

'Why didn't you tell the police in town, or CID?' *Why didn't Cooper tell us?* 'Please stay on the line. Stay with me.'

The woman moaned softly. 'I called Captain Jacobs. I told him. He did nothing with the information, with the truth. I hope you do something. Ellis Cooper didn't kill those three women. I didn't believe my testimony would be enough to save him. And . . . I'm afraid of the consequences.'

'What consequences? Think about the consequences for Sergeant Cooper. He's going to be executed.'

The woman hung up. I couldn't tell much about her, but I was sure she was sobbing. I stood there staring at the phone receiver, not quite believing what I'd just heard. I had just talked to Ellis Cooper's alibi – and now she was gone.

Chapter Seventeen

Around five o'clock, Sampson and I received the terrifically good news that the commanding officer at Bragg was willing to see us at his house on the base. We were to be there at seven-thirty sharp. General Stephen Bowen would give us ten minutes, to share the information we had about the murder case. In the meantime, Sampson got through to Sergeant Cooper at Central Prison. He denied that he'd been with a woman that night. What was worse, Sampson said Cooper wasn't very convincing. But why would he hold the truth back from us? It didn't make sense.

General Bowen's quarters looked to be from the Twenties or Thirties, a stucco house with a Spanish tile roof. Up on the second floor there was a sun porch with glass on three sides, probably the master suite.

A man was watching from up there as we parked in the semicircular driveway. *General Bowen himself?*

We were met at the front door by an officer aide who identified himself as Captain Rizzo. The general's staff included an officer aide, an enlisted aide who was part of the general's security but also worked as the cook, and a driver who was also security.

We stepped into a large foyer with sitting rooms on either side. The décor was eclectic, and probably reflected the general's career around the world. I noticed a beautiful carved cabinet that looked German, a painted screen showing rolling hills and cherry trees from Japan, and an antique sideboard that suggested a possible posting in New England.

Captain Rizzo showed us into a small den where General Stephen Bowen was already waiting for us. He was in uniform. The aide leaned in to me. 'I'll return in exactly ten minutes. The general wants to talk to you alone.'

'Please sit down,' said Bowen. He was tall and solidly built, probably in his mid-fifties. He tented his fingers on top of a well-worn desk that looked like it had been with him for most of his career. 'I understand that you've come down here to try and re-open the Cooper murder case. Why do you think we should reconsider the case? And Cooper's death sentence?'

As concisely as I could I told the general what we had already found out, and also our reactions to the evidence as homicide detectives. He was a practiced listener, who punctuated what I had to say by uttering 'interesting' several times. He seemed open to other points of view and eager for new information. For the moment, I was hopeful.

When I stopped, he asked, 'Is there anything else either

of you wants to add? This is the time for it.'

Sampson seemed unusually quiet and reserved in the general's presence. 'I'm not going to get into my personal feelings for Sergeant Cooper,' he finally spoke, 'but, as a detective, I find it impossible to believe that he'd bring the murder weapon, plus several incriminating photographs, back to his house.'

Surprisingly, General Bowen nodded agreement. 'I do too,' he said. 'But that's what he did. I don't understand why either, but then again, I don't understand how a man could willfully murder three women, as he most definitely did. It was the worst act of peacetime violence I've seen in my career, and gentlemen, I've seen some bad business.'

The general leaned forward across his desk. His eyes narrowed and his jaw tensed. 'Let me tell you something about this murder case that I haven't shared with anyone else. No one. This is just for the two of you. When Sergeant Cooper is executed at Central Prison by the state of North Carolina, I will be there with the families of those murdered women. I'm looking forward to the lethal injection. What that animal did revolts and disgusts me. Your ten minutes are up. Now get the hell out of here. Get the fuck out of my sight.'

His aide, Captain Rizzo, was already back at the door.

Chapter Eighteen

The Three Blind Mice were in Fayetteville again, headed toward Fort Bragg for the first time in several months. Brownley Harris, Warren Griffin and Thomas Starkey were admitted through the security gates on All American Freeway. No problem. They had official business on post; they had an appointment.

The three men were unusually quiet as Starkey drove the dark blue Suburban across the base. They hadn't been at Bragg since the murders of the three women. Not that the place had changed one iota; change happened very slowly in the military.

'This is a trip I personally could do without,' Brownley Harris contributed from the backseat of the Suburban.

'It's not a problem,' said Starkey, taking control as he always did. 'We have a legitimate reason to be here. Be a mistake if we stopped showing our faces at Bragg. Don't disappoint me.'

'I hear you,' said Harris. 'I still don't like being back at the scene of the crime.' He decided that things needed some lightening up. 'You all hear the differential theory of the US Armed Forces – the so-called snake model?' he asked.

'Haven't heard that one, Brownie,' said Griffin, who also rolled his eyes. He knew a joke was coming, probably a bad one.

'Army Infantry comes in after the snake. Snake smells them, leaves the area unharmed. Aviation comes next, has Global Positioning Satellite coordinates to the snake. Still can't find the snake. Returns to base for re-fuel, crew rests and manicures. Field Artillery comes. Kills the snake with massive Line On Target barrage with three Formal Artillery Brigades in support. Kills several hundred civilians as unavoidable collateral damage. All participants, including cooks, mechanics, clerks, are awarded Silver Stars.'

'What about us Rangers?' asked Griffin, playing the straight man.

Harris grinned. 'Single Ranger comes in, plays with the snake, then eats it.'

Starkey snorted out a laugh, then he turned off Armistead Street into the lot for the Corps Head-quarters. 'Remember, this is just business. Conduct yourselves as such, gentlemen.'

Griffin and Harris barked, 'Yes, sir.'

The three of them gathered their briefcases, put on lightweight suit jackets, and tightened their neckties. They were the senior sales team for Hechler and Koch, and they were at Bragg to promote the sale of guns to the Army. In particular, they were trying to build common interest in the gun manufacturer's Personal Defense Weapon (PDW), which weighed just over two pounds, fully loaded, and could 'defeat all known standard issue military body armor'.

'Hell of a weapon,' Thomas Starkey liked to say during his sales pitch. 'If we'd had it in 'Nam, we would have won the war.'

Chapter Nineteen

The meeting went as well as any of them could have hoped. The three salesmen left the Army Corps offices at a little past eight that night, with assurances of support for the PDW. Thomas Starkey had also demonstrated the latest version of the MP5 submachine gun and talked knowledgeably and enthusiastically about his company's fabrications system, which made their gun parts 99.9 percent interchangeable.

'Let's get some cold beers and thick steaks,' Starkey said. 'See if we can get in a little trouble in Fayetteville, or maybe some other town down the line. That's an order, gentlemen.'

'I'm up for that,' said Harris. 'It's been a good day, hasn't it? Let's see if we can spoil it.'

By the time they left Fort Bragg darkness had fallen. 'On the road again . . .' Warren Griffin started in on his theme song, the old Willie Nelson standard that he sang just about every time they started an adventure. They knew Fayetteville, not only from business trips, but from a time when they'd been stationed at Bragg. It was only four years since the three of them had left the Army, where they'd been Rangers: Colonel Starkey, Captain Harris, Master Sergeant Griffin. Seventy-fifth Ranger Regiment, 3rd Battalion, originally out of Fort Benning, Georgia.

They were just entering town when they saw a couple of hookers loitering on a semidarkened street corner. In the bad old days Hays Street in town had block after block of rough bars and strip joints. It used to be known as *Fayettenam*. No more, though. The locals were trying to gentrify the downtown area. A billboard put up by the Chamber of Commerce read: 'Metro Living At A Southern Pace'. Made you want to throw up.

Warren Griffin leaned out the side window of the Suburban. 'I love you, and especially *you*. Stop the car this minute! Oh God, please stop the vehicle. I love you, darling. I'll be back!' he called to the two girls.

Starkey laughed, but he drove on until they reached The Pump, which had been there for at least twenty years. They strolled inside to eat and party. Why work if you couldn't get a reward? Why feel the pain unless you got some gain?

During the next few hours, they drank too many beers, ate twenty-four-ounce steaks with fried onions and mushrooms slathered on top, smoked cigars, and told the best war stories and jokes. Even the waitresses and bartenders got into the act some. Everybody liked Thomas Starkey. Unless you happened to get on his bad side.

They were leaving Fayetteville around midnight when Starkey pulled the Suburban over to the curb. 'Time for a live-fire exercise,' he said to Griffin and Harris. They knew what that meant.

Harris just smiled, but Griffin let out a whoop. 'Let the war games begin!'

Starkey leaned out his window and talked to one of the girls loitering on Hays Street. She was a tall, rail-thin blonde, wobbling slightly on silver platform heels. She had a little, pouty mouth, but it disappeared when she flashed them her best hundred-dollar smile.

'You are a very beautiful lady,' Starkey said. 'Listen, we're heading over to our suite at the Radisson. You be interested in three big tips, instead of just one? We kind of like to party together. It'll be good, clean fun.'

Starkey could be charming, and also respectful. He had an easy smile. So the blonde hooker got into the Suburban. 'You all promise to be good boys,' she said, and smiled that wonderful smile of hers again.

'Promise,' the three of them chorused. 'We'll be good boys.'

'On the road again,' Griffin sang.

'Hey, you're pretty good,' the girl said, and gave him a kiss on the cheek. She was good with men, knew how to handle them, especially soldiers from Fort Bragg, who were usually decent enough guys. Once upon a time, she'd been an Army brat herself. Not so long ago. She was nineteen.

'You hear that? This beautiful lady likes my singing. What's your name, sweetie?' asked Griffin. 'I like you already.'

'It's Vanessa,' said the girl, giving her madeup street handle. 'What's yours? Don't say Willie.'

Griffin laughed out loud. 'Why, it's Warren. Nice to make your acquaintance, Vanessa. Pretty name for a pretty lady.'

They rode out of town, in the direction of I-95. Starkey suddenly pulled the Suburban over after a mile or so and shouted, 'Pit stop!' He let the car roll until it was mostly hidden in a copse of evergreens and prickle bushes.

'The Radisson's not far. Why don't you wait?' Vanessa asked. 'You boys can hold it a little longer, can't you?'

'This *can't* wait,' said Griffin. Suddenly, he had his pistol up tight against the girl's skull.

From the front seat, Brownley Harris had his gun aimed at her chest.

'*De hai tay len dau!*' Thomas Starkey screamed, his voice deep and scary.

Hands on your head.

'*Ban gap nhieu phien phue roi do.*'

You're in serious trouble, bitch.

Vanessa didn't understand a word but she sure got the tone. Bad shit was going down. Real bad shit. Her stomach dropped. Ordinarily, she wouldn't have gotten into a car with three guys, but the driver had seemed so nice. Now why was he yelling at her? What kind of messed-up language was it? What was happening? She thought that she might throw up and she'd had a chili dog and Fritos for dinner.

'Stop, please stop!' Vanessa said, and started to cry. It

was an act, kind of, but it usually worked on the soldiers from Bragg.

Not this time, though. The insane yelling in the car got even louder. The weird language she didn't understand.

'*Ra khoi xe. Ngay bay gro*,' said Thomas Starkey.

Get out of the car. Do it now, bitch.

They were waving their scary guns and pointing, and she finally understood that she was supposed to get out of the car. *Oh my God, were they going to leave her out here as a sick joke? The bastards!*

Or was it worse than that? How much worse could it get?

Then the one in the front seat smacked her with the back of his hand. Why? She was already getting out of the car. Goddamn him! She almost toppled over on her silver platform shoes. Willie Nelson kicked her in the back and Vanessa gasped in pain.

'*Ra khoi xe!*' the man in front screamed again. Who were they? Were they terrorists or something?

Vanessa was sobbing, but she understood she was supposed to run, to hightail it into the dark woods and creepy swampland. *Jesus, God, she didn't want to go in there! There'd be snakes for sure!*

The one from the backseat punched her in the back again, and Vanessa started to run. What choice did she have?

'*Lue do may se den toi!*'

You're going to die.

She heard shouts behind her.

Oh God, God, God, what were they saying? What was going to happen to her? Why had she let them pick her up? Big mistake, big mistake!

Then all Vanessa could think about was running.

Chapter Twenty

'Let her go,' Thomas Starkey said. 'Let's be fair now. We told Vanessa we'd be good.'

So they leaned against the Suburban and let the frightened girl run off into the swamp, gave her a good head start.

Starkey slid on one of the Ranger's new tan berets. It had replaced the black beret of the Special Forces, once the rest of the Army had gone to black. 'Here's the first side bet of the evening. Ole Vanessa will be wearing her platform heels when we catch up with her. Or do you boys think she'll shuck the shoes?' asked Starkey. 'Bets, gentlemen?'

'Shuck 'em for sure,' said Griffin. 'She's dumb, but she's not that stupid. I'll take your bet. Fifty?'

'She'll be wearing the shoes,' pronounced Starkey. 'Girl that pretty working the street, she's dumb as a board. A hundred says so.'

Just then they saw a pair of lights veering off the highway. Someone was driving toward where they'd parked. Now who the hell was this?

'Trooper,' said Starkey. Then he raised his hand in a friendly wave at the slow-moving police car.

'Problem here?' the statie said once he'd rolled up close to the big blue Suburban. He didn't bother to get out of his car.

'Just a little pit stop, Officer. We're on our way to Fort Benning from Bragg,' Starkey said in the calmest voice. In truth, he wasn't nervous about the trooper. Just curious about how this would turn out. 'We're in the Reserves. If the three of us were on the *first* team I guess we'd all be in trouble.'

'I saw your vehicle from the road. Thought I better check to make sure everybody was all right. Nothing but swamp back there.'

'Well, we're fine, Officer. Finish our smokes and hit the road again. Thanks for the concern.'

The state trooper was just about to pull away when a woman's scream came from the woods. There was no mistaking that it was a cry for help.

'Now that's a damn shame, Officer.' Starkey swung his pistol out from behind his back. He shot the trooper point-blank in the forehead. Didn't even have to think about it. 'No good deed goes unpunished.'

He shook his head as he walked to the police car, shut off the headlights. He got into the front, pushing the dead trooper aside, and pulled the car out of sight from the main road.

'Go find the girl,' he said to Harris and Griffin. 'Pronto. She's obviously not too far. And she's still wearing her

platforms, the twit. Go! Go!' he repeated. 'I'll give you chumps a couple of minutes' lead. I want to get this cruiser completely out of sight. Go. Warren is Point. Brownie is Flanker.'

When Colonel Thomas Starkey finally made his move into the woods, there wasn't a false step on his part. He went straight to where the girl had cried out for help and gotten the state trooper killed.

From that point, it was mostly instinct for him. He saw mussed leaves and grass. A broken branch of a bush where she'd passed. He noted his own internal responses – rapid breathing, surging blood flow. He'd been here before.

'*Tao se tim ra may*,' he whispered in Vietnamese. '*Lue do may se den toi*.'

I'm going to find you, honey. You're almost dead.

He was sorry that the chase after the girl had to be rushed, but the dead state trooper was an unexpected development. As always, Starkey had a calm, superaware focus. He was in the zone. Time slowed for him; every detail was precise and every movement controlled. He was moving fast, comfortable and supremely confident in the dark woods. There was just enough moonlight for him to see.

Then he heard laughter up ahead. Saw a light through the branches. He stopped moving. 'Son of a bitch!' he muttered. He moved forward cautiously, just in case.

Harris and Griffin had caught the blonde bitch. They had taken off her black hot pants, gagged her with her own scuzzy underwear, cuffed her hands behind her back.

Griffin was ripping off her silver-sequined blouse. All that was left were the sparkly silver platforms.

Vanessa didn't wear a bra and her breasts were small. Pretty face, though. Reminded Starkey of his neighbor's daughter. Starkey thought again that she was a fine little piece to be selling herself for cheap on the street. *Too bad, Vanessa.*

She struggled and Griffin let her break away, just for the fun of it. But when she tried to run, she tripped and went down hard in the dirt. She stared up at Starkey, who was now standing over her. He thought she was pathetic.

'Why are you doing this?' She was whimpering. Then she said something else through the gag as she tried to push herself up. It sounded like 'I never hurt anybody.'

'This is a game we learned a long time ago,' Starkey said in English. 'It's just a game, honey. Passes the time. Amuses us. Get the paint,' he said to Master Sergeant Griffin. 'I think red for tonight. You look good in red, Vanessa? I think red is your color.'

He looked her right in the eye and pulled the trigger.

Chapter Twenty-One

I got up at around five-thirty my first morning back in Washington. *Same old, same old*, which was fine with me.

I put on a Wizards tee-shirt and ancient Georgetown gym shorts and headed downstairs. The lights in the kitchen were still off. Nana wasn't up yet, which was a little surprising.

Well, she deserved to sleep late every once in a while.

I laced up my sneaks and headed outside for a run. Immediately I could smell the Anacostia River. Not the greatest smell, but familiar. My plan was not to think about Ellis Cooper on death row this morning. So far, I was failing.

Our neighborhood has changed a lot in the past few years. The politicians and business-people would say it's all for the good, but I'm not so sure that's right. There's construction on 395 South, and the Fourth Street on-ramp has been closed forever. I doubt it would happen for this long in Georgetown. A lot of the old brownstones

I grew up with have been torn down.

Town houses are going up which look very Capitol Hill to me. There's also a flashy new gym called Results. Some houses sport hexagonal blue ADT security signs courtesy of the huge Tyco Corporation. Certain streets are becoming gentrified. But the drug dealers are still around, especially as you travel toward the Anacostia.

If you could put on HG Wells time machine glasses, you would see that the original city planners had some good ideas. Every couple of blocks there is a park with clearly delineated paths and patches of grass. Some day the parks will be reclaimed by the people, not just the drug dealers. Or so I like to think.

A *Washington Post* article the other day proclaimed that some people in the neighborhood actually protect the dealers. Well, some people think the dealers do more good things for the community than the politicians – like throwing block parties and giving kids ice-cream money on hot summer days.

I've been here since I was ten and we'll probably stay in Southeast. I love the old neighborhood – not just the memories, but the promise of things that could still happen here.

When I got home from my run the kitchen lights still weren't on. An alarm was sounding inside my head.

Pretty loud, too.

I went down the narrow hallway from the kitchen to check on Nana.

Chapter Twenty-Two

I edged open the door and saw her lying in bed, so I quietly moved into the room. Rosie the cat was perched on the windowsill. She meowed softly. Some watch-cat.

I let my eyes roam. Saw a familiar framed poster depicting jazz musicians by Romare Bearden; it's called 'Wrapping it up at the Lafayette'.

On top of her armoire were dozens of hat boxes. Nana's collection of hats for special occasions would be the envy of any milliner.

I realized I couldn't hear Nana's breathing.

My body tensed and suddenly there was a loud roaring sound inside my head. She hadn't gotten up to make breakfast only a handful of times since I was a kid. I felt the fears of a child as I stood perfectly still in her room.

Oh God, no. Don't let this happen.

When I got close to her bed, I heard shallow breaths. Then her eyes popped open.

'Alex?' she whispered. 'What's happening? Why are you in here? What time is it?'

'Hi there, sweetheart. You okay?' I asked.

'I'm just kind of tired. Feeling a little under the weather this morning.' She squinted her eyes to look at the old Westclox on her night table. 'Seven? Oh my. Half the morning's gone.'

'You want a little breakfast? How about breakfast in bed this morning? I'm buying,' I said.

She sighed. 'I think I'll just sleep in a little longer, Alex. You mind? Can you get the kids ready for school?'

'Sure. Are you positive you're okay?'

'I'll see you later. I'm fine. Just a little tired this morning. Get the children up, Alex.' Rosie was trying to get in bed with Nana, but she wasn't having any of it. 'Scat, cat,' she whispered.

I got the three kids up, or so I thought, but then I had to rouse Jannie and Damon a second time. I put out their favorite cereals, some fruit, and then I made scrambled eggs – overdoing it a little to compensate for Nana's not being there. I warmed Alex's milk then fixed his breakfast and spoon-fed it to him.

The kids marched off to school and I cleaned up after they were gone. I changed Alex's diapers for the second time that morning, and put him in a fresh onesie covered with fire trucks. He was liking this extra attention, seemed to think it was funny.

'Don't get used to this, little buddy,' I told him.

I checked on Nana, and she was still resting. She was fast asleep, actually. I listened to her breathing for a couple of minutes. She seemed all right.

Her bedroom was so peaceful, but not old lady rosy.

There was a fuzzy, very colorful orange and purple rug at the foot of the bed. She said it gave her happy feet.

I took little Alex upstairs to my room, where I hoped to get some work done that morning. I called a friend at the Pentagon. His name's Kevin Cassidy. We had worked a murder case together a few years back.

I told him about the situation at Fort Bragg, and how little time Sergeant Cooper had on death row. Kevin listened, then cautioned me to be extremely careful. 'There are a lot of good folks in the Army, Alex. Good people, well intentioned, honorable as hell. But we like to clean up our own mess. Outsiders aren't usually welcome. You hear what I'm saying?'

'Ellis Cooper didn't commit those murders,' I told him. 'I'm almost certain of it. But I'll take your advice to heart. We're running out of time, Kevin.'

'I'll check into it for you,' he said. 'Let *me* do it, Alex.'

After I got off the phone with the Pentagon, I called Ron Burns at the FBI. I told him about the developing situation at Fort Bragg. The director and I had gotten fairly close during the troubles with Kyle Craig. Craig was a former senior agent I'd helped put away. I still didn't know exactly how many murders he had committed but it was at least eleven, probably much more than that. Burns and I had believed Kyle was our friend. It was the worst betrayal in my lifetime, but not the only one.

Burns wanted to get me over to the Bureau and I was thinking about it.

'You know how territorial local cops can be,' he said.

'The Army is even worse, especially when it comes to a homicide.'

'Even if one of their own is innocent and wrongly accused? Even if he's about to be executed? I thought they didn't leave their own out there to die.'

'If they believed that, Alex, the case would have never gone to trial. If I can help, I will. Let me know. I don't make offers that I don't keep.'

'I appreciate it,' I said.

After I got off the phone, I brought little Alex downstairs for some more milk. I was becoming faintly aware of just how much work was involved every day, every hour of every day, at the house. I hadn't even done any cleaning or straightening up yet.

I decided to check on Nana again.

Gently I opened the door. *I couldn't hear anything.*

I moved closer to the bed.

Finally, I could hear the sound of her breathing. I stood stock-still in her bedroom and, for the first time that I could remember, I worried about Nana.

She was never sick.

Chapter Twenty-Three

Nana finally got up around noon. She shuffled into the kitchen holding a thick new book, *The Bondswoman's Narrative*. I had a hot lunch ready for her and the baby.

She didn't want to talk about how she was feeling and didn't eat much, just a few spoonfuls of vegetable soup. I tried to get her over to Dr Rodman's, but she wasn't having any of it. She *did* let me cook the meals for the rest of the day, and take care of the kids, and clean the house from top to bottom per her explicit instructions.

The next morning I was up before Nana for the second day in a row. It was unheard of in all our years together.

While I waited for her to come to the kitchen, I took in the familiar sights. Paid attention, that is.

The room is dominated by her old Caloric gas stove. It has four burners and a large space she uses to hold goods cooked earlier or cooling. There are two ovens side by side. A large black skillet sits on top of the stove at all times. The refrigerator is also an older model that Nana refuses to give up for a newer one. It's always covered with notes and schedules about our life together: Damon's choir and basketball schedules; Jannie's 'whatever' schedule; emergency phone numbers for Sampson and me; an appointment card for little Alex's next pediatrician checkup; a Post-it on which she has written her latest sage advice: *You will never stumble while on your knees*.

'What are you up to, Alex?' I heard the familiar scuff of her slippers. I turned and saw her standing there, hands on hips, ready for battle, or whatever.

'I don't know. The ghost of breakfast past? How are you feeling, old woman?' I said. 'Talk to me. You okay?'

She winked and nodded her tiny head. 'I'm just fine. How 'bout yourself? You okay? You look tired. Hard work taking care of this house, isn't it?' she said, then cackled, and liked the sound of it so much that she cackled again.

I went across the kitchen and picked her up in my arms. She was so light – under a hundred pounds. 'Put me down!' she said. 'Gently, Alex. I might break.'

'So tell me about yesterday. You going to make an appointment at Dr Rodman's? Of course you are.'

'I must have needed a little extra sleep, that's all it was. It happens to the best of us. I listened to my body. Do you?'

'Yes I do,' I said. 'I'm listening to it now and it's voicing some serious concerns about you. Will you make an appointment with John Rodman, or do I have to make it for you?'

'Put me down, Alex. I'm already seeing the doctor later

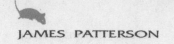

this week. *Regular* visit, no big thing. Now. How do you want your eggs this morning?'

As if to show me how fine she was, Nana said that I should go back to Fort Bragg with Sampson and finish up my business there. She insisted. I did need to go to Bragg at least once more, but not before I got Aunt Tia to come and stay with Nana and the kids. Only after I was sure that everything was under control did I set out for North Carolina.

On the ride I told Sampson what had happened with Nana, and also gave a blow by blow of my day with the kids.

'She's eighty-two, Alex,' he said, but then added, 'She'll probably only be with us for another twenty years or so.' We both laughed, but I could tell John was worried about Nana, too. By his own admission, she's been like a mother to him.

Finally we arrived at Fayetteville, North Carolina, around five in the afternoon. We had to see a woman about an alibi that could maybe save Sergeant Cooper.

Chapter Twenty-Four

We drove to the Bragg Boulevard Estates, less than half a mile from Fort Bragg. The jets were still flying non-stop overhead and the artillery kept pounding away.

Just about everyone at Boulevard Estates worked on the base and lived in what is known as Basic Allowance Housing. BAH is based on rank and pay grade, the size and quality of the residence improving dramatically with rank. Most of the places we saw were small ranch houses. Several of them looked like they needed serious maintenance work. I had read somewhere that over sixty percent of the current Army was married and had children. It looked like that statistic was about right.

Sampson and I walked up to one of the brick ranch houses, and I knocked on the battered and bent aluminum front door. A woman in a black silk kimono appeared. She was heavy-set, attractive. I already knew that her name was Tori Sanders. Behind her, I could see four small children checking out who was at the door.

'Yes? What is it?' she asked. 'We're busy. It's feeding time at the zoo.'

'I'm Detective Cross and this is Detective Sampson,' I told her. 'Captain Jacobs told us you're a friend of Ellis Cooper's.'

She didn't respond. Didn't even blink.

'Mrs Sanders, you called me at my hotel about a week ago. I figured your house had to be within walking distance of the base if Sergeant Cooper stopped here on the night of the murder. I did a little checking. Found out he was here that night. Can we come in? You don't want us standing out here where all your neighbors can see.'

Tori Sanders decided to let us in. She opened the door and ushered us into a small dining area. Then she shooed her kids away.

'I don't know why you're here, or what you're talking about,' she said. Her arms were crossed tightly in front of her body. She was probably in her late thirties.

'We have other options. I'll tell you what we can do, Mrs Sanders,' Sampson spoke up. 'We can go out and ask around the neighborhood about you and Sergeant Cooper. We can also involve CID. Or you can answer our questions here in the privacy of your home. You do understand that Cooper is going to be executed in a few days?'

'God damn you. Both of you!' she suddenly raised her voice. 'You got this all wrong. As usual, the police have it wrong.'

'Why don't you straighten us out then,' Sampson said,

softening his tone some. 'We're here to listen. That's the truth, Mrs Sanders.'

'You want to be straightened out, well then here it is. You want it real? I *did* call you, Detective Cross. That was me. Now here's what I didn't say on the phone. I wasn't cheating on my husband with Sergeant Cooper. My husband asked me to make the call. He's a friend of Ellis's. He happens to believe the man is innocent. So do I. But we have no proof, no evidence that he didn't commit those murders. Ellis *was* here that night. But it was before he went drinking, and he came to see my husband, not me.'

I took in what she had said, and I believed her. It was hard not to. 'Did Sergeant Cooper know you were going to call me?' I asked.

She shrugged her shoulders. 'I have no idea. You'll have to ask Ellis about that. We were just trying to do the right thing for him. You should do the same. The man is on death row, and he's innocent as you or I. He's *innocent*. Now let me feed my babies.'

Chapter Twenty-Five

We were getting nowhere fast and it was frustrating as hell for both of us, but especially Sampson. The clock was ticking so loud for Ellis Cooper I could hear it just about every minute of the day.

Around nine that night, John and I had dinner at a popular local spot called the Misfits Pub, out in the Strickland Bridge shopping center. Supposedly, a lot of non-com personnel from Fort Bragg stopped in there. We were still nosing around for any information we could get.

'The more we know, the less we seem to know.' Sampson shook his head and sipped his drink. 'Something's definitely not right here at Bragg. And I know what you're going to say, Alex. Maybe Cooper is the heart of the problem. Especially if he put the Sanders up to calling you.'

I nursed my drink and looked around the pub. A bar dominated the room, which was crowded, loud and smoky. The music alternated between country and soul. 'Doesn't prove he's guilty. Just that he's desperate. It's hard to blame Cooper for trying anything he can,' I finally said. 'He's on death row.'

'He's not stupid, Alex. He's capable of stirring the pot to get our attention. Or somebody else's.'

'But he's not capable of murder?'

Sampson stared into my eyes. I could tell he was getting angry. 'No, he's not a murderer. I know him, Alex. Just like I know you.'

'Did Cooper kill in combat?' I asked.

Sampson shook his head. 'That was war. A lot of our people got killed too. You know what it's like. You've killed men,' he said. 'Doesn't make you a murderer, does it?'

'I don't know, does it?'

I couldn't help overhearing a man and woman who were sitting next to us at the bar. 'Police found Vanessa in the woods near I-95. Only disappeared last night. Now she's dead, she's gone. Some freaks did her with a hunting knife. Probably Army trash,' the woman was saying. She had a thick Southern accent, and sounded angry, but also frightened.

I turned and saw a florid-faced, redheaded woman in a bright blue halter top and white slacks. 'Sorry, I couldn't help over-hearing. What happened?' I asked. 'Somebody was murdered outside town?'

'Girl who comes in here sometimes. Vanessa. Somebody cut her up,' the redhead said, and shook her head back and forth. The man she was with wore a black silk shirt, cowboy hat, and looked like a failed country and western singer. He didn't like it that the woman was talking to me.

'My name is Cross. I'm a homicide detective from Washington. My partner and I are working a case down here.'

The woman's head shot back. 'I don't talk to cops,' she said, and turned away. 'Mind your own business.'

I looked at Sampson, then spoke in a lowered voice. 'If it's the same killer, he's not being too careful.'

'Or the same *three* killers,' he said.

Someone elbowed me hard in the back. I whirled around and saw a heavy-set, well-muscled blond man in a checkered sport shirt and khakis. He had a 'high and tight'. Definitely military.

'Time you two got the hell out of Dodge,' he said. Two other men stood behind him. *Three of them*. They were dressed in civilian clothes, but they sure looked like Army. 'Time you stopped causing trouble. You hear me?'

'We're talking here. Don't interrupt us again,' Sampson said. 'You hear *me*?'

'You're a big load, aren't you? Think you're a real tough guy?' the front man asked.

Sampson broke into a slow smile that I'd seen before. 'Yeah, I do. He's a tough guy, too.'

The muscular blond tried to shove Sampson off his stool. John didn't budge. One of the blond's buddies came at me. I moved quickly and he swung and missed. I hit him hard in the gut and he went down on all fours.

Suddenly, all three men were on us. 'Your asshole friend's a killer,' the blond yelled. 'He killed women!'

Sampson hit him on the chin and he sunk down on one knee. Unfortunately, these guys didn't stay down once they were hit. Another bruiser joined in and that made four against two.

A shrill whistle sounded inside the bar. I whirled around and looked toward the door. The military police had arrived. So had a couple of eager-looking deputies from the Fayetteville police. They all had batons at the ready. I wondered how they'd gotten here so fast.

They waded in and arrested everybody involved in the bar fight, including Sampson and me. They weren't interested in who'd started it. Our heads bowed, we were escorted out in handcuffs to a black-and-white and shoved down into the squad car.

'First time for everything,' Sampson said.

Chapter Twenty-Six

W e didn't need this crap – not now, especially. We were taken out to the Cumberland County Jail in a small, blue bus that sat ten. Apparently there were only a couple of cells at the jail in Fayetteville. At no time were we offered any professional courtesy because we were homicide detectives from Washington, who just happened to be working on behalf of Sergeant Ellis Cooper.

In case you're ever looking for it, the booking facility at the County Jail is located in the basement. It took about half an hour for the local police to do our paperwork, fingerprints, and take our photographs. We were given a cold shower, then 'put in the pumpkin patch'. That was the guards' clever way of describing the orange jumpsuit and slippers prisoners were made to wear.

I asked what had happened to the four soldiers who'd attacked us and was told it was none of my goddamn business, but that they'd been 'transported to the stockade at Bragg'.

Sampson and I were put in a misdemeanor block in a

dormitory cell, which was also in the basement. It was built for maybe a dozen prisoners, but there were close to twenty of us crowded in there that night. None of the prisoners were white and I wondered if the jail had other holding cells, and if they were segregated, too.

Some of the men seemed to know each other from previous nights they had spent here. It was a civil enough group. Nobody wanted to mess with Sampson, or even me. A guard walked by on checks twice an hour. I knew the basic drill. The prisoners were in charge the other fifty-eight minutes an hour.

'Cigarette?' a guy to my right asked. He was sitting on the floor with his back against a pitted concrete wall.

'Don't smoke,' I said to him.

'You're the detective, right?' he asked after a couple of minutes.

I nodded and looked at him more closely. I didn't think I'd met him, but it was a small town. We had shown our faces around. By this time a lot of people in Fayetteville knew who we were.

'Strange shit going down,' the man said. He took out a pack of Camels. Grinned. Tapped one out. 'Today's Army, man. "An army of one." What kind of bullshit is that?'

'You Army?' I asked. 'I thought they took you guys to the stockade at Fort Bragg.'

He smiled at me. 'Ain't no stockade at Bragg, man. Tell you something else. I was in here when they brought Sergeant Cooper in. He was nuts that night. They printed him down here, then took him *upstairs*. Man was a psycho killer for sure that night.'

I just listened. I was trying to figure out who the man was, and why he was talking to me about Ellis Cooper.

'I'm going to tell you something for your own good. Everybody around here knows he did those women. He was a well-known freak.'

The man blew out concentrated rings of smoke, then he pushed himself off the floor and shuffled away. I wondered what in hell was going on. Had somebody arranged the fight at the bar? The whole thing tonight? Who was the guy who had come over to talk to me? To give me advice *for my own good*?

A short while later, a guard came and took him away. He glanced my way as he was leaving. Then Sampson and I got to spend the night in the crowded, foul-smelling holding cell. We took turns sleeping.

In the morning, I heard someone call our names.

'Cross. Sampson.' One of the guards had opened the door to the holding cell. He was trying to wave away the stink. 'Cross. Sampson.'

Sampson and I pushed ourselves stiffly up off the floor. 'Right here. Where you left us last night,' I said.

We were led back upstairs and taken to the front lobby, where we got the day's very first surprise. Captain Jacobs from CID was waiting there. 'You all sleep well?' he asked.

'That was a setup,' I said to him. 'The fight, the arrest. Did you know about it beforehand?'

'You can go now,' he said. 'That's what you should do. Get your stuff and go home, Detectives. Do yourselves a big favor while you still can. You're wasting time on a dead man's errands.'

Chapter Twenty-Seven

The awful strangeness and frustration continued the day I got back to Washington. If anything, it got even worse. An e-mail was waiting for me in my office at home. The message was from someone who identified himself as 'Foot Soldier'. Everything about it was troubling and impossible for me to comprehend at this point.

It began: *For Detective Alex Cross,*

Your general interest: The Pentagon is currently taking steps to prevent some of the more than one thousand deaths each year in the 'peacetime Army'. The deaths come from car crashes, suicides and murders. In each of the past three years, at least eighty Army soldiers have been murdered.

Specifics to think about, Detective: An Army pilot named Thomas Hoff stationed at Fort Drum near Watertown, New York, was convicted of the slaying of a homosexual enlisted man on post. The convicted man claimed his innocence right up until the moment of his execution. In his defense, Hoff wasn't actually stationed at Drum until three months after the murder was committed. He had visited a friend at Hood prior to the murder, however. His prints were found at the murder scene. Hoff's service record was clean before his conviction for murder. He had been a 'model soldier' until the supposed murder.

Another case for your consideration, Detective. An Army barber, known by his friends as 'Bangs', was convicted of murdering three prostitutes outside Fort Campbell in Kentucky. Santo Marinacci had no criminal record before the killings. His pregnant wife testified that he was home with her on the night of the murders. Marinacci was convicted because of fingerprints and DNA found at the murder scene, and also because the murder weapon, a survival knife, was discovered in his garage. Marinacci swore the knife was planted there. 'For God's sake, he's a barber,' his wife called out during the eventual execution of her husband. Santo Marinacci claimed he was innocent and had been framed up to the moment that he died.

Foot Soldier

I read Foot Soldier's e-mail over again, then I called Sampson at home. I read him the message. He didn't know what to make of it either. He said he'd contact Ellis Cooper as soon as he hung up with me. We both wondered if Cooper might be behind the strange note.

For the rest of the day, I couldn't get the disturbing message out of my head. Information had been passed to me that someone thought was important. No conclusions were reached. Foot Soldier had left that up to me. What was I supposed to make of the murders at Fort Drum and Fort Campbell? The possible frame-up?

That night I took a break for a few hours. I watched

Damon's basketball team play a league game at St Anthony's. Damon scored sixteen points, and he was as smooth an outside shooter as some high school kids. I think he knew it, but he wanted to hear my opinion of his play.

'You had a real good game, Damon,' I told him. 'Scored points, but didn't forget about the rest of your team. Played tough "d" on Number Eleven.'

Damon grinned, even though he tried to hold it back. I had given the right answer. 'Yeah, he's the high scorer in the league. But not tonight.'

After we talked, Damon took off with some of his team-mates, Ramon, Ervin, Kenyon. That was a new one, but I knew I better get used to it.

When I got home, I couldn't stop thinking about Ellis Cooper and the e-mail that had come for me about other murders by Army personnel. According to Sampson, Cooper swore he didn't have anything to do with it. Who then? Someone at Fort Bragg? A friend of Cooper's?

That night in bed I couldn't stop thinking about the damn note.

Innocent men might have been executed.

Sergeant Cooper wasn't the first.

This has happened before.

Who the hell was Foot Soldier?

Chapter Twenty-Eight

I desperately needed to see someone at the Army Court of Criminal Appeals, and the FBI helped me get an appointment with the right person.

The court and its administrative offices were located in a bland-looking commercial building in Arlington. It was considerably nicer inside the building, kind of like a dignified and reserved corporate legal office. Other than the fact that most of the men and women wore uniforms, the normal touches of military culture weren't much in evidence.

Sampson and I were there to see Lt General Shelly Borislow, and we were brought to her office by an aide. It was a lengthy walk – lots of long hallways, typical of government buildings all over the Washington area.

General Borislow was waiting for us when we finally arrived. She stood ramrod straight, and was obviously physically fit. A handsome woman, probably in her late forties.

'Thanks for seeing us,' Sampson said, and shook

General Borislow's hand. I had the feeling that he wanted to handle the meeting, maybe because he had more experience with the Army than I did, but possibly because Ellis Cooper's time was running out.

'I read the transcript of the trial last night,' General Borislow said as we sat around a glass-topped coffee table. 'I also went through the CID notes from Captain Jacobs. And Sergeant Cooper's records. I'm pretty much up to speed. Now, what can I do for you, gentlemen?' I was pleased that the general was the one to bring up gender.

'I have some questions. If you don't mind, General?' Sampson said. He leaned forward so that his elbows rested on his thighs. His eyes were steady on General Borislow, who was just as focused on Sampson.

'Ask any questions you wish. I don't have another meeting until ten. That gives us about twenty minutes to talk, but you can have more time if you need it. The Army has nothing to hide in this matter, I can tell you that much.'

Sampson still held Borislow's eyes. 'Detective Cross and I have worked hundreds of homicide scenes, General. Some things about this one bother us a lot.'

'What, specifically?'

Sampson hesitated, then he went on. 'Before I get into what bothers us, I was wondering if anything about the trial or the investigation bothered you?'

General Shelly Borislow stayed in perfect control. 'A few things, actually. I suppose it could be construed as a little too pat that Sergeant Cooper held on to the murder weapon. It was a valuable souvenir, though, from his years in Vietnam. And a souvenir from the murders themselves.'

'You're aware that Sergeant Cooper's apartment was broken into a day or two before the murders? We saw signs of the break-in and Cooper confirmed it. The knife could have been taken then,' Sampson said.

Borislow nodded. 'That's certainly possible, Detective. But isn't it also possible that the sergeant created the impression that there had been a break-in at his apartment? That's what CID concluded.'

'A boy from the neighborhood saw three men in Tanya Jackson's yard around the time of the murders.'

'The boy could have seen men in the yard. That's true. He also may have seen shadows from trees. It was a dark night, and windy. The boy is ten years old. He gave conflicting accounts of the night to police officers. As I said, Detective, I studied the case thoroughly.'

'Blood that didn't match the murdered women's, or Sergeant Cooper's, was found at the homicide scene.'

General Borislow's demeanor didn't change. 'The judge in the case made the call not to allow that into evidence. If I had been the judge, I would have permitted the jury to hear about the blood. We'll never know about it now.'

'Sergeant Cooper's military record before the murders was nearly perfect,' said Sampson.

'He had an excellent record. The Army is well aware of that. It's one of the things that makes this such a tragedy.'

Sampson sighed. He sensed he wasn't getting anywhere. I did too. 'General, one more question and then we'll leave. We won't even take our allotted time.'

Borislow didn't blink.'Go ahead with your question.'

'It puzzles me that the Army made no real effort to come to Sergeant Cooper's defense. Not before or during the trial. Obviously, the Army isn't going to try and help him now. Why is that?'

General Borislow nodded at the question, and pursed her lips before she answered it. 'Detective Sampson, we appreciate the fact that Ellis Cooper is your friend, and that you've remained loyal to him. We admire that, actually. But your question is easy to answer. The Army, from top to bottom, believes that Sergeant Cooper is guilty of three horrific, cold-blooded murders. We have no intention of helping a murderer go free. I'm afraid that I'm convinced Cooper is a murderer too. I won't be supporting an appeal. I'm sorry that I don't have better news for you.'

After our meeting, Sampson and I were escorted back through the labyrinth of hallways by General Borislow's aide. We were both silent as we walked the long walk to the main lobby.

Once we had left the building and gone outside, he turned to me.'What do you think?'

'I think the Army is hiding something,' I said. 'And we don't have much time to find out what it is.'

Chapter Twenty-Nine

The following morning, Thomas Starkey got a clear picture of just how far things had gone for him. The clarifying incident took place less than two miles from his house in North Carolina.

He had stopped at the local strip mall for copies of *USA Today* and the *Rocky Mount Telegram*, plus some raisin cinnamon bagels from the NY Style deli. It was raining hard that morning and he stood with the newspapers and warm bagels under the overhang at the mall, waiting for the downpour to slow.

When it finally did, he started to wade through deep puddles toward his Suburban. As he did so, he spotted a couple sloshing toward him across the parking lot. They had just gotten out of an old blue pickup and they'd left the headlights on.

'Hi, excuse me. Left your lights on,' Starkey called as they came forward. The woman turned to look. The man didn't. Instead, he started to talk, and it was clear he had a speech impediment. 'Wir frum San Cros head'n La'nce.

Forgath muh wuhlet n'mah pantz . . .'

The woman cut in. 'I'm awful sorry to bother you. We're from Sandy Cross goin' to Laurence,' she said. 'So embarrassing. My brother left his wallet in his other pants. We don't even have money for gas to get back home.'

'Kin you hep's?' asked the sputtering male.

Starkey got the whole thing immediately. They'd left the goddamn truck lights on so he could be the one to make the first verbal contact, not them. The man's speech impediment was a fake and that's what really did it to him. His son Hank was autistic. Now these two shitheels were using a fake handicap as part of their cheap con to get money.

Swiftly, Starkey had his handgun out. He wasn't sure himself what was going to happen next. All he knew was that he was really pissed off. Jesus, he was steamed.

'Get on your knees, both of you,' he yelled, and thrust the gun into the male's unshaven, miserable excuse for a face. 'Now you apologize, and you better talk right or I'll shoot you dead in this fucking parking lot.'

He struck the kneeling man in the forehead with the barrel of his gun.

'Jesus, I'm sorry. We're both sorry, mister. We jus' wanted a few bucks. Don't shoot! Please don't shoot us. We're good Christians.'

'You both stay on your goddamn knees,' Starkey said. 'You stay right there, and I don't want to see you around here again. Ever, *ever*.'

He put his gun back in his jacket as he stomped off toward his car. He got to the Suburban and thanked God his teenage daughter was listening to rock music and not watching what was going on in the parking lot. Melanie was off in her own little world as usual.

'Let's skedaddle home,' Starkey said as he scrunched down into the front seat. 'And Mel, could you turn that damn music *up*?'

That was when his daughter looked up and spotted the couple kneeling in the lot. 'What's the matter with those two?' she asked her father. 'They're like, *kneeling* in the rain.'

Starkey finally managed a thin smile. 'Guess they just been saved, and now they're thanking the Lord,' he said.

Chapter Thirty

On a cold day in early October, Sampson and I made the six-hour trip by car back to Central Prison in Raleigh. We talked very little on the ride down. The clock had run out on Ellis Cooper.

Two days earlier, Cooper had been officially informed of his execution date by North Carolina's Department of Corrections. Then he had been moved to the prison's death watch area. Things were proceeding in an orderly, and deadly fashion.

Sampson and I had been authorized by the Division of Prisons to visit Sergeant Cooper. When we arrived at Central Prison, about a dozen protesters were out in the parking areas. Most were women and they sang gentle folk songs that harked back to the Sixties or even earlier. Three or four held up signs condemning capital punishment.

We hurried inside the prison and could still hear the mournful hymns beyond the heavy stone and mortar walls.

The death watch area at Central had four cells lined up side by side and opened to a day room with a TV and shower. Ellis Cooper was the only prisoner on death watch at that time. Two corrections officers were stationed outside his cell twenty-four hours a day. They were respectful and courteous when we arrived.

Ellis Cooper looked up as we entered the area and seemed glad to see us. He smiled and raised his hand in greeting.

'Hello, Ellis,' Sampson said in a quiet voice as we took chairs outside the cell. 'Well, we're back. Empty-handed, but we're back.'

Cooper sat on a small stool on the other side of the bars. The legs of the stool were screwed into the floor. The cell itself was immaculately clean, and sparsely furnished with a bed, sink, toilet and a wall-mounted writing table. The scene was depressing and desperate.

'Thank you for coming, John and Alex. Thanks for everything that you've done for me.'

'Tried to do,' said Sampson. 'Tried and failed. Fucked up is all we did.'

Cooper shook his head. 'Just wasn't in the cards this time. Deck was stacked against us. Not your fault. Not anybody's,' he muttered. 'Anyway, it's good to see the two of you. I was praying you'd come. Yeah, I'm praying now.'

Sampson and I knew that vigorous legal efforts were still proceeding to try to stop the execution, but there didn't seem much reason to talk about it. Not unless Cooper chose to bring it up, and he didn't. He seemed strangely at peace to me, the most relaxed I'd seen him.

His salt-and-pepper hair was cut short and his prison coveralls were neat and looked freshly pressed.

He smiled again. 'Like a nice hotel in here, y'know. *Luxury* hotel. Four stars, five diamonds, whatever signifies the finest. These two gentlemen take good care of me. Best I could expect under the circumstances. They think I'm guilty of the three murders, but they're pleasant all the same.'

Then Cooper leaned into the steel bars and got as close as he could to Sampson. 'This is important for me to say, John. I know you did your best, and I hope you know that too. But like I said, the deck against me was stacked so goddamn high. I don't know who wanted me to die, but somebody sure did.'

He looked directly at Sampson. 'John, I have no reason in the world to lie to you. Not now, not here on death watch. I didn't murder those women.'

Chapter Thirty-One

Twenty-four hours earlier, Sampson and I had signed an agreement to be searched before we entered the execution room. Now, at one o'clock in the morning, sixteen men and three women were led into the small viewing room inside the prison. One of the men was General Stephen Bowen from Bragg. He'd kept his promise to be there. The US Army's only representative.

At twenty minutes past one in the morning, the black drapes to the execution chamber were opened for the witnesses. I didn't want to be there; I didn't need to see another execution to know how I felt about them. On the order of the prison warden, the lethal injection executioner approached Cooper. I heard Sampson take in a breath beside me. I couldn't imagine what it would be like for him to watch his friend die like this.

The movement of the technician seemed to startle Ellis Cooper. He turned his head and looked into the viewing room for the first time. The warden asked him if he'd like to make a statement.

Cooper's eyes found us and he held contact. It was incredibly powerful, as if he were about to lose us as he fell into the deepest chasm.

Then Ellis Cooper spoke. His voice was reedy at first, but it got stronger.

'I *did not* murder Tanya Jackson, Barbara Green or Maureen Bruno. I would say so if I did, take this final injection like the man I was trained to be. I didn't kill the three women outside Fort Bragg. Someone else did. God bless you all. Thank you, John and Alex. I forgive the United States Army, which has been a good father to me.'

Ellis Cooper held his head up. Proudly. Like a soldier on parade.

The executioner stepped forward. He injected a dose of Pavulon, a total muscle relaxer which would stop Cooper's breathing.

Very soon Ellis Cooper's heart, lungs and brain stopped functioning.

Sergeant Cooper was pronounced dead by the warden of Central Prison at 1:31 A.M.

Sampson turned to me when it was over. 'We just watched a murder,' he said. 'Someone murdered Ellis Cooper, and they got away with it.'

PART TWO

JAMILLA

Chapter Thirty-Two

I was early to meet the flight coming into Gate 74 at Reagan International, and once I was at the airport I didn't know what to do with myself. I was definitely nervous, *good* nervous, with anticipation. Jamilla Hughes was coming to visit.

The airport was crowded at around four on a Friday afternoon. Lots of weary, edgy business-people sitting around ending their workweeks on the computer, or already off the clock at the bar, or reading magazines and popular novels that ranged from Jonathan Frantzen to Nora Roberts to Stephen King. I sat down, then popped up again. Finally I walked close to the large, expansive windows and watched a big American jet slowly taxi to the gate. *Well, here we go. Am I ready? Is she?*

Jamilla was in the second wave of passengers getting off the plane. She had on jeans, a mauve top, and a black leather car jacket that I remembered from our stakeouts together in New Orleans. The two of us had become fast friends on a bizarre homicide case that had started in her hometown of San Francisco, weaved its way through the South, including the Big Easy, then ended up on the West Coast again.

We had been talking about seeing each other ever since, and now we were actually doing it. It was pretty courageous on both of our parts; I just hoped it wasn't dumb. I didn't think so, and I hoped Jam felt the same way.

Jesus, I was twitching as she came walking up to me. She looked great, though. Nice, big smile. What was I so worried about?

'Where are the thick white clouds that are supposed to be covering the city as my plane approached? God, I could see *everything* – the White House, Lincoln Memorial, the Potomac,' Jamilla grinned as she spoke.

I leaned in and gave her a kiss. 'Not every city has mountains of fog like San Francisco. You need to travel more. Your flight okay?'

'Sucked,' Jamilla grinned again. 'I don't like flying much these days, but I'm glad to be here. This is *good*, Alex. You're almost as nervous as I am. We never had trouble talking on stakeouts. We'll be fine. We'll be just fine. Now calm down, so I can calm down. Deal?' She grabbed me in both arms, hugged me, then kissed me lightly, but nicely, on the lips. 'That's much better,' she said, and smacked her lips. 'You taste good.'

'You must like spearmint.'

'No, I like you.'

We were a whole lot more comfortable during the ride into Washington in my old Porsche. We talked about everything that had been happening since we'd last seen each other. At first, it was work stuff, but then we got into the whole terrorist mess, then how my family was, and hers, and as usual neither of us shut up once we got started – which I love.

It was only as I pulled up to the house that things began to feel tense for me again. 'You ready for this?' I asked before we got out of the car.

Jamilla rolled her eyes. 'Alex, I have four sisters and three brothers back in Oakland. Are you ready for *that*?'

'Bring them on,' I said as I grabbed hold of her black leather duffel bag, which obviously held a bowling ball, and headed toward the house. I was holding my breath a little, but I was definitely glad that she was here. I hadn't been this excited in a long time.

'I missed you,' I said.

'Yeah, me too,' said Jam.

Chapter Thirty-Three

Nana had obviously been thinking about the appropriate welcoming dinner for a while. Jamilla offered to help, and of course Nana refused to let her so much as lift a little finger. So Jam trailed her into the kitchen anyway.

The rest of us followed to see what would happen next. Two immovable forces. This was high drama.

'Well all right then, all right,' Nana complained some, but I could tell she was pleased with the company. It allowed her to show off her wares, put us all to work, and test Jamilla at her leisure. She even managed to hum a little of 'Lift Every Voice and Sing' while she worked. And then, so did Jamilla.

'You okay with pork chops in apple gravy, squash casserole, over-creamed potatoes? And you're not allergic to a little cornbread, are you? Or fresh peach cobbler and ice cream?' Nana asked several loaded questions at once.

'Love the pork chops, potatoes, peach cobbler,' Jamilla said as she examined the food. 'Neutral on squash casserole. I make creamed cornbread at home. *My* grandma from Sacramento's recipe. You add creamed corn which makes it extra moist. Sometimes I throw in pork rinds, too.'

'Hmm,' Nana said. 'That sounds pretty good, girl. I'll have to try it.'

'If it ain't broke . . .' Jannie decided to contribute.

'Keep your small mind open,' said Nana, and wagged a crooked pinkie finger at Jannie. 'That's if you ever want it to grow bigger, and don't want to remain a small person all your life.'

'I was just defending your cornbread, Nana,' said Jannie. Nana winked. 'I can take care of myself.'

Dinner was served in the dining room, with Usher, Yolanda Adams and Etta James on the CD player. So far, this was pretty good. Just what the doctor ordered.

'We eat like this every night,' Damon said. 'Sometimes, we even have breakfast out here in the formal dining room,' he told Jamilla. I could tell he already had a little crush on her. Hard not to, I suppose.

'Of course you do, like when the President stops over for tea,' Jamilla said and winked at Damon, then at Jannie.

'He comes here often,' Damon nodded. 'How did you know? My dad tell you?'

'Think I saw it on CNN. We get that on the West Coast, you know. We all have TVs out by our hot tubs.'

Dinner and the small talk were a success – at least I thought so.

The laughter was constant, and mostly relaxed. Little Alex sat in his highchair grinning the whole time. At one point Jamilla pulled Damon out of his seat and they danced a few steps to Aretha's 'Who's Zoomin' Who?'.

Nana finally rose from the table and proclaimed, 'I absolutely forbid you to help with the dishes, Jamilla. Alex can pitch in. That's his job.'

'C'mon, then,' Jamilla said to Jannie and Damon. 'Let's go out front and trade gossip about your daddy. And your Nana! You have questions, I have questions. Let's swap spit. You too, little man,' she said to Alex Jr. 'You're excused from kitchen detail.'

I followed Nana out to the kitchen with about half of the dirty dinnerware stacked in my hands and arms.

'She's pleasant,' Nana said before we got there. 'She's certainly full of life.' Then she started to cackle like one of those pesky crows in the old-time cartoons.

'What's so funny, old woman?' I asked. 'You're really getting a big kick out of yourself, aren't you?'

'I am. Why wouldn't I? You're just dying on the vine to know what I think. Well, surprise, surprise. She's a real sweetheart. I'll give you that, Alex, you pick nice girl-friends. She's a good one.'

'No pressure,' I warned her as I set dirty dishes in the sink and turned on the hot water.

'Why would I do that? I've learned my lesson with you.' Then Nana started to laugh again. She seemed more like her old self. She'd gotten a clean bill of health from her doctor, or so she said.

I went back to the dining room to clear away the rest of the dishes, but I couldn't resist taking a quick peek out the front window to check on Jamilla and the kids.

They were out in the street, tossing around Damon's football. The three of them were laughing. I also noticed that Jamilla had a real good arm, threw a tight, little spiral. She was used to playing with the boys.

Chapter Thirty-Four

Jamilla was staying in the bedroom at the top of the stairs, the room we always kept for special guests – presidents, queens, prime ministers and the like. The kids thought we were doing it for appearances, and we would have, but the unvarnished truth was that Jam and I had never been together that way, never even kissed before the airport reunion. Jamilla was here to find out if things should go any further between the two of us.

She came in through the back door of the kitchen while I was finishing up the dishes. The kids were still playing outside and Nana was straightening up God knows what upstairs. Probably the guest room, but maybe the hall bathroom. Or the linen closet?

'I can't stand it,' I finally said.

'What?' she asked. 'What's wrong?'

'You really want to know?'

'Of course I do. We're buddies, right?'

I didn't answer, but I grabbed hold of Jamilla's shoulders and kissed her on the mouth. Then I kissed her again. I was keeping an eye peeled for the kids.

And Nana, of course.

And Rosie our cat, who is a big gossip too.

Jamilla started to laugh. 'They all think we're doing a lot worse than this – the kids, your grandmother, even that nosey cat.'

'Thinking is different to knowing,' I said.

'I like your family a lot,' Jamilla said as she stared into my eyes. 'I even like the cat. Hiya there, Rosie. You gonna tell everybody about our kisses?'

'I like you,' I said as I held Jamilla in my arms.

'A lot?' she asked as she pulled away. 'You better like me a lot after I came all the way here from San Francisco. God, I hate plane rides these days!'

'Maybe I do like you a lot. I don't see you saying too much. Not a lot of reciprocation going on here.'

She grabbed me again and kissed me harder. She pressed into me and then she slid her tongue into my mouth. I liked that – a lot. I was starting to respond in kind, which probably wasn't a fantastic idea in the kitchen.

'Get a room,' we heard a voice behind us.

Nana was there, but she was laughing. 'Let me call in the kids. I want them to see this too,' she said. 'Let me get my Instamatic camera.'

'She's fooling with us,' I told Jam.

'I know,' she said.

'Heck I am,' said Nana. 'I'm rooting for Alex to get to third base.' She was cackling like a cartoon crow again.

Chapter Thirty-Five

I woke up alone in bed the next morning with the sheets thrown every which way around my body. I was kind of used to the feeling, but I didn't like it anymore than I ever had, especially with Jamilla sleeping just down the hallway in the spare bedroom. I hoped she was okay with how things were going and didn't want to go back to San Francisco already.

I lay in bed for a few minutes, thinking about other people who wake up feeling alone, even though some of them do share a bed with somebody else. Finally, I slid into some loose-fitting clothes, then tiptoed down the hall to check on Jamilla.

I tapped lightly on the door.

'I'm awake. Come in,' I heard her say.

It was a nice sound, her voice – musical, sweet. I pushed against the door and it opened with a soft whine.

'Morning, Alex. I slept great,' Jamilla said. She was sitting up in bed, wearing a white tee-shirt with SFPD printed on it in black. She started to laugh. 'Sexy, huh?'

'Actually, yeah. Detectives can be sexy. Samuel T. Jackson in *Shaft*, Pam Grier in *Foxy Brown*. Jamilla Hughes in the guest bedroom.'

She whispered, 'Come over here, you. Just for a minute. Come *here*, Alex. That's an order.'

I came forward and Jamilla reached out her arms. I slid into them like I belonged there. Kind of nice. 'Where were you when I needed you last night?' I asked her.

'I was right here in the guest room,' she smiled, and winked. 'Listen, I don't want your kids to get the wrong idea either. But.'

I cocked an eyebrow. 'But?' I asked. 'But what?'

'Just but. I'll leave the rest up to you.'

As we were finishing breakfast – in the kitchen, without the cloth napkins – I told Nana and the kids that Jamilla and I were going to tour Washington for the rest of the day. We needed a little time to ourselves. The kids just nodded over their cereal bowls; they'd been expecting as much.

'I won't expect you two home for supper then,' Nana said. 'Is that right?'

'That's right,' I said. 'We'll catch a meal in town.'

'Uh huh,' Nana said.

'Uh huh,' said the kids.

I drove about four miles from the house on Fifth. I pulled into 2020 O Street and stopped the car. Some people might have trouble finding the place, or even any information about the Mansion on O Street. There's no sign hanging outside, no indication that it isn't a private residence. Most guests come to the Mansion because of word of mouth. I happen to know the owner through friends at Kinkead's restaurant in Foggy Bottom.

Jamilla and I went inside, where I registered, and then we were brought upstairs to the Log Cabin room. Along the way, just about every surface, corner, cranny and crevice was filled with antique puppets, lithographs, jewelry in glass cases. We took it all in. Silently.

A strange thing happened to me on our way upstairs. I had the thought, *here I go again*. It almost caused me to stop walking and head back to the car. But something inside told me not to give up, not to shut feelings out, to put my trust in Jamilla.

Neither of us said a word until the bellman was gone.

Chapter Thirty-Six

'**W**ow, I could get used to this in a hurry,' Jamilla whispered when we were alone in the room. 'Let's explore this place. It's beautiful, perfect, Alex. Almost too nice.'

And so we explored.

The Log Cabin room was an amazing two stories that even included a sauna-Jacuzzi. The loft was reached by spiral stairs and had a full kitchen. The walls and floors were wood-paneled to suggest the simply hewn tongue-and-groove design of a cabin. A rough-cut, stone-framed fireplace was there to keep everything cozy. There was also an aquarium.

Jamilla did a quick, gleeful dance. She obviously approved, and so did I, mainly because she was happy. It sure was a whole lot better than the front seats of cars where we'd spent so many hours together during surveillance details in New Orleans.

As we checked out the suite, we explored each other a little, too. We stopped to kiss and I discovered once again that Jamilla had the sweetest-tasting mouth. We held each other and danced in place. We kissed some more and my head began to feel light. I was still nervous, and I couldn't quite figure out why.

Jamilla slowly unbuttoned my denim shirt and I helped her loosen and then slip out of a cream-colored silk blouse. Under her shirt, she wore a plain, thin, silver chain. Very simple and lovely.

Her hands gently unfastened my belt, then loosened my pants. I helped her out of her leather ones. 'Such a gentleman,' she said. Somewhere along the way I kicked off my shoes and she did the same with her sandals.

Which finally, somehow, brought the two of us to the centerpiece of the suite – a king-size bed.

'I like this,' she whispered against my cheek. 'Nicest bed I ever saw.'

The bed was definitely the visual focus of the room. It had four wooden columns suggesting a canopy bed, but without the frills. It was covered with a flannelly comforter and half a dozen throw pillows, which we immediately tossed onto the floor. The room looked even better a little messed-up.

'Music?' Jamilla asked.

'Be nice,' I said. 'You pick something.'

She switched on the CD player and found WPFW, 89.3. Nina Simone's 'Wild Is The Wind' was playing.

'Our song. From now on,' she said.

Jamilla and I kissed again and her mouth was soft. I was happy to see that the homicide inspector had a gentle side. Her lips continued to press into mine and I felt myself melting. Maybe that was why I was afraid. *Here I go again.*

'I'd never hurt you,' she whispered, as if she knew my thoughts. 'You don't have to be afraid. Just don't hurt me, Alex.'

'I won't.'

A few minutes later, we were dancing to 'Just The Two Of Us' and I folded Jam in real close. This was good.

She was strong, but she knew how to be tender. *Another detective. How about that?* We moved well together. My lips brushed the tops of her shoulders, then the hollow in her throat, and just lingered.

'Bite me there. Just a little,' she whispered.

I nipped her gently, slowly. I didn't want to hurry any of this. The first time with someone wasn't like any other. Not always the best, but always different, exciting, mysterious. Jamilla reminded me of my dead wife Maria, and I thought that was a good thing. She was tough on the outside, a city girl, but she could be tender and sweet. The contrast was special, and dramatic enough to give me goosebumps.

I could feel her breasts touch my chest, then her whole body was pressing into me. Our kisses became deeper and more passionate, and lasted longer.

I undid her bra and it slipped to the floor. Then I slid off her panties and she pulled down my shorts.

We stood there and looked at each other for a long time, appraising, admiring I guess, building up anticipation and passion and whatever else was going on between us. I wanted Jamilla badly now, but I waited. *We* waited.

'Disappointed?' she whispered, so low I almost couldn't hear what she said.

JAMES PATTERSON

Her question threw me a little. 'God no. Why should I be? Who could be disappointed with you?'

She didn't say anything, but I thought I knew who she was thinking about. Her ex-husband had said things that had hurt her. I pulled Jamilla to me and her body felt hot all over. She was trembling. We slid down on the bed and she rolled on top of me. She kissed my cheeks, then my lips. 'You sure you're not disappointed?'

'Definitely not disappointed,' I said. 'You're beautiful, Jamilla.'

'In your eyes.'

'Okay. In my eyes, you're beautiful.'

I raised my head to her breasts and she lowered herself to me. I kissed one, then the other, playing no favorites. Her breasts were small, just right. In my eyes. I continued to be amazed that Jamilla didn't seem to know that she was attractive. I knew it was a terrible thing that happened to some women, and some men, too.

I lay my head down and looked at her face, studied it some. I kissed her nose, her cheeks.

She was smiling in a way I'd never seen before. Open and relaxed, beginning to trust, which I loved to see. I felt that I could stare into her deep brown eyes forever.

I eased myself inside Jamilla, and I had a thought that this was just about perfect. I had been right to trust her. Then I had another thought that I hated – *what will spoil it this time?*

Chapter Thirty-Seven

J amilla started to laugh and then she said, 'Phew.' She ran her hand past her forehead.

'What's "phew"?' I asked her. 'Don't tell me you're tuckered out? You look in a lot better shape than that.'

'*Phew*. I was worried about the two of us being together, and now I'm not worried. *Phew*, sometimes men are really self-centered or rough in bed. Or it just feels all wrong.'

I smiled at her. 'Slept with a lot of men, huh?'

Jamilla made a little face. Cute. 'I'm thirty-six years old. I was married for four years, engaged another time. I date some. Not too much lately, but some. How about you? Was I your first?'

'Why? Did it seem like it?'

'Answer the question, smart guy.'

'I was married once, too,' I finally said.

Jamilla lightly punched my shoulder, then she rolled over on top of me. 'I'm really glad I came to Washington. Took a little nerve on my part. I was definitely scared.'

'*Oohh*, Inspector Jamilla Hughes was scared. Well, so was I,' I admitted.

'How come? What scared you about me, Alex?'

'Some women are so self-centered. Or rough in bed—'

Jamilla leaned over and kissed me – a long, lingering kiss – probably to shut me up. I was ready again, and so was she. Jamilla pulled me close and I moved inside her. This time I was on top.

'I am your love slave. Completely submissive,' she whispered against my cheek. 'I'm definitely glad I came to Washington.'

Our second time together was even better than the first, and also edged out the third time. *No, there had been nothing for either of us to be afraid of.*

Jamilla and I stayed at the hotel through the afternoon and into the early evening. It was almost impossible to leave. As it had been right from the start with the two of us, we found it easy to talk about anything on the planet.

'I'll tell you something really strange,' she said. 'And the more I'm with you, the stranger this seems to me. See, my first husband and I could never really talk. Not the way you and I do. And we still got married. I don't know what I was thinking.'

A little while later, Jamilla got up and disappeared into the bathroom. I saw the light go on the telephone on the night stand. She was making a call.

Once a detective . . . oh boy. Here we go.

When she came out, she confessed, 'I had to call work. Murder case I'm on out there is a mess. Nasty stuff. Sorry, sorry. Won't happen again. I promise. I'll be good. Or bad.

Whatever you want me to be.'

'No, no, it's fine. I understand,' I said. I did, of course. Sort of, anyway. I saw so much of myself in Jamilla. The detective! I *think* that was a good thing.

I hugged her and held her close once she got back into bed. Then the truth finally came out. It was my turn to confess. 'Long time ago,' I told her, 'I was at this hotel with my wife.'

Jamilla pulled back a little. She looked deeply into my eyes. 'That's okay,' she said. 'Doesn't mean anything. Except I really love that you were guilty about it. That's nice. I'll always remember that about my trip to Washington.'

'Your first trip,' I said.

'My first trip,' Jamilla agreed.

Chapter Thirty-Eight

Our time together in Washington raced by like a couple of blinks of the eye, and before I knew it Jamilla had to go back to San Francisco. Sunday afternoon at a very crowded Reagan International. Fortunately, my badge got me out to the gate area. I was bummed to see her leave, and I didn't think she wanted to go, actually. The two of us hugged for a long time at the gate and we didn't much care if anyone was staring.

Then Jam had to run to her plane or miss it.

'Why don't you just stay another night?' I asked. 'Lots of planes tomorrow. And the next day. Day after that.'

'I really, *really* liked this,' she said as she pulled away from me and started to back-pedal. 'Bye, Alex. Please miss me. I liked Washington more than I thought I would.'

A flight attendant followed her in and closed the door between us. Jeez, I even liked the way Jamilla ran. She glided. And I did miss her already. I was starting to fall again and that scared me.

That night at home I was up long after midnight. At one

particularly low point I went out to the sun porch and sat at the piano playing a pretty pathetic 'Someone To Watch Over Me', thinking about Jamilla Hughes, romanticizing like hell, loving every painful second of it.

I wondered what was going to happen to the two of us. Then I remembered something Sampson had once said. *Don't ever be Alex's girlfriend. It's dangerous.* Unfortunately, he had been right so far.

A few minutes later, I became aware of banging on the screen door out front. I went around and found Sampson leaning against the doorjamb. He didn't look real good. Actually, he looked awful.

Chapter Thirty-Nine

He was unshaven, his clothes wrinkled, his eyes red and swollen. I had the feeling he'd been drinking. Then I opened the door and smelled liquor all over him, as if he'd taken a bath in the stuff.

'Figured you'd be up,' he slurred out a few words. 'Knew you would be.'

Yeah, he'd been drinking – a lot. I hadn't seen John like this in a long time, maybe ever. He didn't look real happy either.

'C'mon inside,' I said. 'C'mon John.'

'Don't need to go anywhere,' he said loudly. 'Don't need any more help from you. You helped enough, man.'

'What the hell is wrong with you?' I said, and tried to guide him inside the house again.

He shook loose, his long, powerful arms flailing. *'What did I say? I don't need your help!'* he yelled at me. 'You already fucked up enough. The great Dr Cross! Yeah, right. Not this time. Not for Ellis Cooper.'

I took a step back away from him. 'Keep your voice

down. Everybody's sleeping inside. You hear me?'

'Don't tell me what the hell to do. Don't you fucking dare,' he snarled. 'You fucked up. We fucked up, but you're supposed to be so smart.'

Finally I told Sampson, 'Go home and sleep it off.' I shut the door on him. But he pulled it open again, almost took the damn thing off its hinges.

'Don't walk away from me either!' he yelled.

Then he shoved me hard. I let it go, but Sampson pushed again. That was when I lunged at him. I'd had enough of his drunken shit. The two of us tumbled down the wood steps and onto the lawn. We wrestled on the ground and then he tried to throw a punch. I blocked it. Thank God he was too messed-up to throw a straight punch.

'You fucked up, Alex. You let Cooper die!' he yelled in my face as we both struggled to our feet.

I refused to hit him, but he struck out at me again. The punch connected with my cheek. I went down as if I didn't have any legs. I sat there, stunned, my eyes glazing over.

Sampson pulled me up, and by this time he was gasping and wheezing. He tried for a headlock. Christ, he was strong. He connected with a short, hard punch to the side of my face. I went down again but struggled back up. We were both groaning. I hurt where he'd hit me on the point of my cheekbone.

He threw a roadhouse punch that missed by an inch. Then a hard blow caught my shoulder and made it ache. I warned myself to stay away from him. He had me by four inches and forty pounds. He was drunk, angry, insane as I'd ever seen him.

But he wouldn't stop coming at me. Sampson was filled with rage. I had to take him down if I could. Somehow. But how?

Finally I hit him with an uppercut to the stomach. I jabbed his cheek. Drew blood. Then I fired a short right hand into his jaw. That one had to hurt.

'Stop it! Stop it right now! Both of you, stop!'

I heard the voice ringing in my ear. 'Alex! John! Stop this disgraceful behavior. Stop it, you two. Just *stop* it!'

Nana was pulling the two of us apart. She was wedged in between us like a small but determined referee. She'd done it before, but not since I was twelve years old.

Sampson straightened up and looked down at Nana. 'Sorry,' he mumbled. 'I'm sorry, Nana.' He looked ashamed.

Then he stumbled away without saying a word to me.

Chapter Forty

I came down to breakfast the next morning at a little
before six. Sampson was sitting there eating eggs and
his personal favorite, *farina*. Nana Mama was across from
him at the table. Just like old times.

They were talking quietly, as if sharing a deep secret
that no one else should know.

'Am I interrupting?' I asked from the doorway.

'I think we have it sorted out now,' Nana said.

She motioned for me to come sit at the breakfast table.
I poured coffee first, popped in four slices of whole-wheat
toast, and then finally sat across from Nana and Sampson.

He had a big glass of milk propped in front of him. I
couldn't help remembering back to when we were kids.
Two or three mornings a week he'd show up at around
this time to break bread with Nana and me. Where else
could he go? His mom was a junkie. In a way, Nana had
always been like a mother or grandmother to him too. He
and I had been like brothers since we were ten. That's why
the fight the night before was so disturbing.

'Let me talk, Nana,' he said.

She nodded and sipped her tea. I'm pretty sure why I chose psychology for a career, and who my original role model was. Nana has always been the best shrink I've seen. She's wise, and compassionate for the most part, but tough enough to insist on the truth. She also knows how to listen.

'I'm sorry, Alex. I didn't sleep last night. I feel awful about what happened. I was way over the line,' Sampson said. He was staring into my eyes, forcing himself not to look away.

Nana watched the two of us as if we were Cain and Abel sitting at her breakfast table.

'You were over the line all right,' I said. 'That's for sure. You were also crazy last night. How much did you drink before you came over?'

'John told you he was sorry,' Nana said.

'Nana,' he turned to her, then back to me. 'Ellis Cooper was like a brother to me. I can't get over the execution, Alex. In a way, I'm sorry I went to see it. He didn't kill those women. I thought we could save him, so it's my fault. I expected too much.'

He stopped talking.

'So did I,' I said. 'I'm sorry we failed. Let me show you something. Come upstairs. This is about payback now. There's nothing left but payback.'

I brought Sampson to my office in the attic of the house. I had notes on Army murder cases pinned all over the walls. The room looked like the hideout of a madman, one of my obsessive killers. I took him to my desk.

'I've been working on these notes since I met Ellis Cooper. I found two more of these remarkable cases. One in New Jersey, the other in Arizona. The bodies were *painted*, John.'

I took Sampson through the cases, sharing everything. 'During the past year more than sixty soldiers have been murdered.' I finished up.

'Sixty?' Sampson said, and shook his head. 'Sixty murders a year?'

'Most of the violence has to do with sex and hate crimes,' I said. 'Rapes and murders. Homosexuals who've been beaten or killed. A series of vicious rapes by an Army sergeant in Kosovo. He didn't think he'd get caught because there was so much rape and killing going on there anyway.'

'Were any other bodies painted?' he wanted to know.

I shook my head. 'Just the two cases I found, New Jersey and Arizona. But that's enough. It's a pattern.'

'So what do we really have?' Sampson shook his head and looked at me.

'I don't know yet. It's hard to get information out of the Army. Something very nasty going on. It looks like soldiers may have been framed for murders. The first was in New Jersey, the latest seems to be Ellis Cooper. There are definite similarities, John. Murder weapons found a little too conveniently. Fingerprints and DNA used to convict.

'All of these men had good service records. In the Arizona murder-case transcripts, there was a mention of "two or three men" seen near the victim's house before

the homicide took place. There's a possibility that innocent men have been framed and then wrongfully put to
death. Framed, then wrongfully executed. And I know
something else,' I said.

'What's that?'

'These killers aren't brilliant like Gary Soneji or Kyle
Craig. But they're every bit as deadly. They're expert at
what they do, and what they do is kill and get away with
it.'

Sampson frowned and shook his head. 'Not anymore.'

Chapter Forty-One

Thomas Starkey had been born in Rocky Mount, North Carolina, and he still loved the area passionately. So did most of his neighbors. He'd been away for long stretches while he was in the Army, but now he was back to stay, and to raise his family as best he possibly could. He knew that Rocky Mount was a great place to bring up kids. Hell, he'd been brought up here, hadn't he?

Starkey was devoted to his family, and he genuinely liked the families of his two best friends. He also needed to control everything around him.

Just about every Saturday night, Starkey got the three clans together and they barbecued. The exception was the football season, when the families usually had a tailgate party on Friday night. Starkey's son Shane played tailback for the high school. North Carolina, Wisconsin and Georgia Tech were after Shane, but Starkey wanted him to put in a tour with the Army before he attended college. That's what *he* had done, and it had worked out for the best. It would work for Shane, too.

The three men usually did all the shopping and cooking for the Saturday night barbecues and the tailgate parties. They bought steaks, ribs, hot and sweet sausages at the farmers' market. They selected corn on the cob, squash, tomatoes, asparagus. They even made the salads, usually German potato, coleslaw, macaroni and, occasionally, Caesars.

That Friday was no exception, and by seven-thirty the men were in their familiar positions beside two Weber grills, staying downwind from the wafting smoke, drinking beer, cooking every meal 'to order'. Hell, they even cleaned up and did the dishes. They were proud to deliver the food just right, and to get pretty much the same kind of applause given to their sons on football nights.

Starkey's number two, Brownley Harris, tended to intellectualize. He'd attended Wake Forest and then gone to grad school at UNC. 'The irony is pretty thick here, don't you think?' he asked as he gazed at the family scene.

'Fuck all, Brownie, you'd see irony in a turkey shoot, or a clusterfuck in a rice paddy. You think too goddamn much,' Warren Griffin said, and rolled his eyes. 'That's your problem in life.'

'Maybe you just don't think enough,' Harris said, then winked at Starkey, who he considered a god. 'We're going off to kill somebody this weekend, and here we are calmly barbecuing thick sirloin steaks for our families. You don't think that's a little strange?'

'I think you're fucking strange is what I think. We've got a job to do, so we do it. No different than the way it was for a dozen years in the Big Army. We did a job in

Vietnam, in the Persian Gulf, Panama, Rwanda. It's a job. Of course – I happen to love my job. Might be some irony in that. I'm a family man and a professional killer. So what of it? Shit happens, it surely does. Blame the US Army, not me.'

Starkey nodded his head toward the house, a two-story with five bedrooms and two baths he'd built in 1999. 'Girls are coming,' he said. 'Put a lid on it.

'Hey, beautiful,' he called, then gave his wife, Judie, a big hug. Judie 'Blue Eyes' was a tall, attractive brunette who still looked almost as good as she had on the day they were married. Like most of the women in town, she spoke with a pronounced Southern accent, and she liked to smile a lot. Judie even did volunteer work three days a week at the playhouse. She was funny, appreciative, a good lover, and a good life partner. Starkey believed he was lucky to have found her, and she was lucky to have chosen him. All three of the men loved their wives, up to a point. Hell, that was another juicy irony for Brownley Harris to ponder late into the night.

'We must be doing something right,' Starkey said as he held Judie in his arms and toasted the other couples.

'You sure did,' Judie 'Blue Eyes' said. 'You boys married well. Who else would let their husbands sneak off for a weekend every month or so, and trust that they were being good boys out there in the big, bad world?'

'We're always good. Nobody does it better,' Starkey said, and smiled good-naturedly at his closest friends in the world. 'It doesn't get any better than this. It really doesn't. We're the best there is.'

Chapter Forty-Two

On Saturday night the three killers made their way north to a small town in Virginia called Harpers Ferry. During the road trip, Brownley Harris's job was to study maps of the AT, as the Appalachian Trail was called by many of the people who hiked it regularly. The spot where they were headed was a particularly popular place for hikers to stop.

Harpers Ferry was tiny, actually. You could walk from one end of town to the other in less than fifteen minutes. There was a point of tourist interest nearby called Jefferson Rock, where you could see Maryland, Virginia, and West Virginia. Kind of neat.

Starkey drove for the entire trip, no need for any relief. He liked to be at the wheel and in control anyway. He was also in charge of entertainment, which consisted of his *Best of Springsteen* tape, a Janis Joplin, a Doors, a Jimi Hendrix anthology, and a Dale Brown audiobook.

Warren Griffin spent almost the entire trip checking the team's supplies and readying the rucksacks in back. When he was finished, the packs weighed around forty pounds, a little more than half of what they used to carry on their re-con missions in Vietnam and Cambodia.

He had prepared the packs for a 'hunt and kill', the kind of ambush Colonel Starkey had planned for the Appalachian Trail. Griffin had packed standard-issue canteens; LRPs – meals which were pronounced 'lurps'; hot sauce to kill the taste of the LRPs; a tin can for coffee. Each of them would have a K-Bar, the standard military combat knife; cammo sticks, with two colors of greasepaint; boony hats; poncho liners that could do double duty as ground cover; night-vision goggles; Glocks as well as an M-16 rifle fitted with a sniper scope. When he was finished with the work, Griffin uttered one of his favorite lines, 'If you want to get a good belly laugh out of God, just tell Him about your plans.'

Starkey was the TL, or Team Leader. He was in control of every aspect of the job.

Harris was the Point Man.

Griffin was Rear Security, still the junior guy after all these years.

They didn't have to do the 'hunt and kill' exactly like this. They could have made it a whole lot easier on themselves. But this was the way Starkey liked it, the way they had always committed their murders. It was 'the Army way'.

Chapter Forty-Three

They made camp about two clicks from the AT. It was dangerous for them to be seen by anybody so Starkey established an NDP, a Night Defense Position, for the camp. Then they each kept watch in two-hour shifts. *Nostalgia rules.*

When Starkey took his shift, he passed the time thinking not so much about the job looming ahead of them, but the job in general. He, Harris and Griffin were professional killers and had been for over twenty years. They'd been assassins in Vietnam, Panama, the Gulf War, and now they were assassins for hire. They were careful, discreet and expensive. The current job was their most lucrative and involved several murders over a period of two years. The curious thing about it was they didn't know the identity of their employer. They were given new targets only after the previous job was completed.

As he stared into the dark, restless woods, Starkey wanted a cigarette, but he settled for an Altoids. Those little fuckers kept you awake. He found himself thinking about the blonde bitch they had offed near Fayetteville, pretty Vanessa. The memory got him hard and that helped the time pass. While they were still in Vietnam, Starkey had discovered that he liked to kill. The murders gave him a powerful feeling of control and elation. It was like electricity was passing through his body. He never felt guilt, not anymore. He killed for hire; but he also killed in between jobs, because he wanted to, and liked it.

'Strange, scary stuff,' Starkey muttered as he rubbed his hands together. 'Scare myself sometimes.'

The three of them were up and ready by five the next morning, which was shrouded in a thick, bluish-gray fog. The air was cool, but incredibly fresh and clean. Starkey figured the fog wouldn't burn off until at least ten.

Harris was in the best physical shape of the three, so he was designated as the scout. He wanted the job anyway. At fifty-one, he still played in a men's basketball league and did triathlons twice a year.

At 5:15 he set off from camp at a comfortable jogging pace. Christ, he loved this shit.

Nostalgia.

Harris found that he was wide awake and alert once he was on the move. He was operating beautifully after just a few minutes on the trail. The hunt and kill was a satisfying combination of business and pleasure for him, for all three of them.

Harris was the only person around this early on the AT, at least this particular stretch of it. He passed a four-person dome tent. Probably some white-bread family. Most likely 'section hikers' as opposed to 'through hikers' who would take up to six months to do the entire trail, finally ending at a place called Katahdin, Maine. Around the dome tent he noticed a camp stove and fuel bottles, ratty shorts and tee-shirts laid out to air. *Not a target*, he decided, and moved on.

Next, he came upon a couple in sleeping bags laid just off the trail. They were young, probably 'go see the world' types. They slept on inflatable air mattresses. All the comforts of home.

Harris got up close, no more than ten yards from them, before he finally decided to move on. He could tell the girl was a looker, though. Blonde, cute face, maybe twenty. Just watching her sleep with her boyfriend got his jets going pretty good. They were a definite maybe.

He saw a second couple already up and exercising near their tent about a quarter mile farther on. They had high-tech internal frame packs, $200 hiking boots, and looked like snooty city slicks. He liked them as potential targets, mainly because he *disliked* them so much immediately.

Not far past the couple's camp, he came upon a single male hiker. This guy was definitely in for the long haul. He had a high-tech pack which looked light and tight. He would probably be carrying dried food, trail mix, protein drink powder – fresh food was too heavy and difficult to haul around on your back all day. His wardrobe would be no frills too – nylon shorts, tank tops, maybe long under-wear for the cold nights.

Harris stopped and watched the single hiker's camp for a couple of minutes. He let his heartbeat slow and con-trolled his breathing. Finally, he slipped right into the man's camp. He wasn't afraid, and he never doubted himself. He took what he needed. The hiker never stirred from his sleep.

Harris checked his sports watch and saw it was only 5:50. So far, so good. He walked back to the trail, then he began to jog again. He felt invigorated, excited about the hunt and kill out here on the nature trail. Man, he wanted to kill somebody bad. Man or woman, old or young, it didn't much matter.

The next camp he came upon was close – another couple, still asleep in a two-person dome tent. Harris couldn't help thinking how easy it would be to take them out right now. Ducks on a pond. Everybody was so vulnerable and trusting out here. What a bunch of loonies. Didn't they ever read the funny papers? There were killers on the loose in America, lots of them.

A little less than a mile beyond, he reached the camp of another family. Someone was already up.

He hid in the pine trees and watched. A fire had been started and was throwing up sparks. A woman of about forty was futzing around with a rucksack. She wore a red Speedo swimsuit and seemed in good physical shape – well-muscled arms and legs; a nice ass, too. She called out, 'Wakee, wakee!'

Moments later, two shapely teenage girls emerged from the larger tent. They had on one-piece bathing suits, and they were slapping their lithe bodies with their arms and hands, trying to get warm in a hurry, trying to 'wakee, wakee'.

'Mama bear and two baby bears,' Brownley Harris

muttered. 'Interesting concept.' Maybe too close to the murders at Bragg, though.

He watched as the three women huddled for a moment around the fire, then took off at a run. Soon he could hear a chorus of war whoops and screams, then laughter and loud splashes as they hit the small brook that ran directly behind their camp.

Brownley Harris moved quickly and silently through the trees until he reached a choice point where he could watch the mother and her pretty daughters frolic in the cold stream. They sure reminded him of the women in the massacre in Fayetteville, outside Fort Bragg. Still, they could be the secondary target.

He returned to his camp at a little past six-thirty. Griffin had prepared breakfast: eggs, bacon, plenty of coffee. Starkey was sitting in a familiar lotus position, thinking and plotting. He opened his eyes before Harris announced himself. 'How'd you do?' he asked.

Brownley Harris smiled. 'We're right on schedule, Colonel. We're good. I'll describe the targets while we eat. Coffee smells good. Hell of a lot better than napalm in the morning.'

Chapter Forty-Four

Starkey took full command that morning. Unlike the other hikers on the AT, he kept his men deep in the woods, unseen by their fellow travelers or anyone else.

It wasn't hard to do. In their past lives they'd spent days, sometimes weeks, being invisible to enemies who were out to find and kill them, but who frequently ended up getting killed themselves. One time it had been a team of four homicide detectives in Tampa, Florida.

Starkey demanded that they treat this like a real-life combat mission, in real-life war. Total silence was imperative. They used hand signals most of the time. If someone had to cough, he did so in his neck rag, or in the crook of an arm. Their rucksacks had been packed tight by Sergeant Griffin so that nothing shook or rattled as they walked.

The three of them had slathered on bug juice, then laid on the cammo. They didn't smoke a cigarette all day.

No mistakes.

Starkey figured that the kill would take place some-where between Harpers Ferry and an area known as Lowdown Heights. Parts of the trail were densely forested there, an endless green tunnel that would be good for their purposes. The trees were mostly deciduous, leafy, no conifers. A lot of rhododendron and mountain laurel. They noticed everything.

They didn't actually make camp that night, and were careful not to leave evidence that they had been in the woods at all.

Brownley Harris was sent on another scouting mission at seven-thirty, just before it got dark. When he returned, the sun was gone and darkness had fallen like a shroud over the AT. The woods had a kind of jungle feel, but it was only an illusion. A state road ran about half a mile from where they were standing.

Harris reported in to Starkey. 'Target One is approx-imately two clicks ahead of us. Target Two is less than three. Everything's still looking good for us. I'm pumped.'

'You're always ready for a hunt and kill,' said Starkey. 'But you're right, everything's working for us. Especially this friendly, trust-your-neighbor mindset all these rec-reational hikers have.'

Starkey made the command decision. 'We'll move to a point midway between Targets One and Two. We'll wait there. And remember, let's not get sloppy. We've been too good for too long to blow it all up now.'

Chapter Forty-Five

A three-quarter moon made the going easier through the woods. Starkey had known about the moon beforehand. He wasn't just a control freak; he was obsessive about details because getting them wrong could get you killed, or caught. He *knew* they could expect mild temperatures, low wind and no rain. Rain would mean mud, and mud would mean a lot of footprints, and footprints would be unacceptable on their mission.

They didn't speak as they moved through the woods. Maybe it wasn't necessary to be so cautious out here, but it was habit, the way they had been conditioned for combat. A simple rule had always been drummed into them: *remember how you were trained, and don't ever try to be a hero.* Besides, the discipline helped them to concentrate. Their focus was on the killings that would soon take place.

The three men were in their own private worlds as they walked: Harris fantasized about the actual kills with real-life faces and bodies; Starkey and Griffin stayed very real time, and yet they hoped that Harris wasn't pulling their chain with his description of the targets. Starkey remembered one time Brownley had reported the prey was a Vietnamese schoolgirl, whom he went on to describe in elaborate detail. But when they got to the kill zone, a small village in the An Lao Valley, they found an obese woman well into her seventies, with black warts all over her body.

Their reveries were cut short by a male voice piercing the air.

Starkey's hand flew up in warning.

'Hey! Hey! What's going on? Who's out there?' the voice called. 'Who's there?'

The three of them stopped in their tracks. Harris and Griffin looked at Starkey, who kept his right arm raised. No one answered the unexpected voice.

'Cynthia? Is that you, sweetie? Not funny if it is.'

Male. Young. Obviously agitated.

Then a bright yellow light flashed in their direction, and Starkey walked forward in its path. 'Hey,' was all he said.

'What the hell? You guys Army?' the voice asked next. 'What are you doing out here? You training? On the Appalachian Trail?'

Starkey finally flicked on his Maglite flashlight. It lit up a white male in his early twenties, khaki walking shorts down around his ankles, a thick roll of toilet paper in one hand. Skinny kid. Longish black hair. A day's growth on his face. Not a threat.

'We're on maneuvers. Sorry to barge in on you like this,' Starkey said to the young man squatting before him. He chuckled lightly, then turned to Harris. 'Who the hell is he?' he whispered.

'Couple Number Three. Shit. They must have fallen behind Target Two.'

'All right then. Change of plan,' Starkey said. 'I'll take care of this.'

'Yes, sir.'

Starkey felt a coldness in his chest and knew that the others probably did too. It happened in combat, especially when things went wrong. The senses became heightened. He was acutely aware of everything going on, even at the periphery of his eyesight. His heartbeat was strong, even, steady. He loved these intense feelings, just before it happened.

'Can I get a little privacy here?' the shitter asked. 'You guys mind?'

A brighter light suddenly flashed on – Brownley Harris was shooting another video movie.

'Hey, is that a fucking camera?'

'Sure is,' Starkey said. He was on top of the crouching, shitting man before he knew what was happening. He picked the victim up by his long hair and slit his throat with the K-Bar.

'What's the woman like?' Griffin turned to Harris, who was still shooting with the hand-held camera.

'Don't know, you horny bastard. The girlfriend was sleeping this morning. Never saw her.'

'Boyfriend wasn't bad-looking,' said Griffin. 'So I'm hopeful about the chick. Guess we'll soon find out.'

Chapter Forty-Six

Sampson and I were riding on I-95 again, heading toward Harpers Ferry, Virginia. There had been a brutal double murder on the Appalachian Trail near there. So far, it didn't make sense to the FBI or the local police. But it made perfect sense to us. *The three killers had been there.*

We hadn't had this much time to talk in a long while. For the first hour we were cops discussing the murder victims, two hikers on the AT, and any possible connection to Ellis Cooper or the victims in Arizona and New Jersey. We had read the investigating detective's notes. The descriptions were bleak and horrific. A young couple in their twenties, a graphic artist and an architect, had had their throats slit. Innocents. No rhyme or reason for the murders. Both of the bodies had been marked with red paint, which was why I got the call from the FBI.

'Let's take a break from the mayhem for a while,' Sampson finally said. We had reached the halfway point of our ride south.

'Good idea. I need a break, too. We'll be knee-deep in the shit soon enough. What else is going on? You seeing anybody these days?' I asked him. 'Anybody serious? Anybody fun?'

'Tabitha,' he said. 'Cara, Natalie, LaTasha. You know Natalie. She's the lawyer with HUD. I hear your new girlfriend from San Francisco came to visit last weekend. *Inspector* Jamilla Hughes, *Homicide*.'

I laughed. 'Who told you about that?'

John furrowed his brow. 'Let's see. Nana told me. And Damon. And Jannie. Little Alex might have said something. You thinking about settling down again? I hear this Jamilla is something else. Is she too hot for you to handle?'

I continued to laugh. 'Lot of pressure, John. Everybody wants me to get hooked up again. Get over my unlucky recent past. Settle down to a nice life.'

'You're good at it. Good daddy, good husband. That's how people see you.'

'And you? What do you see?'

'I see all that good stuff. But I see the dark side, too. See, part of you wants to be old Cliff Huxtable. But another part is this big, bad, lone wolf. You talk about leaving the police department, maybe you will. But you like the hunt, Alex.'

I looked over at Sampson. 'Kyle Craig told me the same thing. Almost the same words.'

Sampson nodded. 'See? Kyle's no dummy. Sick, twisted bastard, but not dumb.'

'So, if I like the hunt so much, who's going to settle down first? You or me?'

'No contest. My role models on families are bad ones. You know that. Father left when I was three. Maybe he had his reasons. My mother was never around much. Too busy hooking, shooting up. They both knocked me around. Beat up on each other, too. My father broke my mother's nose three times.'

'Afraid you'll be a bad father?' I asked. 'Is that why you never settled down?'

He thought about it. 'Not really. I like kids fine. Especially when they're yours. I like women, too. Maybe that's the problem – I like women too much,' Sampson said, and laughed. 'And women seem to like me.'

'Sounds like you know who you are anyway.'

'Good deal. Self-knowledge is a start,' Sampson said, and grinned broadly. 'What do I owe you, Dr Cross?'

'Don't worry about it. I'll put it on your tab.'

I saw a road sign up ahead: Harpers Ferry, two miles. A man was being held there for murder.

A former Army colonel with no past record.

And currently a Baptist minister.

I wondered if anyone had seen three suspicious-looking men in the area of the murder? And if one of them had been filming what happened?

Chapter Forty-Seven

Sampson and I met with Reverend Reece Tate in a tiny room inside the modest jailhouse in Harpers Ferry. Tate was a slight, balding man with shaped sideburns down to the bottoms of his earlobes; he didn't look much like a former soldier. He had retired from the Army in 1993 and now headed a Baptist congregation in Cowpens, South Carolina.

'Reverend Tate, can you tell us what happened to you yesterday on the Appalachian Trail?' I asked him after identifying who we were. 'Tell us everything you can. We're here to listen to your story.'

Tate's suspicious eyes darted from Sampson to me. I doubt he was even aware of it, but he kept scratching his head and face as he looked around the small room. He also looked terribly confused. He was obviously nervous and scared and I couldn't blame him for that, especially if he'd been set up and framed for a double murder he didn't commit.

'Maybe you can answer a few of my questions first,' he

155

managed. 'What are homicide detectives from Washington DC doing here in Virginia? I don't understand that. Or anything else that's happened in the last two days.'

Sampson looked at me. He wanted me to explain. I began to tell Tate about our connection to Ellis Cooper and the murders that had taken place near Fort Bragg.

'You actually believe that Sergeant Cooper is innocent?' he asked when I was finished.

I nodded. 'Yes, we do. We think he was framed, set up. But we don't know the reason yet. We don't know why and we don't know who.'

Sampson had a question. 'You and Ellis Cooper ever meet while you were in the Army?'

Tate shook his head. 'I was never stationed at Bragg. I don't remember a Sergeant Cooper from 'Nam. No, I don't think so.'

I tried to remain low key. Reece Tate was an uptight, buttoned-down and formal man, so I kept our conversation as non-threatening as I possibly could.

'Reverend Tate, we've answered your questions. Why don't you answer a few of ours? If you're innocent of these murders, we're here to help you out of this mess. We'll listen, and we'll keep an open mind.'

He looked thoughtful for a moment before he spoke. 'Sergeant Cooper, he was judged guilty, I assume. Is he in prison? I'd like to talk with him.'

I looked at Sampson, then back at Reece Tate. 'Sergeant Cooper was executed in North Carolina recently. He's dead.'

Tate shook his head in a soft, low arc. 'My God, my God

in heaven. I was just taking a week off, giving myself a break. I love to camp and hike. It's a carryover from my days in the Army, but I always loved it. I was a Boy Scout, an Eagle Scout in Greensboro. Sounds kind of ridiculous, under the circumstances.'

I let him talk. The Eagle Scout in him wanted to, *needed* to get this out.

'I've been divorced for four years. Camping is my only decent escape, my release. I take off a couple of weeks a year, plus a few weekends when I can grab them.'

'Did anybody know you were planning this trip?'

'Everyone at our church knew. A couple of friends and neighbors. It wasn't any big secret. Why should it be?'

Sampson asked, 'Did your ex-wife know?'

Tate thought about it, then he shook his head. 'We don't communicate very much. I might as well tell you, I beat Helene up before we divorced. She may have driven me to it, but I hit her. It's on me, my fault. No excuse for a man to ever strike a woman.'

'Can you tell us about the day of the murders. Go through as much of what you did as you can remember,' I said.

It took Tate about ten minutes to take us through the day in detail. He said he woke up at about seven and saw that the morning was fogged in. He was in no hurry to get on the trail and so he had breakfast at camp. He started hiking by eight-thirty and covered a lot of ground that day. He passed two families and an elderly couple along the way. The day before, he'd seen a mother and her two daughters and hoped to catch up with them, but it didn't happen. Finally he made camp at around six.

'Why did you want to catch up with the three women?' Sampson asked.

Tate shrugged. 'Just crazy daydreams. The mother was attractive, early forties. Obviously, they all liked to hike. I thought maybe we could hike together for a while. That's pretty common on the AT.'

'Anybody else you saw that day?' Sampson asked.

'I don't remember anybody unusual. I'll keep thinking. I have the time in here. And the motivation.'

'All right, so there were the families, the elderly couple, the mother and her two daughters. Any other groups you saw on the trail? Males hiking together? Any single hikers?'

He shook his head. 'No, I don't remember seeing anybody suspicious. Didn't hear any unusual noises during the night. I slept well. That's one benefit of hiking. Got up the next morning, hit the road by seven-thirty. It was a beautiful day, clear as a bell and you could see for miles. The police came and arrested me around noon.'

Reverend Tate looked at me. His small eyes were pleading, searching for understanding. 'I swear, I'm innocent. I didn't hurt anybody in those woods. I don't know how I got blood on some of my clothes. I didn't even wear those clothes the day those poor people were murdered. I didn't kill anybody. Somebody has to believe me.'

His words chilled me through and through. Sergeant Ellis Cooper had said virtually the same thing.

Chapter Forty-Eight

My last case as a homicide detective. A real tricky one. I'd been thinking about it pretty much non-stop for the past few days and it weighed on my mind during the numbing ride home from Harpers Ferry, Virginia.

I still hadn't given notice at work. Why not? I continued to take on homicide cases in DC, though most weren't challenging. A small-time drug dealer had been killed in the projects, but nobody cared. A twenty-year-old woman had killed her abusive husband, but it was clearly in self-defense. At least to me it was. Ellis Cooper was dead. And now a man named Reece Tate was accused of murders that he probably didn't commit.

That weekend I used air miles and took a flight out to Tempe, Arizona. I'd scheduled a meeting with Susan Etra, whose husband had been convicted of murdering two gay enlisted men. Mrs Etra was suing the Army for wrongful death. She believed her husband was innocent, and that she had enough evidence to prove it. I needed to find out if Lieutenant Colonel James Etra might have been framed for murder, too. How many victims were there?

Mrs Etra answered her front door and seemed very uptight and nervous. I was surprised to see a poker-faced man waiting in the living room. She explained that she had requested her lawyer be present. *Great.*

The lawyer was darkly tan, with slicked-back white hair, an expensive-looking charcoal-gray suit and black cowboy boots. He introduced himself as Stuart Fischer from Los Angeles. 'In the interest of possibly getting to the truth about her husband's wrongful arrest and conviction, Mrs Etra has consented to talk with you, Detective. I'm here to protect Mrs Etra.'

'I understand,' I said. 'Were you Lieutenant Colonel Etra's lawyer at his trial?' I asked.

Fischer kept his game face. 'No, I wasn't. I'm an entertainment attorney. I do have experience with homicide cases, though. I started in the DA's office in Laguna Beach. Six years down there.'

Fischer went on to explain that Mrs Etra had recently sold her husband's story to Hollywood. Now I was the one who had to be careful.

For a half-hour or so, Susan Etra told me what she knew. Her husband, Lieutenant Colonel Etra, had never been in any trouble before. As far as she knew he'd never been intolerant of gays, men or women. And yet he had supposedly gone to the home of two gay enlisted men and shot them dead in bed. At the murder trial, it was alleged that he was hopelessly in love with the younger of the two men.

'The murder weapon was an Army service revolver. It

was found in your home? It belonged to your husband?' I asked.

'Jim had noticed the revolver was missing a couple of days before the murder. He was very organized and meticulous, especially when it came to his guns. Then, suddenly, the gun was conveniently back in our house for the police to find.'

Lawyer Fischer apparently decided I was harmless enough and he left before I did. After he was gone, I asked Mrs Etra if I could take a look at her husband's belongings.

Mrs Etra said, 'You're lucky that Jim's things are even here. I can't tell you how many times I've thought about bringing his clothes to a local charity group like Goodwill. I moved them into a spare bedroom. Far as I've gotten.'

I followed her down the hall to a spare room. Then she left me alone. Everything was neat and in its place, and I had the impression that this was how Susan and James Etra had lived before murder and chaos destroyed their lives. The furniture was an odd mix of blond wood and darker antiques. A war table against one wall was covered with collectible pewter models of cannons, tanks and soldiers from various wars. Next to the models was a selection of guns in a locked display case. They were all labeled.

1860 Colt Army revolver, .44 caliber, 8-inch barrel.

Springfield Trapdoor rifle, cartridge, used in the US/Indian Wars. Has original bayonet and leather sling.

Marlin rifle, circa 1893, black powder only.

I opened the closet next. Lt Colonel Etra's clothes were

divided between his civvies and Army uniforms. I moved on, checking the various cabinets.

I was rummaging through the drawers of a highboy when I came upon the straw doll.

My stomach tightened. The creepy doll was the same kind I'd found at Ellis Cooper's place outside Fort Bragg. Exactly the same – as if they'd been bought at the same place. By the same person? *The killer?*

Then I found the watchful, lidless eye in another drawer. It seemed to be watching me. Vigilant, keeping its own nasty secrets.

I took a deep breath, then I went outside and asked Mrs Etra to come to the spare room. I showed her the straw doll and the all-seeing eye. She shook her head and swore she'd never seen either before. Her eyes revealed her confusion, and fear.

'Who *was in my house?* I'm sure that doll wasn't here when I moved Jim's things,' she insisted. 'I'm positive. How could they have gotten here? Who put those dreadful things in my house, Detective Cross?'

She let me take the doll and the eye. She didn't want them around, and I couldn't blame her.

Chapter Forty-Nine

Meanwhile, the murder investigation continued on another front. John Sampson turned his black Mercury Cougar off Route 35 in Mantoloking on the Jersey Shore and headed in the general direction of the ocean. Point Pleasant, Bay Head and Mantoloking were connecting beach communities and, since it was October, they were fairly deserted.

He parked on East Avenue and decided to stretch his legs after the drive up from Washington.

'Jesus, what a beach,' he muttered under his breath as he walked up a public access stairway and reached the crest of the dunes. The ocean was right there, less than forty yards away, if that.

The day was just about perfect. Low seventies, sunny, cloudless blue sky, the air unbelievably clear and clean. Actually, he thought, it was a better beach day than people got for most of the summer, when all these shore towns were probably jammed full of beachgoers and their transportation.

He liked the scene stretching out before him a lot. The quiet, pretty beach town made him feel relaxed. Hard to explain, but recently his days on the job in DC seemed tougher and more gruesome than usual. He was obsessing about Ellis Cooper's death, his *murder*. His head was in a real bad place lately. That wasn't true here, and it had happened instantly. He felt that he could hear and see things with unusual clarity.

He figured he better get to work, though. It was almost three-thirty, and he had promised to meet Billie Houston at her house at that time. Mrs Houston's husband had allegedly killed another soldier at nearby Fort Monmouth. The victim's face had been painted white and blue.

Let's do it, he told himself as he opened a slatted gate and walked toward a large, brown-shingled house on a path strewn with seashells. The beach house and the setting seemed too good to be true. He even liked the sign: *Paradise Found.*

Mrs Houston must have been watching for him from inside the beach house. As soon as his foot touched down on the stairs, the screen door swung open and she stepped outside to meet him.

She was a small African-American woman, and more attractive than he'd expected. Not movie-star beautiful, but there was something about her that drew his attention and held it. She was wearing baggy khaki shorts with a black tee-shirt, and was bare-footed.

'Well, you certainly picked a nice day for a visit,' she said, and smiled. Nice smile, too. She was tiny, though, probably only five feet tall, and he doubted that she weighed much more than a hundred pounds.

'Oh, it isn't like this every day?' Sampson asked, and managed a smile himself. He was still recovering from his surprise at Mrs Houston as he mounted her creaking, wooden porch steps.

'Actually,' she said, 'there are a lot of days like this one here. I'm Billie Houston. But of course you knew that.' She put out her hand. It was warm and soft in his, and so small.

He held her hand a little longer than he'd meant to. Now why had he done that? He supposed it was partly because of what she'd been through. Mrs Houston's husband had been executed nearly two years earlier, and she'd proclaimed his innocence loudly and clearly until the end, and then some. The story felt familiar. Or maybe it was because there was something about the woman's ready smile that made him feel comfortable. She impressed him about as much as the town and the fine weather had. He liked her immediately. Nothing not to like. Not so far anyway.

'Why don't we walk and talk on the beach,' she suggested. 'You might want to take off your shoes and socks first. You're a city boy, right?'

Chapter Fifty

Sampson did as he was told. No reason the murder investigation, this interview anyway, couldn't have a few nice perks. The sand felt warm and good against his bare feet as he followed her down the length of the big house, then up and over a tall, broad dune covered with white sand and waving beach grass.

'Your house is sure something else,' he said. 'Beautiful doesn't begin to do it justice.'

'I think so,' she said, and turned to look back at him with a smile. 'Of course, this isn't my house. My place is a couple of blocks inland. One of the small beach bungalows you passed driving in. I house-sit for the O'Briens while Robert and Kathy are in Fort Lauderdale for the winter.'

'That's not such bad duty,' he said. Actually, it sounded like a great deal to him.

'No, it's not bad at all.' She quickly changed the subject. 'You wanted to talk to me about my late husband, Detective. Do you want to tell me why you're here? I've been on pins and needles since you called. Why did you want to see me? What do you know about my husband's case?'

'Pins and needles?' Sampson asked. 'Who says pins and needles anymore?'

She laughed. 'I guess I do. It just came out. Dates and locates me, right? I grew up on a sharecropper's farm in Alabama, outside Montgomery. Not giving you the date. So *why* are you here, Detective?'

They had started down a sandy hill sloping toward the ocean which was all rich blues and greens and creamy foam. It was unbelievable – hardly a soul either way he looked up or down the shoreline. All of these gorgeous houses, practically mansions, and nobody around but the seagulls.

As they walked north he told Mrs Houston about his friend Ellis Cooper, and what had happened at Fort Bragg. He decided not to tell her about the other murders of military men.

'He must have been a very good friend,' she said when Sampson had finished talking. 'You're obviously not giving up easily.'

'I *can't* give up. He was one of the best friends I ever had. We spent three years in Vietnam together. He was the first older male in my life who wasn't just out for himself. You know, the father I never had.'

She nodded, but she didn't pry. Sampson liked that. He still couldn't get over how petite she was. He had the thought that he could have carried her around under his arm.

'The other thing is, Mrs Houston, I am totally convinced that Ellis Cooper was innocent of those murders. Call it sixth sense, or whatever, but I'm sure of it. He told me so just before they executed him. I can't get past that. I just can't.'

She sighed, and he could see the pain in her face. He could tell she hadn't gotten over her husband's death and how it had happened, but she still hadn't intruded on his story. That was interesting. She was obviously very considerate.

He stopped walking, and so did she.

'What's the matter?' she finally asked.

'You don't talk about yourself easily, do you?' he asked.

She laughed. 'Oh, I do. When I get going, I do. Too much sometimes, believe me. But I was interested in what you had to say, how you would say it. Do you want me to tell you about my husband now? What happened to him? Why I'm sure he was innocent, too?'

'I want to hear everything about your husband,' Sampson said. 'Please.'

'I believe Laurence was murdered,' she began. 'He was killed by the state of New Jersey. But somebody else wanted him dead. I want to know who murdered my husband, as much as you want to know who killed your friend, Ellis Cooper.'

Chapter Fifty-One

S ampson and Mrs Billie Houston stopped and sat in the sand in front of a sprawling ocean house that must have at least a dozen bedrooms. It was empty now, boarded up and shuttered, and that seemed such a monumental waste to Sampson. He knew people in DC who lived in abandoned tenements with no windows and no heat and no running water.

He couldn't peel his eyes away. The house was three stories high with wraparound decks on the upper two. A large sign posted on the dune near the house read: *These dunes are protected. Stay on walkway. $300 fine.* These people were serious about their property, or its beauty, or both, he thought to himself.

Billie Houston stared out at the ocean as she began to speak.

'Let me tell you about the night the murder happened,' she said. 'I was a nurse at the Community Medical Center in Tom's River. I got off my shift at eleven and arrived home at about half past. Laurence almost always waited up for me. Usually we'd catch up on each other's day. Sit on the couch. Maybe watch a little TV together, mostly comedies. He was a big man like you, and always said he could carry me around in his pocket.'

Sampson didn't interrupt, just listened to her story take shape.

'What I remember the most about that night was that it was so *ordinary*, Detective. Laurence was watching *The Steve Harvey Show* and I leaned in and gave him a kiss. He sat me on his lap and we talked for a while. Then I went in to change out of my work clothes.

'When I came out from the bedroom, I poured myself a glass of Cabernet, and asked him if he wanted me to make popcorn. He didn't. He'd been watching his weight, which sometimes ballooned in the winter. He was in a playful mood, jokey, very relaxed. He wasn't tense, wasn't stressed in any way. I'll never forget that.

'The doorbell rang while I was pouring my glass of wine. I was up anyway, so I went to get it. The military police were there. They pushed past me into the house and arrested Laurence for committing a horrible murder that night, just a few hours earlier.

'I remember looking at my husband, and him looking at me. He shook his head in absolute amazement. No way he could have faked that look. Then he said to the police, "You officers are making a mistake. I'm a sergeant in the United States Army". That's when one of the cops knocked him down with his baton.'

Chapter Fifty-Two

I was trying to forget that I was on a case. Carrying around a nasty straw doll and lidless evil eye. In pursuit of killers. Relentless as I had ever been.

I walked into the lobby of the Wyndham Buttes Resort in Tempe and there was Jamilla. She had flown east from San Francisco to meet me. That had been our plan.

She was wearing an orange silk blouse with a deeper orange sweater around her shoulders, slender gold bracelets and tiny earrings. She looked just right for the 'valley of the sun', which is what I'd heard the metropolitan area of Phoenix, Scottsdale, Mesa, Chandler and Tempe was called.

'I suspect you already know this,' I said as I walked over and gave her a big hug, 'but you look absolutely beautiful. Took my breath away.'

'I did?' she asked, and seemed surprised. 'That's a nice way to start our weekend.'

'And I'm not the only one who thinks so. Everybody in the lobby is checking you out.'

She laughed. 'Now I know you're putting me on.'

Jamilla took my hand and we walked across the lobby. Suddenly, I stopped and spun her around into my arms. I looked at her face for a moment, then I gave her a kiss. It was long and sweet because I'd been saving it up on the drive over.

'You look pretty good yourself,' she said after the kiss. 'You always look good. Tell you a secret. The first time I saw you in San Francisco Airport you took *my* breath away.'

I laughed and rolled my eyes. 'Well we better take this upstairs, get a room, before we get in trouble down here.'

Jamilla leaned in and gave me another quick kiss. 'We could get in a whole lot of trouble.' And then another kiss. 'I don't do things like this, Alex. What's happening to me? *What* has come over me?'

One more hug and then we headed for the hotel elevators.

Our room was on the top floor with a view of the Phoenix skyline and a waterfall cascading into a mountainside swimming pool. In the distance, we could see jogging and hiking trails, tennis courts, and a golf course or two. I told Jamilla that a nearby football field we could see must be Sun Devil Stadium. 'I think Arizona State plays there.'

'I want to know all about Tempe and Arizona State football,' Jamilla said, 'but later on.'

'Oh, all right.'

I touched my fingers to her blouse, which was brushed silk. 'This feels nice.'

'It's supposed to.'

I slowly ran my hands over the shirt, Jamilla's shoulders, the tips of her breasts, her stomach. I massaged her shoulders and she leaned up against me and let out a long, 'Mmmm, yessssss, please and thank you.' It was like an impromptu dance, and neither of us knew exactly what was going to happen next. So nice to be back with her again.

'There's no hurry,' she whispered, 'is there?'

'No. We have all the time in the world. You know, this is called entrapment in police circles.'

'Yes, it is. I'm fully aware of that. It's also an ambush. Maybe you ought to just surrender.'

'All right, I surrender, Inspector.'

There was nothing except the two of us. I had no idea where this was going but I was learning to just go along, to enjoy each moment, not to worry too much about the destination.

'You have the softest touch of anyone,' she whispered. 'Unbelievable.'

'So do you.'

'You seem surprised.'

'A little bit,' I admitted. 'It's probably because I saw your tough-as-nails side when we were working together.'

'Is that a problem for you? My tough side?'

'No. It isn't,' I told her. 'I like your tough side. As long as you don't get too rough with me.'

Jam immediately pushed me back onto the bed, then fell on top of me. I kissed her cheeks, then her sweet lips. She smelled and tasted so good. I could feel the pulse under her skin. *There's no hurry.*

'I was a tomboy when I was a kid in Oakland. Baseball player, fast-pitch softball,' she said. 'I wanted my father and my brothers to approve of me.'

'Did they?'

'Oh yeah. Are you kidding? I was all-state in baseball and track.'

'Do they still approve?'

'I think so. Yeah, they do. My pop's a little disappointed I'm not playing for the Giants,' she said, and laughed. 'He thinks I could give Barry Bonds a run.'

Jamilla helped me with my pants while I unhooked her skirt. I shivered, couldn't control it. *All the time in the world.*

Chapter Fifty-Three

When his interview with Mrs Billie Houston was finished, it was too late for Sampson to head back to Washington, plus he liked the atmosphere at the shore, so he checked into Conover's Bay Head Inn, a bed and breakfast in town that Billie had recommended.

He had just stepped into his room on the third floor when the phone rang. He wondered who could be calling him here?

'Yeah?' he spoke into the receiver. 'John Sampson.'

There was a short silence.

'This is Billie. Mrs Houston.'

He sat down on the edge of the bed and found that he was surprised, but he was smiling. He definitely hadn't expected the call, hadn't expected to hear from her again. 'Well, hi. I haven't spoken to you . . . in minutes. Did you forget to tell me something?'

'No. Well, yes I did, actually. Here you are helping Laurence, and I do absolutely nothing to make your visit more comfortable. Would you have dinner at the house tonight? I've already got food in, so please don't say no. What do you have to lose? I'm a good cook, by the way.'

Sampson hesitated. He wasn't sure this was such a good idea. It wasn't that he thought dinner with Billie Houston would be a chore. It was just, well, a potentially uncomfortable situation, maybe a conflict of interest.

Still, the way she'd put it, what choice did he have? And what real harm could it do?

'That's a fine idea. I'd like to have dinner at the house. What time should I come by?'

'Whatever suits you is fine. It's nothing fancy, Detective. I'll start up the grill as soon as you arrive.'

'How about an hour? Is that all right? I'm John, by the way. Not Detective.'

'I think you told me that. You already know I'm Billie, and if you don't mind, I prefer that to Mrs Houston. I'll see you in about an hour.'

She hung up, and Sampson held onto the receiver for another few seconds. Now that he thought about it, dinner with Billie Houston didn't seem like a bad idea. He was looking forward to it as he stepped out of his clothes and headed for the shower.

Nothing fancy sounded pretty good.

Chapter Fifty-Four

S ampson picked up a small bouquet of flowers and a bottle of red at Central Market in Bay Head. As he got to the beach house, he wondered if he was overdoing it. *Flowers? Wine? What was going on here?*

Was he feeling guilty about the fact that this woman's husband might have been murdered? Or that she was a widow before her time? Or did it have something to do with Ellis Cooper? Or was this just about Billie Houston and himself?

He went round to the screen door that led into the kitchen of the beach house. He rapped his knuckles lightly on the wooden frame.

'Hi? Billie?' he called out.

Billie? Was that how he should be talking to her?

He had no idea why, but he was concerned for her safety. Yet no one would want to hurt Billie Houston now, would they? Still, he felt what he felt. The real killers were out there somewhere. Why not here in New Jersey?

'Door's open. C'mon in,' she called. 'I'm out on the porch.'

He came in through the kitchen and saw her setting a small dining table on the open front porch facing the ocean. Beautiful spot for dinner. Adirondack chairs, a wicker rocker painted navy blue to match the shutters.

He could see the ocean over the top of the dunes and the constantly waving sea grass.

But his eyes went back to her. She had on a crisp white shirt with faded Levi's, no shoes again. Her hair was clipped back in a ponytail. She'd put on a little lipstick, just a touch.

'Hi there. I thought that we'd eat out here. It's not too cold for you, is it?' she asked with a wink.

Sampson stepped out onto the spacious wood porch. The breeze was coming from inland, but it was comfortable outside. He could smell the ocean, but also sea lavender and asters in the air.

'It's just about perfect,' he said. That was true. The temperature was just right, as was the table she'd set, and the view of the ocean was definitely something else. There sure wasn't anything like this in Southeast DC.

'Let me do something to help,' he said.

'Good idea. You can chop vegetables and finish up the salad. Or you can cook on the grill.'

Sampson found himself smiling. 'Not much of a choice there. I'll do the salad. Nah, I'm kidding. I'd be happy to grill. Just so long as I don't have to wear a hat or apron with a snappy slogan on it.'

She laughed. 'Don't have any of those. You passed a CD player on your way from the kitchen. I left a bunch of CDs out. Pick what you like.'

'This a test?' he asked.

Billie laughed again. 'No, you already passed all your tests. That's why I asked you to supper. Stop worrying about me and you. We won't break. This is going to be fun. Better than you think.'

Chapter Fifty-Five

She was right about the night being special. It embarrassed him, but he just about forgot Ellis Cooper for several hours. Sampson was usually quiet unless he knew somebody pretty well. Part of it was shyness, because he'd always been so tall and stood out in every social group. But he was honest enough with himself to know he didn't want to waste time on people who didn't mean anything to him, and never would.

Billie was different and he knew it, from the first time she spoke to him. The surprising thing about her was that he liked hearing her talk about anything. Her daily routine in Mantoloking; her two grown children – Andrew, a freshman at Rutgers, and Kari, a senior at Monmouth; the ocean tides and how they affected surf-casting for blues; a half dozen other things. In addition to the house-sitting, she still worked full-time as a nurse. She was in the Emergency Clinic and specialized in adult trauma. She'd flown in Med-Evac helicopters to the larger trauma units in Newark and

Philadelphia. Once upon a time, she'd even worked as a MASH unit nurse.

They didn't discuss her husband until after dinner. Sampson brought the subject up again. It had gotten cooler and they'd moved back into the living room. Billie started a fire, which was crackling and popping and warming things up inside.

'Do you mind if we talk about Laurence for a few more minutes?' he asked as they sat together on a small couch near the fire. 'We don't have to do this now if you don't want to.'

'No, it's okay. It's fine, really. That's why you came here.'

Suddenly, something caught Sampson's eye. He rose up from the couch and walked to a glass case near the fireplace. He reached inside and took out a straw doll.

Now this was definitely very strange. He examined it closely. He was sure it was a replica of the one he'd seen in Ellis Cooper's house. It scared him because it was in Billie's house. *What was the doll doing here?*

'What is it?' she asked. 'What is that creepy doll? I don't remember seeing it before. Is something wrong? You look so serious suddenly.'

'I saw this same doll at Ellis Cooper's house,' he admitted. 'It's from Vietnam. I saw lots of them in villages over there. Something about evil spirits and the dead. These dolls are bad medicine.'

She came over to the glass cabinet and stood beside him. 'May I see, please?' She examined the straw doll and shook her head. 'It looks like something Laurence might have brought home, I suppose. A souvenir.

Memento mori. I honestly don't remember ever seeing it, though. Isn't that strange. It reminds me – the other day I found a big, ugly eye in that same cabinet. It was so . . . *evil* I tossed it.'

Sampson held her gaze. 'Strange coincidence,' he said, shaking his head. He was thinking that Alex refused to believe in coincidences. 'As far as you remember, your husband never mentioned Sergeant Ellis Cooper?' he asked.

Billie shook her head. She seemed a little spooked now. 'No. He rarely talked about the war. He didn't like it when he was there. He liked it even less once he came back and had time to think about his combat experiences.'

'I can understand that. When I got back to DC I was stationed at Fort Myers in Arlington for a couple of months. I came home in my dress greens one Saturday. I got off a bus in downtown Washington. A white girl in bellbottom jeans and sandals came up and spat on my uniform. She called me a baby murderer. I'll never forget that for the rest of my life. I was so angry I turned and walked away as fast as I could. The hippie girl had no idea what happened over there, what it's like to get shot at, to lose friends, to fight for your country.'

Billie clasped her hands together and slowly rocked back and forth. 'I don't know what to tell you about Laurence. I think you probably would have liked him. Everybody did. He was very responsible, a good father to our children. He was a thoughtful, loving husband. Before he died, and I'm talking twenty minutes before he was executed, I sat with him in the prison. He stared into my eyes and said, "I did not kill that young man. Please make sure our kids know that. Make sure, Billie." '

'Yeah,' Sampson said. 'Ellis Cooper said something like that, too.'

It got quiet in the living room. A little uncomfortable for the first time.

Finally, Sampson was compelled to speak. 'I'm glad you called, Billie. Tonight was great for me. Thank you. I need to go now. It's getting late.'

She was standing beside him and she didn't move. Sampson leaned down and kissed her cheek. God, she was so tiny.

'You *do* think I'll break,' she said, but then she smiled. 'That's all right.'

She walked him out to his car. They felt compelled to talk again, mostly about the night sky over the ocean, how expansive and beautiful it was.

Sampson got into the Cougar and Billie started to walk back to the house. He watched her, and he felt sorry that the night was ending and he'd probably never see her again. He was also a little worried about her. How had the straw doll gotten into her house?

She stopped at the stairs to the house, one hand on the banister. Then, almost as if she'd forgotten something, she walked back to his car.

'I, uhm,' she said, then stopped. She seemed nervous for the first time since they'd met. Unsure of herself.

Sampson took her hands in his. 'I was wondering if I could have another cup of coffee,' he said.

She laughed lightly and shook her head. 'Are you always this gallant?'

Sampson shrugged. 'No,' he said. 'I've never been this way in my whole life.'

'Well, c'mon back inside.'

Chapter Fifty-Six

It was almost midnight and Jamilla and I were up to our necks in the shimmering mountain pool that looked down on Phoenix in the distance and on the desert up closer. The sky over our heads seemed to go on forever. A big jet took off from Phoenix and all I could think of was the tragedy at the World Trade Center. I wondered if any of us would ever be able to look at a jet in the sky without having that thought.

'I don't want to get out of this water. Ever,' she said. 'I love it here. The desert sky goes on and on.'

I held her close to me, felt her strong heart beating against my chest. The night air was cool and it made being in the pool feel even better.

'I don't want to leave here either,' I whispered against her cheek.

'So why do we do what we do? Live in the big city? Hunt killers? Work long hours for low pay? Obsess on murders?'

I looked into her deep brown eyes. Those were good questions, ones I'd asked myself dozens of times, but especially during the past few months. 'It always seems like a good idea at the time. But not right now.'

'You think you can ever quit? Get past the adrenalin? The need to feel that what you do matters. I'm not sure that I can, Alex.'

I had told Jamilla that I was probably going to leave the police force in Washington. She nodded and said she understood, but I wondered if she really did. How many times had she faced down killers? Had any of her partners died?

'So,' she said, 'we've been beating all around it. What do you think about us, Alex? Is there hope for two cops off the beat?'

I smiled. 'I think we're doing great. Of course, that's just me.'

'I think I agree,' she smiled. 'Too early to tell for sure, right? But we're having fun, aren't we? I haven't thought about being a detective all day. That's a first.'

I kissed her lips. 'Neither have I. And don't knock fun. I could use a lot more of it in my life. This beats solving homicides.'

'Really, Alex?' She grinned and pulled me close against her. 'Is this good for you. Well, it's good for me, too. That's enough for right now. I love being here. I love tonight. And I trust you, Alex.'

I couldn't have agreed more.

At a little before midnight.

In the mountainside pool overlooking Phoenix and the sprawl of the desert.

'I trust you, too,' I said as the big American Airlines jet passed right over our heads.

PART THREE

THE FOOT SOLDIER

Chapter Fifty-Seven

I got back to Washington on Sunday night at eleven. There was more of a bounce in my step and a smile plastered on my face. I'd forgotten about the rigors of the murder investigation for a couple of days and Jamilla was the reason why.

Nana was waiting up in the kitchen. What was this? She sat at the table without her usual cup of tea and with no book to read. When she saw me come in, she waved me over and gave me a hug. 'Hello, Alex. You have a good trip? You say hello to Jamilla for me? You better.'

I looked down into her brown eyes. They seemed a little sad. Couldn't hide it from me. 'Something's wrong.' Fear had grabbed at me already. Was she sick? How sick?

Nana shook her head. 'No, not really, sweetheart. I just couldn't sleep. So tell me about the trip. How was Jamilla?' she asked, and her eyes brightened. Nana definitely liked Jamilla. No hiding that either.

'Oh, she's good and she says hello too. She misses everybody. I hope I can get her to come East again, but you know, she's a California girl at heart.'

Nana nodded. 'I hope she comes back,' she said. 'Jamilla is a real strong woman. You've met your match with that one. I won't hold it against her that she's from out West. Anyway, I guess Oakland is more like DC than San Francisco. Don't you think?'

'Oh, absolutely.'

I continued to look into Nana's eyes. I didn't get it. She wasn't giving me a hard time like she usually does. What was up? We were quiet for the next minute or so. Unusual for us. We usually jabber back and forth until one of us surrenders.

'You know, I'm eighty-two years old. I never felt like I was seventy, or seventy-five, or even eighty. But Alex, suddenly I feel my age. I'm *eighty-two*. Give or take.'

She took my hand in hers and squeezed it. The sadness was back in her eyes, maybe even a little fear. I felt a lump in my throat. Something was wrong with her. What was it? Why wouldn't she tell me?

'I've had a pain lately, in my chest. Shortness of breath. Angina or whatever. Not so good, not so good.'

'Have you seen Dr Rodman? Or Bill Montgomery?' I asked.

'I saw Kayla Coles. She was in the neighborhood treating a man a few houses down from us.'

I didn't understand. 'Who's Kayla Coles?'

'Dr Kayla makes house calls in Southeast. She's organized about a dozen doctors and nurses who come into the neighborhood to help people here. She's a fabulous doctor and a good person, Alex. She's doing a lot of good in Southeast. I like her tremendously.'

I bristled a little.'Nana, you're not some charity case. We have money for you to see a doctor of your choice.'

Nana squeezed her eyes shut.'Please. Listen to me. And pay attention to what I'm saying. I'm eighty-two and I won't be around forever. Much as I'd like to be. But I'm taking care of myself so far, and I plan to keep doing it. I like and trust Kayla Coles. She *is* my choice.'

Nana got up slowly from the table, kissed me on the cheek and then she shuffled off to bed. At least we were fighting again.

Chapter Fifty-Eight

L ater that night, I went up to my attic office. Everyone was asleep and the house was quiet.

I liked working when it was peaceful like this. I was back on the Army case; I couldn't get it out of my mind. The bodies painted in bright colors. The eerie straw dolls. The even spookier all-seeing eyes. Innocent soldiers punished by wrongful executions.

And who knew how many more soldiers might be scheduled for execution?

There was plenty of material to go through. If even some of these executions were linked, it would be a huge bombshell for the Army. I continued my research, did some spade work on the straw doll and the evil eye. I did a search on Lexus-Nexus, which held information from most local and national newspapers and the major international ones. A lot of detectives underestimate the usefulness of press research, but I don't. I have solved crimes using information passed to the press by police officers.

I read reports about a former PFC in Hawaii. He'd been accused of murdering five men during a sex-slavery-and-torture spree that occurred from 1998 to 2000. He was currently on death row.

I moved on. I felt I had no choice but to keep going on the case.

An Army captain had killed two junior officers in San Diego less than three months ago. He'd been convicted and was awaiting sentencing. His wife was lodging an appeal. He'd been convicted on the basis of DNA evidence.

I made a note to myself: *Maybe talk to this one.*

My reading was interrupted by the sound of footsteps peppering the stairs up to the attic.

Someone was coming up.

In a hurry.

Adrenalin fired through my system. I reached into a desk drawer and put my hand on a gun.

Suddenly Damon burst into the room. He was soaked with sweat and looked like hell. Nana had told me he was asleep in his room. Obviously that hadn't been the case. He hadn't even been in the house, had he?

'Damon?' I said as I rose. 'Where have you been?'

'Come with me, Dad. Please. It's my friend. Ramon's sick! Dad, I think he's dying.'

Chapter Fifty-Nine

We both ran down to my car and Damon told me what had happened to his friend Ramon on the way. His hands were shaking badly as he spoke.

'He took E, Dad. He's been doing E for a couple of days.'

E was one of the latest drugs of choice around DC, especially among high school and college kids at George Washington and Georgetown.

'Ramon hasn't been going to school?' I asked.

'No. He hasn't been going home either. He's been staying at a crib down by the river. It's in Capitol Heights.'

I knew the river area and I headed there with a red lamp on my car roof and a siren bleating. I had met Ramon Ramirez, and I knew about his parents: they were musicians, and addicts. Ramon played baseball with Damon. He was twelve. I wondered how deeply Damon was involved, but this wasn't the time for questions like that.

I parked, and Damon and I walked into a dilapidated

row house down near the Anacostia. The house was three stories and most of the windows were boarded.

'You been in this place before?' I asked Damon.

'Yeah, I was here. I came to help Ramon. I couldn't just leave him, could I?'

'Was Ramon conscious when you left him?' I asked.

'Yeah. But his teeth were clenched together and then he was throwing up. His nose was bleeding.'

'Okay, let's see how he is. Keep up with me.'

We hurried down a dark hallway and turned a corner. I could smell the stench of garbage and also a recent fire.

Then I got a surprise. Two EMS techs and a doctor were in a small room; they were working over a boy. I could see Ramon's black sneakers and rolled-up cargo pants. Nothing moved.

The doctor rose from her kneeling position over Ramon. She was tall and heavy-set, with a pretty face. I hadn't seen her around before. I walked up to her, showed my badge, which didn't seem to impress her much.

'I'm Detective Cross,' I said. 'How is the boy?'

The woman focused hard on me. 'I'm Kayla Coles. We're working on him. I don't know yet. Someone called nine-one-one. Did you make the call?' She looked at Damon. I realized she was the doctor Nana had talked about.

Damon answered her question. 'Yes, ma'am.'

'Did you take any drugs?' she asked.

Damon looked at me, then at Dr Coles. 'I don't do drugs. It's dumb.'

'But your friends do? Do you have dumb friends?'

'I was trying to help him. That's all.'

Dr Coles' look was severe, but then she nodded. 'You probably saved your friend's life.'

Damon and I waited in the bleak, foul-smelling room until we heard news that Ramon would make it. This time. Kayla Coles stayed there the whole time. She hovered over Ramon like a guardian angel. Damon got to say a few words to his friend before they took him to a waiting ambulance. I saw him clasp the boy's hands. It was nearly two in the morning when we finally made our way out of the row house.

'You okay?' I asked.

He nodded, but then his body started to shake, and he finally began to sob against my arm.

'It's all right. It's all right,' I consoled him. I put my arm around Damon's shoulders and we headed home.

Chapter Sixty

Thomas Starkey, Brownley Harris and Warren Griffin took separate flights to New York City, all leaving out of Raleigh-Durham Airport. It was safer and a lot smarter that way, and they always worked under the assumption that they were the best, after all. They couldn't make mistakes, especially now.

Starkey was on the five o'clock out of North Carolina. He planned to meet the others at the Palisade Motel in Highland Falls, New York, just outside the United States Military Academy at West Point. There was going to be a murder there. Two murders, actually.

Then this long mission was over.

What was it Martin Sheen's commanding officer had told him in *Apocalypse Now*? *'Remember this, Captain. There is no mission. There never was a mission.'* Starkey couldn't help thinking that this job had been like that for them – a long haul, a relentless nightmare. Each of the murders had been complicated. This was Starkey's fourth trip to New York in the past two months. He still didn't even know who he was working for; he'd never met the bastard.

In spite of everything, he felt confident as the Delta flight took off that evening. He talked to the flight attendant, but avoided the kind of innocent flirting he might do under other circumstances. He didn't want to be remembered, so he stuck his face in a Tom Clancy thriller he'd picked up at the airport. Starkey identified with Clancy characters like Jack Clark and John Patrick Ryan.

Once the jet leveled off and drinks were served, Starkey went over his plan for the final murders. It was all in his head; nothing ever written down. It was in Harris's and Griffin's heads, too. He hoped they didn't get in any trouble before he got to the Point tonight. There was a raunchy strip club in nearby New Windsor called The Bed Room, but they'd promised to stay at the hotel.

Finally, Starkey sat back, closed his eyes and started doing 'the math' again. It was a comforting ritual, especially now that they were close to the end.

$100,000 apiece for the first three hits.

$150,000 for the fourth.

$200,000 for the fifth.

$250,000 for West Point.

$500,000 bonus when the entire job was done.

It was almost over.

And Starkey still didn't know who was paying for the murders, or why.

Chapter Sixty-One

Sharp, steep cliffs of granite overlooked the Hudson River at West Point. Starkey knew the area well. Later that night he drove down the main drag in Highland Falls, passing cheesy-looking motels, pizza shops, souvenir stands. He went through Thayer Gate with its turreted sentry tower and stone-faced MP on guard. *Murder at West Point*, he thought. *Man oh man.*

Starkey put the job out of his mind for another few moments. He let impressions of West Point wash over him. Impressions and memories. Starkey had been a cadet here, been a first-year plebe like the two youngsters he saw jogging back to barracks now. In his day he'd shouted the cadet motto 'Always the hard way, sir!' over a thousand times if he'd shouted it once.

God, he loved it here: the attitude, the discipline, the whole physical plant.

The Cadet Chapel stood high on a hillside overlooking the Plains. A cross between a medieval cathedral and a fortress, it still dominated the entire landscape. The campus was filled with mammoth gray-stone buildings and emphasized the fortress effect. An overwhelming sense of solidarity and permanence. *Soon to be shaken badly.*

Harris and Griffin were waiting for him on the grounds. For the next hour, they took turns watching the Bennett house on Bartlett Loop, an area of West Point reserved for officers and their families. The house was redbrick with white trim and plenty of ivy creeping the walls. Smoke curled lazily from the stone chimney. It was a four-bedroom, two-bath unit. On the housing map it was designated as Quarters 130.

Around nine-thirty the three killers reconnoitered on the seventeenth fairway of the West Point golf course. They didn't see anyone on the hilly course that formed one of the boundaries of the military academy. Route 9-W was just to the west.

'This might be easier than we thought,' Warren Griffin said. 'They're both home. Relaxing. Guard down.'

Starkey looked at Griffin disapprovingly. 'I don't think so. There's a saying here, "Always the hard way, sir". Don't forget it. And don't forget that Robert Bennett was Special Forces. This isn't some big city architect having a sleep-over on the Appalachian Trail.'

Griffin snapped to attention. 'Sorry, sir. Won't happen again.'

Just before ten o'clock, the three of them made their way through the bramble and woods that bordered the backyard of Quarters 130. Starkey pushed back a stubborn branch of a pine tree and saw the house.

Then he spotted Colonel Robert Bennett in the kitchen. War-hero, father of five, husband for twenty-six years, former Special Forces in Vietnam.

Bennett was holding a goblet of red wine and seemed to be supervising the preparation of a meal. Barbara Bennett stepped into view. She was doing the real work. Now she too took a sip of his wine. Robert Bennett kissed the back of her neck. They seemed loving for a couple married well over twenty years. *That's too bad*, Starkey thought, but kept it to himself.

'Let's do it,' he said. 'The last piece in the puzzle.'

And it truly was a puzzle – even to the killers.

Chapter Sixty-Two

Robert and Barbara Bennett were just sitting down to dinner when the three heavily armed men burst through the back door into the kitchen. Colonel Bennett saw their guns, camouflage dress, and also noted that none of the men wore masks. He saw *all of the faces* and knew this couldn't be worse.

'Who are you? Robert, who are they?' Barbara stuttered out a few words. 'What's the meaning of this?'

Unfortunately, Colonel Bennett was afraid that he knew exactly who they were, and maybe even who had sent them. He wasn't sure, but he thought he recognized one of them from a long time ago. He even remembered a name – *Starkey. Yes, Thomas Starkey. Good God, why now? After all these years?*

One of the intruders pulled shut the colorful curtains on the two kitchen windows. He used a free arm to sweep the dinner plates, chicken, salad and wine glasses onto the kitchen floor. Bennett understood this was for dramatic effect.

Another man held an automatic weapon pressed to Barbara Bennett's forehead.

The kitchen was totally silent.

Colonel Bennett looked at his wife and his heart nearly broke. Her blue eyes were stretched wide and she was trembling. 'It's going to be all right,' Bennett said in the calmest voice he could manage.

'Oh, is it, Colonel?' Starkey spoke for the first time. He signaled the third intruder, and the man grabbed the front of Barbara's white peasant blouse and tore it off. Barbara gasped and tried to cover herself. The bastard then yanked off her bra. It was for effect, again, but then the man stared at Barbara's breasts.

'Leave her alone! Don't hurt her!' Bennett yelled, and it sounded like a command, as if he were in a position to give them.

The one he knew to be Starkey hit him with the butt of his handgun. Bennett went down and thought that his jaw was broken. He almost blacked out, but managed to stay conscious. His cheek was pressed into the cold tile of the kitchen floor. He needed a plan – even a desperate one would do.

Starkey stood directly over him. And now it got insane. He spoke in Vietnamese.

Colonel Bennett understood some of the words. He'd done enough interrogations during the war, when he'd run several Kit Carson scouts in Vietnam and Laos.

Then Starkey spoke in English. 'Be afraid, Colonel. You'll suffer tonight. So will your wife. You have sins to pay for. You know what they are. Tonight your wife will know about your past, too.'

Colonel Bennett pretended to pass out. When one of the gunmen leaned over him, he pushed off the floor and grabbed at his handgun. Getting the gun was the only thought in Bennett's brain. *He had it!*

But then he was struck viciously on the head. Then on the shoulders and back. He was being screamed at in Vietnamese as the severe beating continued. He saw one of the bastards punch his wife right in the face. For no reason at all.

'Stop it. Don't hurt her for Christ sakes.'

'May se nkin co ay chet,' Starkey yelled in Vietnamese.

Now you get to watch her die.

'Trong luc tao hoi may.'

While I interrogate you, pig.

'May thay cank nay co quen khong, Robert?'

Does that sound familiar, Robert?

Starkey then forced his pistol inside Colonel Bennett's mouth. 'Remember this, Colonel? Remember what happens next?'

Chapter Sixty-Three

Sampson and I got to West Point at a little past five o'clock on Friday evening. All hell had broken loose there.

I'd received an urgent heads-up from Ron Burns at the FBI. There'd been a murder-suicide at the Point that had immediately aroused suspicions when the news got to Quantico. A highly decorated colonel had supposedly killed his wife, then himself.

Sampson and I flew into Stewart Field in Newburgh, then I drove eighteen miles by car to West Point. We had to park our rented car and walk the last several blocks to the officers' housing.

The streets were roped off and closed to through traffic. The press was on hand, but they were being kept away by military police. Even the cadets couldn't help looking curious and concerned.

'You're getting chummy with Burns and the FBI,' Sampson said as we walked to the murder scene on Bartlett Loop. 'He's giving a lot of help.'

'He has it in his head that I might want to work with them,' I told Sampson.

'And? Might you?'

I smiled at Sampson, didn't confirm or deny.

'I thought you were getting out of police work, sugar. Wasn't that the big master plan?'

'I don't know anything for sure right now. Here I am though, headed to another completely fucked-up murder scene with you. Same shit, different day.'

'So you're still hooked, Alex. Bad as ever, right?'

I shook my head. 'No, I'm not *hooked* on the case, John. I'm helping you out. Remember how this started? Payback for Ellis Cooper?'

'Yeah, and you're also hooked. You can't figure out this puzzle. That makes you angry. And curious as hell. That's who you are, Alex. You're a hunter.'

'I yam what I yam,' I shook my head and finally smiled, 'said Popeye the sailor man. The killers were here, John. The three of them were here.'

Chapter Sixty-Four

The Bennett house was roped off and secured. Sampson and I identified ourselves to a nervous-looking MP at the perimeter of the crime scene. I could tell that he'd never seen anything like this before. Unfortunately, I had.

After we put on disposable paper boots, we were permitted to climb three stone steps that led into the house. Then we went looking for a CID officer named Pat Conte. The Army was 'cooperating' because of the other cases. They'd also let in a couple of FBI techs to show their good faith.

I found Captain Conte in the narrow hallway leading from the living room. The murders had apparently taken place in the kitchen. Techies were dusting for fingerprints and photographing the scene from every angle.

Conte shook hands and then he told us what he knew, or thought that he knew at this point.

'All I can give you so far is the obvious. From the looks of things, Colonel Bennett and his wife were engaged in an argument that seems to have turned violent. For a while, she must have given as good as she got. Then Bennett retrieved his service revolver. He shot her in the temple, then shot himself. Friends say that he and his wife were close, but that they fought a lot, sometimes violently. As you can see, the shooting took place in the kitchen. Some time last night.'

'That's what you think happened?' I asked Conte.

'At this point, that's my statement.'

I shook my head and felt my anger rising. 'I was told that because of the possible connection between these deaths and the others that we could expect cooperation here.'

Captain Conte nodded. 'That's what you just got, my full cooperation. Excuse me, I have work here.' He walked away.

Sampson shrugged as we watched the CID officer shuffle off. 'Can't say that I blame him too much. I wouldn't want you and me messing around at my crime scene either.'

'So, let's go mess around.'

I went over to see if I could get anything from the FBI people, the *Evidence Response Team*, also known as ERTs. They were being their usual thorough selves in the kitchen, where the murders had taken place. Given the normal level of dislike for the FBI, it's remarkable how much respect is given to ERTs. The reason is, they're very, very good.

Two members of the ERTs were taking Polaroid shots in the kitchen. Another, wearing a white coverall called a 'bunny suit', was looking for fibers and hairs using an alternative light source. Everybody had on rubber gloves and paper booties over their shoes. The head man was named Michael Fescoe, and I had already met him down on the Appalachian Trail, where he had supervised the crime scene investigation in the woods.

'CID giving you their full cooperation too?' I asked.

He scratched his light brown crew cut. 'I can tell you my version, and it's a little different from Captain Conte's.'

'Please,' I said.

Fescoe began, 'The killers, whoever they were, did a thorough job with both the setup and the cleanup. They've done this before. They're professionals through and through. Just like the killers in Virginia.'

'How many of them?' I asked.

Fescoe held up three fingers. 'Three men. They surprised the Bennetts at dinner. And then they murdered them. These men, they bring force to bear without conscience. You can quote me on that.'

Chapter Sixty-Five

It was time to celebrate! The war was over. Starkey, Harris and Griffin ordered obscenely large, very rare Porterhouse steaks topped with jumbo shrimp at Spark's restaurant on West Forty-sixth Street in Manhattan. For anyone with wads of the green stuff, there was no better place to get happy in a hurry than in New York City.

'Three years, but it's finally over,' said Harris, and raised a glass of cognac, his fourth after-dinner drink of the evening.

'Unless our mysterious benefactor changes his mind,' cautioned Starkey. 'It could happen. One more hit. Or maybe a complication that we didn't plan on. Which doesn't mean we shouldn't party tonight.'

Brownley Harris finished his cheesecake and dabbed his mouth with a cloth napkin. 'Tomorrow we go home to Rocky Mount. The good life. That's not so terrible bad. We're finally out of the game, undefeated and unscored on. Nobody can touch us now.'

Warren Griffin just grinned. He was pretty well plowed.

They all were, except Starkey, who said, 'But tonight, we party. We damn well deserve it. Just like the old days, Saigon and Bangkok, Hong Kong. The night is young, and we're full of mischief, piss and vinegar.' He leaned in close to his friends. 'I want to rape and pillage tonight. It's our right.'

After they left the restaurant, the three friends strolled to East Fifty-second, between First and York. The brownstone they stopped at was a walk-up that had seen better days. Four stories. No doorman. Starkey knew it as 'Asia House'.

He rang the front buzzer and waited for the intercom. He had been here before.

A woman answered in a sultry voice. 'Hi. May I have your code please, gentlemen.'

Starkey gave it in Vietnamese. *Silver. Mercedes Eleven.*

They were buzzed inside. '*Xin moi len lau. Cac em dang cho,*' the voice said in Vietnamese. The ladies are waiting, and they are stunning.

'So are we,' Thomas Starkey said, and laughed.

Starkey, Harris and Griffin climbed the flight of red-carpeted stairs. As they reached the first landing, a plain gray door opened.

An Asian girl, slender and young, no more than eighteen, and gorgeous, stood legs akimbo in the doorway. She had on a black bra and matching panties, thigh-high stockings, sling backs with high-heels.

'Hi there,' she said in English. 'I'm Kym. Welcome. You're very good-looking men. This will be fun for us, too.'

'You're very beautiful, Kym,' Starkey said in Vietnamese.

'And your English is flawless.' He then pulled out a revolver and pointed it between the girl's eyes. 'Don't say another word or you die. Right here, right now, Kym. Your blood all over the carpet and those walls.'

He shoved the girl into a living room, where three other girls were seated on two small couches. They were also young, Asian, very pretty. They wore silk negligees, lavender, red and pink, with color-coordinated high-heels and stockings. Victoria's Secret.

'Don't speak, ladies. Not a word,' Starkey said, and pointed his gun at one then the other.

'Shhh,' Brownley Harris held a finger to his lips. 'Nobody gets hurt. We don't want that either. Trust me, my little Asian dolls.'

Starkey threw open the door at the rear of the living room. He surprised an older woman, probably the voice over the intercom, as well as a husky bouncer in gym shorts and black tee-shirt with CRUNCH stenciled on it. They were greedily eating Chinese food out of cardboard containers.

'Nobody gets hurt,' Starkey said in Vietnamese as he shut the door behind him. 'Hands up high.'

The man and woman slowly raised their hands, and Starkey shot them dead with the silenced revolver. He wandered over to some high-tech equipment and calmly removed a tape. The surveillance camera at the front entrance had recorded their arrival, of course.

Starkey left the slumped, bloody bodies and returned to the living room. The party had begun without him. Brownley Harris was kissing and fondling the pretty young girl who had answered the door. He had lifted Kym up and held her tiny mouth pressed against his. She was too frightened to resist.

'*May cai nay moi dem lai nhieu ky niem,*' Starkey said, and smiled at his friends, but also at the women.

Memories are made of this.

Chapter Sixty-Six

They had done this many times before, and not just in New York. They'd 'celebrated' victories in Hong Kong, Saigon, Frankfurt, Los Angeles, even in London. It had all started in South Vietnam when they were just boys in their teens and early twenties, when the war was on and the madness was everywhere around them. Starkey called it 'blood lust'.

The four Asian girls were terrified, and that was the thrill for Starkey. He totally got off on the look of fear in their eyes. He believed that all men did, though few would admit it.

'*Bon tao muon lien hoan!*' he shouted.

We want to party now!

'*Chi lien hoan, the thoi.*'

It's a celebration.

Starkey found out the girls' names: Kym, Lan, Susie and Hoa. They were pretty, but Kym was truly beautiful. A slender body with small breasts; delicate features – the best of a complicated heritage that could be

Chinese, French and Indian.

Harris found bottles of Scotch and champagne in a small kitchen. He passed the hootch around and made the girls drink, too.

The alcohol calmed them, but Kym kept asking about the owner. Occasionally, the bell rang downstairs. Kym's English was the best and she was told to say that the girls were busy for the night – a private party. 'Come back another time, please. Thank you.'

Griffin took two of the girls upstairs to another floor. Starkey and Harris looked at each other and rolled their eyes. At least he'd left two pretty ones for Brownley and himself. Kym and Lan.

Starkey asked Kym to dance. Her eyes were gleaming slants of dark purple. Except for her three-inch heels, she was naked now. An old song by the Yardbirds played on the radio. As he danced, Starkey remembered that Vietnamese women had a thing about their height, at least when they were around American men. Or maybe it was American men who had a thing about height? Or length?

Harris was speaking in English to Lan. He handed her a bottle of champagne. 'Drink,' he said. 'No, drink it down there, babe.'

The girl understood, either the words or lewd gestures. She shrugged, then dropped onto the couch and inserted the champagne bottle in herself. She poured the champagne, then comically wiped her lips. 'I was thirsty!' she said in English.

The joke got a good laugh. Broke the tension.

'*Ban cung phai wong nua,*' the girl said.

You drink, too.

Harris laughed and passed the bottle to Kym. She lifted one leg and put it inside without sitting down. She kept it there while she danced with Starkey, spilling champagne all over the carpet and her shoes. Everybody was laughing now.

'The bubbles tickle,' Kym said. 'I have an itch inside me now. You want to scratch it?' she asked Starkey.

The switchblade seemed to come from nowhere. Kym jabbed it at Starkey without actually stabbing him. She screamed, 'You go! Leave right now. Or I cut you bad!'

Then Starkey had his gun out again. He was so cool and calm. He reached and shut off the loud music. Silence. And dread. Incredible tension in the room. Everywhere except on Thomas Starkey's face.

'*Dung, dung!*' cried Kym. '*Hay dep sung ong sang mot ben di bo.*'

No, no! Put the gun away.

Starkey moved toward little Kym. He wasn't afraid of the switchblade, almost as if he knew he wasn't going to die like this. He twisted the knife out of her hand, then he held the revolver against the side of her skull.

Tears ran down the girl's smooth cheeks. Starkey brushed them away. She smiled up at him. '*Hay yew toi di, ank ban,*' she whispered.

Make love to me, soldier man.

Starkey was there in the apartment, but his head was in Vietnam. Kym was shaking and he loved that, the total control he felt, the evil he was capable of, the electricity it could bring into his system.

He looked at Harris and his friend knew. He just *knew*.

They fired the guns simultaneously.

The girls flew back against the wall and then slid down onto the floor. Kym was shaking all over, very close to death. 'Why?' she whispered.

Starkey just shrugged at her.

Upstairs there were two more *pffthts*. The sound of falling bodies, Susie and Hoa. Warren Griffin had been waiting for them. He knew, too.

It was just like in the An Lao Valley, Vietnam.

Where the madness had started.

Chapter Sixty-Seven

When we finished up at Colonel Bennett's house, Sampson and I checked into the Hotel Thayer, right on the grounds of West Point. I continued to think about the three killers and how they kept getting away. *Force without any conscience.* That was what Agent Fescoe had called it.

In the morning I met Sampson for breakfast in the hotel dining room overlooking the majestic Hudson, which appeared almost steely gray in the distance and was topped by whitecaps. We talked about the grisly Bennett murders and wondered if they were connected to the others, and if the killers had changed their pattern.

'Or maybe there are more murders that we just don't know about,' Sampson said. 'Who knows how many have been killed at this point, or how far back the murders go?' He poured himself another steaming cup of coffee. 'It has to come down to the three killers. They were here, Alex. It has to be the same three men.'

I couldn't disagree with him. 'I have to make a few calls,

then we're out of here. I want to make sure the local police are checking into whether anybody actually saw three men who don't belong on the grounds or in Highland Falls.'

I went upstairs to my room and called Director Burns. He wasn't in, so I left a message. I wanted to call Jamilla, but it was too early in California so I logged onto my computer and sent her a long e-mail.

Then I found that I had a new message. *Now what?*

It turned out to be from Jannie and Damon. They were breaking my chops about being away from home again, even for a night. When was I coming back? Would they get a neat souvenir from West Point? How about a shiny new sword for each of them? And one for little Alex, too.

There was a second message for me.

It wasn't from the kids.

Or Jamilla.

Detective Cross. While you are at West Point, you ought to see Colonel Owen Handler. He teaches political science. He might have some answers for you. He's a friend of the Bennetts. He might even know who killed them.

I'm just trying to be helpful. You need all the help you can get.

Foot Soldier.

Chapter Sixty-Eight

The three killers had been right here. I couldn't get the
thought out of my head, but the feeling was in my
bones, my blood.

Sampson and I walked along the main drag toward
Thayer Hall. Several cadets were out practicing for parade
on the Plains. As we got closer, I saw that wooden pegs
were driven into the ground to show the cadets exactly
where to turn their faultlessly sharp corners. I had to
smile. It reminded me that so many things in life were an
illusion. Maybe even the 'facts' I was collecting on this
case.

'So what do you think about this help we're getting?
The mad e-mailer? The Foot Soldier?' Sampson asked. 'I
don't like it, Alex. It's too convenient, too pat. This whole
case is about being set up.'

'You're right, we don't have any reason to trust the
information we're getting. So I don't. On the other hand,
we're here. Why not talk to Colonel Handler? It can't
hurt.'

Sampson shook his head. 'I wish that was so, Alex.'

I had called the History Department immediately after I received the 'helpful' e-mail from Foot Soldier. I was told that Colonel Handler had a class that met from eleven until noon. We had twenty minutes to kill, so we took in a few sights: Washington Hall, a cavernous three-story building where the entire Corps of Cadets could sit simultaneously for meals; the Eisenhower and MacArthur Barracks; the Cadet Chapel; plus several incomparable river vistas.

Cadets flowed past us lickity-split on the sidewalk. They wore long-sleeved gray shirts with black ties, gray trousers with a black stripe, brass belt buckles shined to perfection.

Everybody was moving in double time! It was contagious.

Thayer Hall was a huge gray building that was virtually windowless. Inside, the classrooms all looked identical, each with desks arranged in a horseshoe so that everyone was in the front row.

Sampson and I waited in a deserted hallway until Handler's class was finished and the cadets filed out.

They were incredibly orderly for college students, which didn't surprise me, but it was still impressive to watch. Why aren't students in all universities orderly? Because no one demands it? Well hell, who cares? But it was a striking scene. All these young kids with so much purpose and resolve. On the surface anyway.

Colonel Handler trailed his students out of the class-room. He was a burly man, around six feet one with short-cropped, salt-and-pepper hair and a full beard. I already knew he'd served two tours of duty in Vietnam, had an MA from the University of Virginia and a doctorate from Penn State. That much was on the West Point web-site.

'We're Detectives Cross and Sampson,' I said as I walked up to him. 'Could we talk to you for a moment?'

Handler grimaced. 'What's this about, Detectives? One of our cadets in trouble?'

'No, no,' I shook my head. 'The cadets seem beyond reproach.'

A smile broke across Handler's face. 'Oh, you'd be surprised. They only look blameless, Detective. So if it isn't one of our charges, what is it you'd like to talk to me about? Robert and Barbara Bennett? I've already spoken to Captain Conte. I thought CID was handling that.'

'They are,' I told him. 'But the murders might be a little more complicated than they appear. Just like the cadets here at West Point.'

As concisely as I could, I told Handler about the other murder cases that Sampson and I had been investigating. I didn't tell him about the e-mail from the Foot Soldier that had led us to him. As I spoke, I noticed a professor in the classroom next to Handler's. He had a bucket with water and a sponge, and he was actually washing the blackboard before the next class. All the classrooms had identical buckets and sponges. Hell of a system.

'We think there's a connection to something pretty bad that took place in Vietnam,' I said to Colonel Handler. 'Maybe the murders actually started there.'

'I served in Southeast Asia. Two tours,' Handler volunteered. 'Vietnam and Cambodia.'

'So did I,' said Sampson. 'Two tours.'

Suddenly, and for no apparent reason, Colonel Handler seemed nervous. His eyes narrowed and darted around the hallway. The cadets were gone now, no doubt rushing off to Washington Hall for lunch.

'I'll talk to you,' he finally said, 'but not on the grounds. Pick me up at my place tonight. It's Quarters ninety-eight. We'll go somewhere else. Come by at eight sharp.'

He looked at Sampson and me, and then Colonel Handler turned and walked away.

In double time.

Chapter Sixty-Nine

I had the feeling that we were close to something important, at West Point, and maybe with Colonel Handler. It was something ineffable that I'd seen in his eyes when the subject had turned to Vietnam. *Maybe the murders started there.*

The colonel had made reservations at what he called an 'extraordinarily misplaced' northern Italian restaurant in Newburgh, Il Cenacolo. We were on our way there, riding the Storm King Highway, a winding rollercoaster with incredible views of the Hudson, which stretched out hundreds of feet below.

'Why didn't you want to talk to us closer to home?' I finally asked the colonel.

'Two of my best friends were just murdered there,' Handler said. He lit up a cigarette, blew out a stream of smoke. It was pitch black outside and the mountainous road had no lights to guide our way.

'You believe the Bennetts were murdered?' I asked.

'I *know* they were.'

'Do you know why?'

'I might. You've heard of the blue wall of silence with the police? In the Army, it's the same, only the wall is gray. It's higher, thicker, and has been here for a hell of a long time.'

I had to ask another question. I couldn't hold back. 'Are you Foot Soldier, Colonel? If you are, we need your help.'

Handler didn't seem to understand. 'What the hell is Foot Soldier? What are you talking about?'

I told him that a mysterious someone had been periodically slipping me information, including Handler's own name. 'Maybe you thought it was time we met face to face,' I said.

'No. I *may* be a source for you now. But it's only because of Bob and Barbara Bennett. I'm not Foot Soldier. I never contacted you. You came to see me. Remember?'

As convincing as he sounded, I didn't know whether to believe him, but I had to pursue the identity of Foot Soldier. I asked Handler for names, others who might be helpful in the investigation. He gave me a few, some Americans, even a couple of South Vietnamese who might be willing to help.

Handler spoke from the darkened backseat of the sedan. 'I don't know who's been contacting you, but I'm not so sure that I'd trust whoever it is. Right about now, I'm not sure that I'd trust anyone.'

'Not even you, Colonel?'

'*Especially* not me,' he said, and laughed. 'Hell, I'm a college professor.'

I glanced up into the rearview mirror and saw a single

pair of headlights approaching. I hadn't noticed much traffic so far and most of it had been speeding in the opposite direction, heading south.

Suddenly Sampson raised his voice and turned to Handler. 'Why don't you tell us what's really going on, Colonel? How many more have to die? What do you know about these murders?'

That's when I heard a gunshot, then the sound of glass breaking. The car behind was already on us, and passing on the right shoulder.

My eyes darted and I saw a driver, then a gunman leaning out the window of the backseat.

'Get down!' I yelled at Handler and Sampson. 'Cover up!'

More shots came from the pursuing car. I swerved the wheel violently to the left. We skidded hard across double-yellow lines, heading for the cliffs, and the Hudson River far below. Handler yelled, *'Watch it, Jesus! Watch it!'*

We hit a straight part of the highway, thank God. I stomped on the accelerator, picked up some speed. But I couldn't lose the other car.

He was in the right-hand lane now.

I was in the *wrong* lane, the one meant for oncoming traffic.

Sampson had gotten to his gun and returned fire. More shots struck our car.

The other sedan stayed right with us. I couldn't shake loose. I was doing over ninety on a twisty road built for fifty or sixty. On my right side was a shoulder and then the mountain wall; on my left, a sheer drop down toward the Hudson River and certain death.

I was going too fast to see faces in the other car. Who the hell was it?

Suddenly I stomped on the brakes and our car skidded badly. Then it fishtailed! We wound up facing in the opposite direction, south.

I took off that way. Back toward West Point.

I floored it again, got back up to ninety in an awful hurry.

I passed two cars heading north, both blaring their horns at me. I couldn't blame them. I was over the double line and racing at about forty miles an hour over the speed limit. They must have thought I was drunk, or mad, or both.

When I was sure no one was following, I slowed down.

'Handler? Colonel?' I called out.

He didn't answer. Sampson hung over the backseat to check on him. 'He's been hit, Alex.'

I pulled to the side of the road and turned on the interior lights. 'How bad? Is he alive?'

I saw that Handler had been shot twice. Once in the shoulder. And once in the side of the head.

'He's dead,' Sampson said. 'He's gone.'

'You all right?' I asked.

'Yeah,' he said. 'I wasn't the target, and that boy in the car could shoot. He was after Handler. We just lost our first real lead.'

I wondered if we had lost Foot Soldier as well.

Chapter Seventy

T here's nothing like an attempt on your life to get you properly focused – and to get the blood boiling.

It was an exercise in futility, but Sampson and I rushed Owen Handler to the ER at West Point Hospital. He was pronounced dead at around nine. I'm certain he was dead when we brought him in. The shooter in the other car was a chillingly good marksman, a professional killer. *Had three men actually been in the pursuing car? I didn't think so*.

We were questioned by the local police and also CID officers from West Point. Captain Conte even came to see us, spouting off his concern for our safety, but also playing twenty questions with us, almost as if we were suspects. Conte informed me that the commanding officer at West Point, General Mark Hutchinson, was personally supervising the investigation now. Whatever that was supposed to mean.

Then General Hutchinson actually showed up at the hospital. I saw him speaking to Captain Conte, then a few other grim-faced officers gathered in the hallway. But

Hutchinson never came over to see Sampson and I. Not a word of condolence or concern.

How goddamn strange, and inconsiderate. It was maddening. *The gray wall of silence,* I thought, remembering Owen Handler's words. General Mark Hutchinson left the hospital without making contact with us. I wasn't going to forget that.

All the while I was at West Point Hospital, I couldn't get one thought out of my head: *There is nothing like an attempt on your life . . . to get your blood boiling.* I was shaken by the attack on Colonel Handler, but I was also angry as hell.

Wasn't that part of the motive behind the massacres at My Lai and others like it? Anger? Fear? The need for retribution? Unthinkable things happened during combat. Tragedies were inevitable. They always had been. What was the Army trying to cover up now? Who had sent the killers after us tonight? Who had murdered Colonel Handler, and why?

Sampson and I spent the night at the Hotel Thayer again. General Hutchinson decided to put MPs on the second floor to protect us. I didn't think it was necessary. If the gunmen had been after us, they wouldn't have driven off and left us alive.

I kept thinking: *two* men had been in the car that attacked us.

There had been *three* men involved in the earlier killings.

I couldn't get that fact out of my head either.

Three, not two.

Eventually, I called Jamilla and shared everything that had happened with her. Detective to detective, friend to friend. She didn't like the actions of General Hutchinson and the Army either. Just talking it through with her helped tremendously.

I was thinking about doing it more often, like maybe every night.

Finally, I fell asleep on that thought.

Chapter Seventy-One

The following morning the New York papers were filled with a story about the murder of four call girls, a madam and a bouncer on the East Side of Manhattan. The women were Vietnamese and Thai, and because of that I talked to the detective in charge of the investigation in Manhattan. So far, the NYPD was nowhere on the grisly case. I thought about going to New York, but there were other pressing things on my mind.

There was an important lead I hadn't even begun to satisfactorily check out. The Foot Soldier. Who the hell was he? Or she? And why had Foot Soldier contacted me by e-mail? What was the mystery person trying to tell me?

Owen Handler had given me a few names, and once I returned to Washington, I dug around until I tracked a few of them down. The most interesting to me was Tran Van Luu, a former Kit Carson scout who was now living in the United States.

There was a catch, a big one. Tran Van Luu was on death

row in Florence, Colorado. He'd been found guilty of murdering nine people in Newark and New York City. I knew a little about the federal prison at Florence and had even been there once. *That was the second catch.* Kyle Craig was imprisoned there, my old nemesis. Kyle was also on death row.

The Florence ADX was one of the so-called 'supermax' prison facilities. Thirty-six states now had them. Death row was located in the Security Housing Unit, a kind of prison within a prison. It turned out to be a bland, sand-colored building with extraordinarily heavy security inside and out. That was comforting, since Kyle Craig was being held inside, and Kyle had nothing but disdain for prison security.

Two heavily armed guards accompanied me to death row. As we walked down the otherwise empty, fluorescent-lit hallways, I heard none of the usual chaotic noise of a prison. My mind was somewhere else anyway.

I had arrived in Colorado around noon. Everything was running smoothly on the home front, and hopefully I'd be back in DC that night. Nana wasn't missing any opportunities, though. Before I left the house she sat me down and told me one of her story-parables. She called it *The story of the thousand marbles.* 'I heard this on NPR, Alex. It's a true story, and I'm passing it along to you for what it's worth. Seems there was this man who lived in Southern California, around San Diego I believe it was. He had a family, nice family, and he worked very hard, long hours, lots of weekends. Sound familiar?'

'Probably familiar to a lot of people,' I said. 'Men and women. Go ahead, though, Nana. This hardworking man with the extraordinarily nice family living outside San Diego. What happened to him?'

'Well anyway, this man had a kindly grandfather who adored both him and his family. He'd noticed that his grandson was working too hard, and he was the one who told him about the marbles. He told it this way. He said that the average life span for men was around seventy-five years. That meant thirty-nine hundred Saturdays – to play when you were a kid, and to be with your family when you got older and wiser.'

'I see,' I said. 'Or to play once you got older. Or even to give lectures to anyone who'll listen.'

'Shush, Alex. Now, listen. So the grandfather figured out that his grandson, who was forty-three, had about sixteen hundred and sixty Saturdays left in his life. Statistically speaking. So what he did was he bought two large jars and filled them with beautiful cat's-eye marbles. He gave them to his grandson. And he told him that every Saturday, he should take one marble out of the jar. Just one, and just as a reminder that he only had so many Saturdays left, and that they were precious beyond belief. Think about that, Alex. If you have the time,' said Nana.

So here I was at a supermax prison – on a Saturday. I didn't think I was wasting the day, not at all. But Nana's message had sunk in anyway.

This was my last murder case. It had to be. This was the end of the road for Detective Alex Cross.

I focused my mind on the baffling case as I walked toward the cell of Tran Van Luu. He would make my trip worth at least one marble.

Or so I had to hope.

Chapter Seventy-Two

Tran Van Luu was fifty-four years old and he informed me that he spoke Vietnamese, French and English fluently. His English was excellent and I couldn't help thinking that he looked more like a college professor than a prison inmate convicted of several murders. Luu wore gold wire-rim glasses and had a long, gray goatee. He was philosophical – about everything apparently. But was he the Foot Soldier?

'Nominally, I am a Buddhist,' he said as he sat in a cell that was only seven by twelve feet. A bed, a stool and a fixed writing shelf filled more than half of the space. The fixtures were all made of poured concrete so they couldn't be moved or disassembled by the inmates.

'I will give you some history,' he said. 'The back story.'

I nodded. 'That would be a good place to start.'

'My birthplace is Gon Track Village in the Quang Bihn Province, just north of what was the DMZ. This is one of the country's poorest provinces, but they are all relatively poor. I started work in my family's rice fields at five.

Everyone was always hungry, even though we grew food. We had one real meal a day, usually yams or cassava. Ironically, our rice was handed over to the landlord. All loyalty was to family, including ancestors, a plot of land and the village. Nationalism was non-existent, a Western notion imported by Ho Chi Minh.

'My family moved south in nineteen sixty-three and I enlisted in the Army. The alternative was starvation, and besides, I had been brought up to hate the Communists. I proved to be an excellent scout and was recommended to MAC-V/Recondo school run by US Army Special Forces. This was my initial encounter with Americans. I liked them at first.'

'What happened to change that?' I asked Luu.

'Many things. Mostly I came to understand that many of the Americans looked down on me and my country-men. Despite repeated promises, I was left behind in Saigon. I became a boat person.

'I finally got to America in seventy-nine. Orange County in California, which has a very large Vietnamese population. The only way we could survive was to recreate the family/village structure from our own country. I did so with a gang – the Ghost Shadows. We became successful, at first in California, then in the New York area, including Newark. They say I murdered members of rival gangs in New York and Jersey.'

'Did you?' I asked Luu.

'Oh, of course. It was justifiable, though. We were in a war.' He stopped talking. Stared at me.

'So now you're here in a supermax prison. Have you

received a date for the execution?'

'No. Which is very humorous to me. Your country is afraid to execute convicted murderers.'

'It's comical? Because of things you saw in Vietnam?'

'Of course. That is my frame of reference.'

'Atrocities committed in the name of military activity.'

'It was war, Detective.'

'Did you know any of these men in Vietnam: Ellis Cooper, Reece Tate, James Etra, Robert Bennett, Laurence Houston?'

Luu shrugged. 'It was a long time ago. Over thirty years. And there are so many American surnames to remember.'

'Colonel Owen Handler?'

'I don't know him.'

I shook my head. 'I think you do. Actually, Colonel Handler was in charge of the MAC-V/Recondo school when you were there being trained as a Kit Carson scout.'

Luu smiled for the first time. 'Believe it or not, Detective Cross, the scouts didn't usually get to meet the man-in-charge.'

'But you met Colonel Handler. He remembered you to the day he was killed. Can you help me stop the murders?' I asked Luu. 'You know what happened over there, don't you? Why did you agree to see me?'

He gave another indifferent shrug. 'I agreed to see you . . . because my good friend asked me to. My friend is Kyle Craig.'

Chapter Seventy-Three

I could feel a cold spot where my heart was supposed to be. This couldn't all be leading to Kyle Craig. I had put him here in Florence for all the murders he had committed – and now, somehow, he'd gotten me to come and visit.

'Hello, Alex. I thought you'd forgotten all about me,' Kyle said when he saw me. We met in a small interviewing room near his cellblock. My head was full of paranoid thoughts about the 'coincidence' of seeing him again. He couldn't have set this up. Not even *he* could do that.

Kyle had changed physically, so much so that he resembled one of his older brothers, or maybe his father, more than himself. When I had been pursuing him, I'd met everyone in Kyle's family. He'd always been gaunt, but in prison he had lost at least twenty pounds. His head was shaven and he had a tattoo on one side of his skull: it was part dragon, part snake. He actually looked like a killer now.

'Sit down, Alex. I missed you even more than I thought

I would. Sit, please. Let's talk the talk. Catch up with the catch up.'

'I'll stand, thanks. I'm not here to make small talk, Kyle. What do you know about these murders?'

'They've all been solved by the police or the Army, Alex. The guilty have been charged, and in some cases executed. Just as I will be eventually. Why waste your time on them? I'm a hundred times more interesting. You should be studying me.'

His words were delivered in a low-key manner, but they went through me like a powerful electric current. Was Kyle the missing goddamn connection? He couldn't be behind the murders? They had started long before he'd been arrested. *But did that really matter?*

'So, you don't know anything that can help me? Then I'm leaving. Have a nice life.'

Kyle raised a hand. 'I'd like to help, Alex. I mean that sincerely. Just like the old days. I miss it. The chase. What if I *could* help?' he asked.

'If you can, then do it, Kyle. Do it right now. We'll see where it goes from there.'

Kyle leaned back in his chair. Finally, he smiled, or maybe he was laughing at me? 'Well, since you didn't ask, it's better here in prison than I could have hoped. Believe it or not, I'm a minor celebrity. And not just among my peers. Even the kick-ass guards cater to my wishes. I have lots of visitors. I'm writing a book, Alex. And, of course, I'm figuring out some way to get out of here. Trust me, I will some day. It's just a matter of time. It almost happened a month ago. *This* close. I would have come to visit, of course. You and Nana and those sweet children.'

'Does Luu know *anything*?' I asked.

'Oh, absolutely. He's very well read. Speaks three languages fluently. I like Luu very much. We're dear friends. I also like Ted Kaczynski; Yu Kikimura, the Japanese terrorist; and Ramon Matta, formerly with the Medellin cartel. Interesting inmates, fascinating lives, though more conservative than I would have expected. Not Ted, but the others.'

I'd had enough. Of Kyle Craig. Luu. Florence.

'I'm going,' I said. I started to walk away.

'You'll be back,' Kyle whispered. 'Or maybe I'll come and visit you next time. At any rate, best of luck with your fascinating murder case.'

I turned back. 'You'll be in here for the rest of your life. Not too long, I hope.'

Kyle Craig laughed heartily. More than ever, he gave me the creeps.

Chapter Seventy-Four

As John Sampson drove into Bay Head, New Jersey, he felt his spirits rise dramatically, and the very pleasant sensation inside made him smile to himself. He was doing a lot of that lately. Hell, he was going to ruin his tough guy image if he kept this shit up much longer.

He drove along Route 35, past sprawling beach houses, Central Market, and a couple of picturesque, whitewashed churches. This part of the Jersey shore was quiet and undeniably pretty. He couldn't help but appreciate the serenity and the well-preserved beauty. A slight breeze from the ocean blew through the open windows of his Cougar. Geraniums and rose hips bloomed along the side of the road, obviously planted by the village itself.

What was not to like? He was glad to be here again.

Long ways from DC, he found himself thinking. *And it's not all bad. For a change of pace anyway. For a break from all the murders.*

During the drive up from DC, Sampson had tried to convince himself that this excursion to the Jersey shore

was all about Ellis Cooper and the other murders, but that
wasn't the whole truth. Coop was definitely a big part of
it, but this was also about Billie Houston.

He thought about her all the time. What was it about
that wisp of a woman?

Actually, he knew at least part of the answer. From the
moment he'd met her, he was completely comfortable.
She was the female friend he'd been hoping to meet for a
long time. It was hard to describe the feeling, but he knew
he'd never had it before. He felt that he could tell Billie
things about himself that he'd held inside for a long time.
He trusted her already. When he was with her he could
come outside of himself, leave the castle he had con-
structed to guard the person he really was from being
hurt.

On the other hand, John Sampson had never had a
successful long-range relationship with any woman.
Never been married, not even seriously tempted. So he
wasn't going to delude himself, or get too soppy and
sentimental about Billie. He had good reasons to be here
in Jersey. A few more questions had to be asked about her
husband's time in Vietnam. He and Alex had learned
things from Owen Handler that needed filling in. He *was*
going to solve these murder cases. Somehow, some way.

Well, hell, that cynical little introspection had sure
dampened his spirits, and any burgeoning romance in his
soul.

Then he happened to see her up ahead on East Avenue.
Yep, it was her!
Billie was climbing out of her light green convertible

with an armful of groceries. He'd called ahead and said he might be coming.

Now who had she been shopping for? Did she expect him to stay for dinner? Oh brother, he needed to calm himself down. *Slow down. You're on the job, that's all. This is just police business.*

Then Billie saw his car and waved her free arm, and he found himself leaning out of the window of the Cougar, calling up the street, 'Hey there, little one.' *Hey there, little one?*

What the hell had happened to smooth and cool and detached John Sampson? What was happening to him?

And why did he feel so good about it?

Chapter Seventy-Five

B illie understood that she and John Sampson needed to talk about her husband and his murder. That was why he'd come back, probably the only reason. She made a pitcher of sweetened iced tea, and they went out to the oceanside porch. Might as well be comfortable. *Try not to make an ass out of herself.*

'Another perfect day in paradise,' he said, and smiled brilliantly. Billie couldn't keep herself from staring a little at the policeman. He was strong and good-looking and his smile was dazzling whenever it came. She had the sense that he didn't smile enough, and wondered why that was. What had happened to him growing up in Washington? And then living and working there? She wanted to know everything about him, and that natural curiosity was something that had been missing since Laurence had died.

Don't make this into something it isn't, she reminded herself. *He's a policeman on a murder case. That's all this is. You just have a silly crush on him.*

'Average day in paradise,' she laughed. Then she got a little more serious. 'You wanted to talk some more about Laurence. Something else happened, didn't it? That's why you're back here.'

'No, I came to see you.' *There was that amazing smile of his again.*

Billie took a little swing at the air with her hand. 'Sure you did. Anyway – your murder case?'

He told her about the recent deaths of Robert and Barbara Bennett in West Point, and then the shooting of Colonel Owen Handler. He shared his and Alex's theory that three men might be responsible for at least some of the murders. 'Everything seems to point back to Vietnam. Something incredible happened, something so bad that it's probably the root cause of all these murders in the present. Your husband may have been involved in some way. Maybe he didn't even know it, Billie.'

'He didn't like to talk about his experiences over there.' She repeated what she'd told him during his first visit. 'I always respected that. But then something strange happened. Several years ago, he brought home books about the war. *Rumors Of War* was one that I remember. He rented the movie *Platoon*, which he'd always insisted he wouldn't watch. He still didn't want to talk about the war, though. Not to me anyway.'

Billie sat back in the navy blue wicker rocker she'd chosen. She stared out at the ocean. Several gulls floated over the tall dunes. Picture pretty. Miles away, she could see the blurred outline of an ocean liner on the horizon.

'He always drank, but during those last years, he drank

much more. Hard liquor, wine. He wasn't ever abusive, but I felt he was drifting farther and farther away.

'One night around dusk he took off down the beach with his fishing pole and a pail for anything he might catch. It was early September, and the bluefish were running. He could have caught them with his pail.

'I waited for him to come back, but he didn't. Finally, I went out looking for him. Most of these houses on the beach empty out after Labor Day. That's the way it is here. I walked south a mile or so. I was getting a little scared.

'I had brought a flashlight, and as I headed back, I turned it on and worked my way up closer to the dunes and the deserted beach houses. That was where I found him.

'Laurence was laying in the sand beside his fishing pole and the bait bucket. He'd finished off a pint of whiskey. Looked like a street bum who'd lost his way and wound up sleeping it off on the beach.

'I lay down beside him and held him in my arms. I asked him to please tell me why he was so sad. He *couldn't*. It broke my heart that he couldn't tell me. All he said was that "you can't outrun your past". It looks like he was right.'

Chapter Seventy-Six

They talked about Vietnam, and her husband's Army experiences after the war, until Sampson was starting to get a headache. Billie never complained. Around four in the afternoon they took a break and watched the high tide coming in. It amazed Sampson that the long stretch of beach could be so empty on such a sunny and blue-skied day.

'Did you bring a suit?' she asked, and smiled.

'Actually, I did throw a suit in the car,' Sampson said, and returned her smile.

'Want to take a swim?'

'Yeah. Be nice.'

They slipped into their suits and met back on the front porch. She had on a black one-piece. He figured she must do a lot of swimming, or maybe worked out. She was little, but she didn't look like a young girl. She was probably in her early forties.

'I know I look okay,' Billie said, and twirled around. 'So do you. Now let's hit the water before you chicken out on me.'

'Chicken out? You know I'm a homicide detective?'

'Uh-huh. Water's sixty-seven today, tough guy.'

'What? Is that cold?'

'You'll soon find out.'

They walked to the top of the dune in front of the house. Then they broke into a full-out run. Sampson was laughing, mostly at himself, because he didn't *do* this kind of thing.

They high-stepped their way through the low surf like kids on vacation, ignoring that the water was in the sixties, cold as hell, absolutely freezing.

'You *can* swim?' Billie asked as a huge swell moved toward them. She thought she saw him nod.

'John?' she asked again.

'I can swim. Can *you*?'

Then they both dove under the wave as it crested high above their heads. A short way out past the first wave, they re-surfaced. Billie started to stroke her way out to a point past the breakers. Sampson followed, and he was a good, strong swimmer. That delighted her for some reason.

'Sometimes, kids from the cities,' she said as they bobbed heads together, 'they don't learn to swim.'

'That's true. I have this good friend. When we were growing up in DC, his grandmother made sure we knew how. She used to take us to the city pool. She said, "You swim, or you drown".'

Then Sampson found himself taking Billie in his arms. She used a forefinger to wipe beads of water off his face. Her touch was gentle. So were her eyes. Something was going on here and whatever it was, he didn't know if he was ready for it.

'What?' Billie asked.

'I was just going to say,' he said, 'that you're surprising in a lot of ways.'

She closed her eyes for a second, nodded. Then she opened her eyes again. 'You're still here. Good. I'm glad you came back. Even if you came to interrogate me.'

'The reason I came was to see you. I told you.'

'Whatever you say, John.'

Nobody but Alex and Nana called him John.

They swam back toward shore and played in the creamy surf for a while. Even though it was late afternoon they took a walk to the south, passing more large houses that were shut up tight for the coming winter. They fell into a nice rhythm along the way. They had to stop and kiss at each house.

'You're getting kind of corny,' Billie finally said. 'It becomes you. You have a tender side, John Sampson.'

'Yeah. Maybe I do.'

They ate dinner on the front porch again. Sampson put on the radio. Afterward, they snuggled in the loveseat, and again he was struck by how tiny she was. She fit against him, though.

'One Night With You' came on the radio. Luther Vandross. Sampson asked her to dance. He couldn't believe it – *I just asked Billie to dance on the porch.*

He tucked her in close. She fit nicely standing up, too. They moved well together, totally in synch. He listened to her breathing and could feel her heartbeat as well.

An old Marvin Gaye tune came on the radio and they danced to that, too. It all seemed dreamlike to him. Completely unexpected.

Especially when they went upstairs together at around ten-thirty. Neither of them said a word, but Billie took his hand and led him into the bedroom. A three-quarter moon was lighting the whitecaps. A sailboat lazily drifted by out beyond the line of surf.

'You okay?' she whispered.

'I am much more than okay. Are you, Billie?'

'I *am* Billie. I think I wanted this to happen from the first time I saw you. You ever done this before?' she asked. There was that sly grin of hers again. She was playing with him, but he liked it.

'First time. I've been saving myself for the right woman.'

'Well, let's see if I'm worth the wait.'

Sometimes, he could be in a hurry, and that would be okay, the way of the world in Washington, but not tonight. He wanted to explore Billie's body, to get to know what pleased her. He touched her everywhere; kissed her everywhere. Everything about her seemed right to him. *What's happening here? I came to ask this woman about some murders. Murders! Not love-making in shimmering moonlight.*

He could feel her small breasts rising and falling, rising and falling. He was on top of her, supporting his weight on his hands.

'You won't hurt me,' she whispered.

'No, I won't.'

I won't. I couldn't hurt you. And I won't let anybody hurt you.

She smiled, rolled over, and then slid up on top of him. 'How's that? Is that better for you?'

He ran his strong hands up and down her back and over her buttocks. She hummed 'One Night With You'. They began to move together, really slowly at first. Then faster. And faster still. Billie rose and fell hard on him. She liked it that way.

When they finally collapsed with the pleasure of it all, she looked into his eyes. 'Not bad for your first time. You'll get better.'

Later, Sampson lay in the bed with Billie snuggled up against his side. It still made him smile to see how small she was. Small face, small hands, feet, breasts. And then the thought hit him – stunned him: he was at peace for the first time in years. Maybe ever.

Chapter Seventy-Seven

I was pumped up to see Nana and the kids when I got home from my trip to Florence prison that night. It was only seven and I'd been thinking we might go to the IMAX theater, or maybe the ESPN Zone – some nice treat for the kids.

As I climbed the front steps of the house, I spotted a note stuck onto the screen door, flapping in the breeze.

Uh-oh.

Messages left at the house always make me a little queasy. There'd been too many bad ones during the past few years.

I recognized Nana's handwriting: *Alex, we've gone to your Aunt Tia's. Be back by nine or so. Everybody misses you. Do you miss us? Of course you do – in your own way. Nana and the kids.*

I'd noticed that Nana Mama had been unusually senti-mental lately. She said she was feeling better, back to her old self again, but I wondered if that was true. Maybe I should talk to her doctor, but I didn't like interfering in her business. She'd been doing an excellent job of taking care of herself for a long time.

I shuffled on into the kitchen and grabbed a cold beer from the fridge.

I saw a funny drawing of a pregnant stork that Jannie had stuck up on the door. Suddenly, I felt lonely for everybody. The thing about kids for some people – for me anyway – is that they complete your life, make some kind of sense out of it, even if they do drive you crazy sometimes. The gain is worth the pain. At least in our house it is.

The telephone rang and I figured it was Nana.

'Hooray, you're home!' came a welcome voice. *Well, surprise, surprise.* It was Jamilla, and that cheered me right up. I could picture her face, her smile, the bright shine in her eyes.

'Hooray, it's *you*. I just got home to an empty house,' I said. 'Nana and the kids deserted me.'

'Could be worse, Alex. I'm at work. Caught a bad one on Friday. Irish tourist got killed in the Tenderloin district. So tell me, what was a fifty-one-year-old *priest* from Dublin doing in one of the seediest parts of San Francisco at two in the morning? How did he get strangled with a pair of extra-large pantyhose? My job to find out.'

'Sounds like you're enjoying yourself anyway.' I found myself smiling. Not at the murder, but at Jamilla's enthusiasm for the Job.

Jamilla was still laughing. 'Well, I do enjoy a good mystery. How's your case going? Now that sucker is nasty. I've been thinking about it in my free moments.

Somebody "murdering" Army officers by framing them for crimes they didn't commit.'

I brought her up to speed, detective to detective, then we talked about more pleasant subjects, like our time together in Arizona. Finally, she said she had to run, to get back to her case. I thought about Jam after I hung up the phone. She loved police work, and she said so. I did too, but the demons were getting to me.

I grabbed another beer out of the fridge, then I headed upstairs. I was still ruminating about Jamilla. Nice thoughts. Nothing but blue skies . . .

I opened the bedroom door, then I just stood there, shaking my head back and forth.

Sitting on my bed were two large glass jars. Pretty ones. Maybe antiques. They were filled with what looked to be hundreds of cat's-eye marbles.

I went over to the bed. Took one out.

I rolled the marble between my thumb and forefinger. I had to admit that it felt precious.

The Saturdays I still had left.

How did I plan to use them?

Maybe that was the biggest mystery of all.

Chapter Seventy-Eight

I had the feeling that I was being followed around in Washington during the next few days. *Watched.* But I couldn't seem to catch them at it. They were either very good, or I was completely losing it.

On Monday I was back at work. All that week I put in my time at the precinct, on the Job. I made sure I spent extra hours at home with the kids before I did overtime in my office in the attic. A colonel named Daniel Boudreau at the Pentagon was cooperating somewhat. He'd sent me Army records from the Vietnam War. Lots of paperwork that appeared not to have been looked at in years. He also suggested I contact the Vietnamese Embassy. They had records, too.

I read through the old files until I couldn't stay awake any longer and my head was throbbing severely. I was searching for anything that might link Ellis Cooper, Reece Tate, Laurence Houston, James Etra, Robert Bennett, or even Tran Van Luu to the string of murders.

I found no connection, nothing remotely promising. Was that possible?

None of the men had ever served together in Asia.

Late that night I got another e-mail from the Foot Soldier. Jesus Christ. Obviously, he wasn't Owen Handler. So who was sending the messages? Kyle Craig? Was he still trying to play with my head? How could he get the messages out of a supermax prison?

Somebody was sending them and I didn't like it. I also didn't trust the information I was getting. Was I being set up, too?

Detective Cross,

I am a little disappointed in your progress. You get on a good track, then you get off it. Look back at where you've been already. The answers are all in the past. Isn't that always the way it works out?

The note was signed *Foot Soldier.*

But there was something else at the bottom of the page. A very disturbing icon – *a straw doll.* Just like the ones we'd found.

After work on Wednesday of that week I visited the Vietnamese Embassy on Twentieth Street in Northeast. The FBI had made a call for me. I arrived at a little before six and went up to the fourth floor. I was met there by a translator named Thi Nguyen. At her desk were four large boxes of old records kept by the government of her country.

I sat in her small office and Thi Nguyen read passages to me. She didn't want to be doing this, I could tell. I supposed she'd been ordered to work late. On a wall

behind her was a sign: *Embassy Of The Socialist Republic of Vietnam*. Also a portrait of Ho Chi Minh.

'There's nothing here, Detective. Nothing new,' she complained as she went through dusty files that were over thirty years old. I told her to please stay with it. She would sigh loudly, adjust her odd, black-rimmed glasses, and sullenly dig into another file. This pouty ritual went on for hours. I found her incredibly unpleasant.

At around nine o'clock, she looked up in surprise. 'There's something here,' she said. 'Maybe this is what you're looking for.'

'Tell me. Don't edit, please. Tell me exactly what you're reading.'

'That's what I've been doing, Detective. According to these records, there were unauthorized attacks on small villages in the An Lao Valley. Civilians seem to have been killed. This happened half a dozen times. Somebody must have known about it. Maybe even your Military Advisory Council.'

'Tell me everything that's in there,' I repeated. 'Please don't leave anything out. Read from the texts.'

The boredom and exasperation she had shown before were gone. Suddenly the translator was attentive, and also seemed a little frightened. What she was reading now was disturbing her.

'There are always unfortunate incidents during a war,' she lectured me. 'But this is a new pattern in the An Lao Valley. The killings seem to have been organized and methodical. Almost like your serial killers here in America.'

'There are serial killers in Asia, too,' I said.

Ms Nguyen bristled at my comment. 'Let me see. There were formal complaints made to your government and the US Army by officers in the ARVN. Did you know that? There are also repeated complaints from what was then called Saigon. This was a murder case, according to the ARVN. Murder, not war. The murder of innocent civilians, including children.' She frowned and shook her head. 'There's more about the precise pattern of the murders. Men, women and children, innocent villagers were killed. Often the bodies were painted.'

'Red, white, blue,' I said. 'The painting was a calling card left by the killers.'

Ms Nguyen looked up in alarm. 'How did you know? Did you already know about these horrible murders? What is your role in all this?'

'I'll tell you when we're finished. Don't stop now. Please. This could be what I've been looking for.'

About twenty minutes later, Ms Nguyen came upon something that I asked her to read a second time. 'A team of Army Rangers was sent into the An Lao Valley. It's unclear, but it seems they were dispatched to the area to investigate the murders. I'm sorry, Detective. It's also unclear here whether they succeeded or not.'

'Do you have any names?' I asked. 'Who was on this team?' I could feel the adrenalin ripping through my body now.

Ms Nguyen sighed and shook her head. Finally, she rose from her desk. 'There are more boxes on the fifth floor. Come with me, Detective. You say that people are still being killed?'

I nodded, then I followed Thi Nguyen upstairs. There was an entire wall of boxes and I helped her carry several of them down to her office.

The two of us worked late on Wednesday, then again on Thursday night, and we even got together during her lunch hour on Friday. She was hooked now, too. We learned that the Rangers sent to the An Lao Valley were military assassins. Unfortunately, none of the paperwork had been organized according to dates. It had just been thrown into boxes and left to collect dust, never to be read by anyone again.

Around two-fifteen on Friday we opened another few boxes crammed with papers pertaining to the investigation in the An Lao Valley.

Thi Nguyen looked up at me. 'I have names for the assassins,' she said. 'And I think I have a code name for the operation. I believe it was called *Three Blind Mice*.'

PART FOUR

EXIT WOUNDS

Chapter Seventy-Nine

I had three names now – three men who had been dispatched to the An Lao Valley to stop the murder of civilians there. I needed to be extremely careful with the information, and it took Sampson and I another week to track the men down and find out as much as we could about them.

The final confirmation that I needed came from Ron Burns at the FBI. He told me that the Bureau had suspected these men of doing two other professional hits: one a politician in Cincinnati, the second a union leader's wife in Santa Barbara, California.

The names were:

Thomas Starkey.

Brownley Harris.

Warren Griffin.

The Three Blind Mice.

The following weekend, Sampson and I went to Rocky Mount, North Carolina. We were chasing men who had played a part in mysterious violence in the An Lao Valley thirty years before. What in hell had really happened there? Why were people still dying now?

Less than five miles outside the city limits of Rocky Mount, tracts of farmland and crossroad county grocers still dominated the landscape. Sampson and I drove out into the country, then back to town again, passing the Rocky Mount-Wilson Airport and Nash General Hospital, as well as Heckler and Koch where Starkey, Harris and Griffin worked as the sales team for several military bases, including Fort Bragg.

Sampson and I entered Heels, a local sports bar, at around six o'clock. Race-car drivers as well as a few basketball players from the Charlotte Hornets frequented the place, so it was racially mixed. We were able to fit into the crowd, which was noisy and active. At least a dozen TVs blared from raised platforms.

The sports bar was less than a mile from Heckler and Koch US, where some of these men and women worked. Other than the thriving high-tech business community, Heckler and Koch (pronounced 'Coke') was one of the largest places of employment in town, just behind Abbott Laboratories and Consolidated Diesel. I wondered if the gun company might have some connection to the murders. Probably not, but maybe.

I struck up a conversation with a plant supervisor from H and K at the bar. We talked about the plight of the Carolina Panthers, and then I worked in the subject of the gun manufacturer. He was positive about his company, which he referred to as 'like a family' and 'definitely one of the best places to work in North Carolina, which is a good state to work in'. Then we talked about guns, the MP5 submachine gun in particular. He told me the MP5 was used by the Navy SEALS and elite SWAT teams, but it had also found its way into inner-city gangs. I already knew that about the MP5.

I mentioned Starkey, Harris and Griffin, casually.

'I'm surprised Tom and Brownie aren't here already. They usually stop in on a Friday. How do you know those boys?' he asked, but didn't seem surprised that I did.

'We served together a long time ago,' said Sampson. 'Back in sixty-nine and seventy.'

The supervisor nodded. 'You Rangers too?' he asked.

'No, just regular Army,' said Sampson. 'Just foot soldiers.'

We talked to some other H and K employees, and they spoke positively about the company. The guys we talked to knew Starkey, Harris and Griffin, and everybody knew they'd been Rangers. I got the impression that the three men were popular and might even be local heroes.

Around quarter past seven, Sampson leaned in close and whispered into my ear. 'Front door. Look who just blew in,' he said. 'Three business suits. Don't much look like killers.'

I turned slowly and looked. *No, they didn't look like killers.*

'But that's what they are,' I said to Sampson. 'Army assassins who look like the nicest guys in the bar, maybe in all of North Carolina.'

We watched the three of them for the rest of the night – just watched the trio of hit men.

Chapter Eighty

Sampson and I were staying out at a Holiday Inn near the Interstate. We were up the next morning by six.

We had a potentially heart-stopping, but rather tasty breakfast at a nearby Denny's (omelets and 'home fries covered and smothered'). Then we planned out our big day. We'd learned the night before that Heckler and Koch had a big family-style picnic going that afternoon. We were planning to crash it. Cause a little trouble if we could.

After breakfast we took a spin past the houses of the three murder suspects. A slick DC group we liked called Maze was playing from the CD. Nice contrast to the folksiness of Rocky Mount. City meets country.

The killers' houses were in upscale developments called Knob Hill, Falling River Walk, and Greystone. It looked as if a lot of young professionals with families lived there. The new South. Quiet, tasteful, civilized as hell.

'They know how to blend in,' Sampson said as we drove by Warren Griffin's two-and-a-half story Colonial. 'Our three killer boys.'

'Good at what they do,' I said. 'Never been caught. I really want to have a chat with them.'

Around eight, we went back to the Holiday Inn to get ready for the picnic and whatever else might happen today. It was hard to believe that the three killers fit so well into Rocky Mount. It made me wonder about pretty, innocent-looking small towns and what might be lurking behind their façades. Maybe nothing, maybe a whole lot of everything.

Sampson and I were originally from North Carolina, but we hadn't spent that much time here as adults, and unfortunately, most of it had been working on a couple of celebrated murder cases. The gun-company picnic was scheduled to start at eleven, and we figured we would show up at around one when the crowds were large. We knew from the night before that just about everybody from H and K, from the mailroom to stockroom to the corporate suite, would be on hand for the big day.

That included Starkey, Harris, Griffin – and their families.

And of course, Sampson and I.

It was time for a little payback.

Chapter Eighty-One

It was a hot, humid day and even the cooks at the company picnic were checking the grill infrequently. They much preferred to stay in the shade and sip cold Dr Pepper soft drinks in their *'BBQ from Heaven'* aprons. Everybody seemed to be taking it easy, having a good time on a pretty Saturday. *Another cat's-eye marble bites the dust.*

Sampson and I sat under an ancient, leafy oak tree and listened to the symphony of local birds. We drank iced tea from Lucite cups that looked like real glass. We wore *H and K Rules* tee-shirts and looked as if we belonged, and always had.

The smell of ribs was strong in the air. Actually, the smoke from the grills was probably keeping the bugs from becoming an immediate problem.

'They sure know how to cook those ribs,' Sampson said.

They did, and so did I. Ribs, to cook properly, need indirect heat, and the fires had been built with two piles of charcoal – one in front, one in the back, but none in the middle where the racks with the ribs had been placed. I

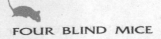

had learned about ribs, and all kinds of cooking, from Nana. She'd wanted me to be as good in the kitchen as she was. That wasn't going to happen real soon, but I was decent, at least. I could fill in when needed.

I even knew that there was a standing argument in the grilling world about the relative merits of the 'dry rub' versus the 'wet mop'. The dry rub was a mixture of salt, pepper, paprika and brown sugar, which was said to have both the heat and the sweetness to bring out the true flavor of the meat. The wet-mop mix had a base of apple cider, with added shallots, jalapeno peppers, ketchup, brown sugar and tomato paste. I liked the mop *and* the rub just fine – so long as the meat was cooked until it just about fell off the bone.

'Everybody is having such a good, all-American time,' Sampson said as we sat and watched the world go by. 'Remind me to tell you about Billie in Jersey.'

'Billie?' I asked. 'Who's Billie?'

'Tell you later, partner. We're working now. On the trail of three stone-cold killers.'

That we were. We were busy watching the families of Starkey, Harris and Griffin from a safe distance. I noticed that Thomas Starkey looked our way once or twice. Had he spotted us? If he had, he didn't seem overly concerned.

'You think they're the ones who killed Colonel Handler? Think they know who we are, sugar?' Sampson asked.

'If they don't, they probably will soon.'

Sampson didn't seem to mind. 'That's your big plan? Get us killed down here in Rocky Mount?'

'They won't do anything with their families around,' I said.

'You sure?'

'No,' I said. 'I'm not sure. But that's what my gut tells me.'

'They're killers, Alex.'

'Professional killers. Don't worry, they'll pick their spot.'

'Oh, I'm not worried,' Sampson said. 'I'm just anxious to get it on with these boys.'

As the afternoon progressed, we talked casually to some more H and K employees and their families. The people were easy to talk to and we were real friendly. Most of them said they liked where they worked a lot. Sampson and I passed ourselves off as new to the company and nobody questioned it. In fact, most everyone was cordial and welcoming, almost to a fault. Hard not to like the folks in Rocky Mount, most of them anyway.

Lunch was followed by team sports and other competitive games: swim races, volleyball, soccer, softball, and organized contests for the kids.

Starkey, Harris and Griffin eventually headed off toward one of the adjoining softball fields.

Sampson and I followed at a distance.

Let the games begin.

Chapter Eighty-Two

'Need a couple more to fill out this team. You big fellows play any ball?' asked an old man wearing a dusty Atlanta Braves shirt and ball cap. 'You're welcome to join in. It's a friendly little game.'

I glanced over at Sampson. He smiled and said, 'Sure, we'll play some ball.'

The two of us were put on the same team, which seemed the more ragtag and needier of the two. Starkey, Harris and Griffin were on the other team. Our worthy opponents for the friendly game.

'Looks like we're the underdogs,' Sampson said.

'We're not down here to win a softball game,' I said.

He grinned. 'Yeah, and we're not here to lose one either.'

The game was good-natured on the surface, but everything was heavily stacked against our team. Starkey and Harris were good athletes, and everybody on their team seemed decent and knew how to play. Our group was uneven, and they exploited our weaknesses. We were behind by two runs after the first inning, and four runs after the third.

As we jogged off the field to take our turn at bat, Sampson patted my butt. 'Definitely not down here to lose,' he said.

Sampson was scheduled to bat third that inning. I would be up fourth if somebody got on base. A skinny, older Mexican man led off with a bunt single and got razzed by our macho opponents for not having any *cojones*. The next batter, a big-bellied accountant, blooped a single just over the second baseman's head. More semi-good-natured razzing came from our opponents.

'Rather be lucky than good,' our guy yelled back from first base as he slapped his big beer belly.

Now Sampson stepped to the plate. He never took a practice swing, just touched the rubber base with the tip of the longest and heaviest bat he could find on the rack.

'Big power hitter. Better move back those fences!' Starkey called from shortstop. He looked like a ballplayer, moved easily and fluidly at bat and in the field, bent the peak of his cap just so.

Sampson just stood there with the bat on his shoulder. Nobody except me knew what to expect from the big man, and even I couldn't always tell with him. The two of us had played a lot of ball together when we were kids. Sampson had been an all-city receiver as a junior in high school, but he didn't go out for the football team in his senior year. He was an even better baseball player, but he never played organized ball after Little League.

I stood on deck, trying to figure how he would play it.

Actually, there weren't any fences at the field, so he couldn't hit one out of the park if he wanted to. So what would he do?

The first pitch floated up to the plate, fat and juicy, but Sampson never took his bat off his shoulder. It was hard to imagine a more tempting pitch would come his way.

Warren Griffin was doing the pitching for their team. He was a decent-enough athlete, fielded his position well.

'Didn't like that one?' he called to Sampson. 'What's the matter with it?'

'No challenge.'

Griffin smiled. He signaled for Harris to come out to the mound. Brownley Harris was doing the catching, and he looked like a slightly shorter version of the old Red Sox great, Carlton Fisk. *Pudge.*

On the next pitch, Griffin wound up and delivered a windmill-style fastball toward home plate. He was real quick, what they call sneaky fast.

But so was Sampson.

He dropped his bat and sent a near-perfect drag bunt down the third-base line. They were so surprised, he could have walked to first base and made it easily. He was on, the bases full.

'Up to you, sugar,' Sampson called from first base. He was grinning at me, winking, pointing an imaginary six-gun my way.

I started to smile as I strolled to the plate. He'd put me on the spot, just like he'd planned it.

'You like a challenge, too?' Warren Griffin called from the pitcher's mound.

'You a bunter or a hitter?' Starkey taunted from his spot at shortstop.

The catcher, Brownley Harris, settled in behind me. 'What's it going to be, hot-shot? How you want it?'

I looked back at him. 'Surprise me,' I said.

Griffin set up for a windmill-style pitch so I figured he was coming with heat. *What the hell?* I thought. *Just a friendly little game.*

The fast pitch came in a little high, but it was close enough to my power wheel that I couldn't resist taking a whack. The bat cracked and the ball shot straight over the pitcher's head, still picking up speed and altitude. It flew over the center fielder's head, too. Our team of misfits was going crazy, screaming and cheering from the bench. Suddenly, there was some joy in Mudville.

I was on my horse, rounding the bases. Starkey gave me a look as I touched second and raced past him. It was as if he knew something. *Did he?*

I made it to third and saw Sampson ahead of me; he was waving me home. I didn't even look toward the outfield – I was coming no matter what happened out there.

I curled around third base, and then I accelerated. I probably hadn't moved this fast in years.

I was really motoring.

Brownley Harris was waiting for me at home plate – but where was the ball? I was moving like a runaway train when I saw the throw from the outfield skipping through the infield on two hops. Hell, it was going to beat me home. Goddamn it.

Harris held his ground as he took the perfect throw from the center fielder. He had me dead to rights.

I kept barreling toward him. Harris was blocking home plate with his beefy body. If I hit him hard it might shake the ball loose. His dark, hooded eyes held mine. He was ready for impact, whatever I could give him. He looked like he'd played some football; still looked tough and in shape. Army Ranger. Killer. His eyes bordered on mean.

I was bearing down on Harris and, as I got close, I lowered my shoulder. Let him see what was coming his way.

Then, at the last possible instant, I went wide and low. I did a pretty hook-slide around the catcher. With my left hand I touched home plate between his thick legs and muddy cleats.

'Safe!' the umpire yelled and spread his arms wide.

As I was getting up, I caught sight of Harris out of the corner of my eye. He was moving toward me fast. This could be trouble. No more friendly little game.

His right arm suddenly shot forward and he slapped me 'five'.

'Nice play,' he said. 'You got us that time, partner. Be ready for you next time. Hell, we're all on the same team anyway, right? H and K all the way.'

Jesus, he actually seemed like a nice guy.

For a killer.

Chapter Eighty-Three

'You run pretty good for a washed-up cop in his early forties,' Sampson said as we walked through a dusty lot filled mostly with minivans and trucks. We'd seen enough at the company picnic. After our show of respectability we'd lost the softball game by seven runs, and it could have been even worse.

'At least I don't have to bunt to get on base,' I said.

'Last thing they expected, sugar. Worked, didn't it? Pissed'm off, too.'

'We lost the game.'

'But not the war,' said Sampson.

'This is true. Not the war. Not yet anyway.'

I drove from the picnic site out to the Falling River Walk development. I parked right around the corner from Thomas Starkey's house. It was redbrick with white trim on the windows, black shutters. The lot looked to be about an acre and was landscaped with rhododendron, hemlock and mountain laurel. It was well kept. We walked past a mass of yellow chrysanthemums to the side door.

'This how it's going to be from here on?' Sampson asked. 'Breaking and entering in broad daylight?'

'They probably know who we are,' I said. 'Know we're here for them.'

'Probably. Rangers are the premier light-infantry unit in the Army. Most are good guys, too. "Rangers lead the way." That's been their motto since Omaha Beach, D Day. Tip of the spear.'

'How about in Vietnam?' I asked.

'Lots of Rangers over there. They performed the heavy re-con missions. Seventy-fifth Ranger Regiment, three battalions. Exemplary soldiers, the best. Most of them. Probably had the best military assassins, too.'

It took me less than a minute to get inside the side door of the Starkey house, which led into a small laundry room that reeked of bleach and detergent. We didn't hear any alarm going off, but that didn't mean we hadn't tripped one coming inside.

'Could the three of them still be in the Army? Special assignment?' I asked.

'The thought had crossed my mind. I hope this isn't about something the Army is trying to hide.'

'But you think it might be?'

'Like I said – I hope it's not. I *do* like the Army, sugar. Hoo-hah!'

The house was only a few years old, and it was immaculate and strikingly ordered inside. Two fieldstone fireplaces on the first floor, vaulted ceilings, a game room with a wet bar and a pool table. I figured the house was probably around five thousand square feet and cost maybe four hundred thousand. Thomas Starkey lived pretty well for a salesman. So did Griffin and Harris from the look of their new houses.

Everything was neat and clean; even the kids' toys were stacked and arranged on shelves. Starkey and his wife sure ran a tight ship.

The kitchen was high tech, with a big Below Zero refrigerator. Shiny, stainless-steel All-clad pots and pans hung above the work station. A giant cast-iron skillet had a place of pride on the right back burner of the stove.

Off the master bedroom was a small room that turned out to be Starkey's den. Lots of Army souvenirs and pictures. I looked at the photographs on the walls, saw Harris and Griffin in several. *But none of the men whom they had set up.* I didn't really expect to see Ellis Cooper in a picture on Thomas Starkey's wall, but that didn't stop me from hoping.

Sampson was opening desk drawers and examining the contents of several cabinets built into the wall. He came to a closet with a padlock on it. He looked over at me.

I shrugged. 'Go for it. That's what we're here for.'

'No turning back now.'

He took out his Glock and smashed down with the butt. The padlock held, but he had snapped the hinge off the wall. Obviously, the lock was just to keep out Starkey's kids, and maybe his wife.

'Dirty pictures,' Sampson said as he rummaged around inside. 'Skin magazines, some nasty bondage. One with really young girls. Here the women are shaved. Lots of Asian girls. Fancy that. Maybe they did those girls in New York.'

He checked the closet for false sides. 'Nothing. Just the sleazy porn collection. He's not the husband and daddy of the year, but I guess we knew that already.'

I kept looking, but I didn't think I'd find anything incriminating. 'He must keep the good stuff somewhere else. I guess we should go. Leave everything the way it is. I want Starkey to know we were here.'

'Might get Tom in some trouble with the missus,' Sampson said, and winked.

'Good deal. He should be in trouble with somebody.'

Sampson and I walked back through the house and out the side door again. Birds were chirping in the trees. How sweet. The sun was a brilliant white-gold orb in blue skies. Nice town, Rocky Mount.

A blue GMC Suburban was parked out front. Starkey, Harris and Griffin were waiting for us.

Three Blind Mice.

Also, three against two.

Chapter Eighty-Four

No point in being subtle. Sampson and I took our guns out. We held them with the barrels down, not pointed at anyone. The three of them didn't appear to be armed. *Just a friendly little game, right.*

'Nothing's going to happen here,' Starkey called to us. 'This is where my wife and children live. It's a good neighborhood. Decent people in all these houses up and down the street.'

'And it's also where you keep your porn collection,' I said. 'S&M, bondage. Memories of your sweethearts from the war.'

He smiled thinly, nodded. 'That too. You're detectives, right? DC? Friends of Sergeant Ellis Cooper. Seems to me that you're a long ways from home. Why don't you go back to Washington? It's safer there than here in Rocky Mount. Believe it or not.'

'We know what you've done,' I told him. 'Most of it anyway. We don't know why yet. That'll come. We're getting close. The An Lao Valley in Vietnam? What happened there, Colonel Starkey? It was real bad, right? Things got out of control. Why is Three Blind Mice still working?'

Starkey didn't deny the murders or anything else I said. 'There's nothing you can do to us. Like I said, I think you should go home now. Consider this a friendly warning. We're not bad guys. We're just doing our job.'

'What if we don't go?' Sampson asked. 'What if we continue the investigation here in Rocky Mount? You killed a friend of mine.'

Starkey clasped his hands together, then he looked at Harris and Griffin. I could tell they weren't into friendly warnings.

'Don't come near any of our houses again,' Starkey said. His eyes were cold and hard. The assassin. *We're not bad guys. We're a whole lot worse than that.*

Brownley Harris pushed himself away from the hood of the Suburban. 'You hear what the man said? You two niggers listening? You *oughtta* be. Now clear the fuck out of here and don't ever come back. You don't come to a man's house with this shit. Not the way it's done, you hear? You fucking hear me?'

I smiled. 'You're the hothead. That's good to know. Starkey is the leader. So what does that make you, Griffin? You just muscle?'

Warren Griffin laughed out loud. 'That's right. I'm just muscle. And artillery. I'm the one who eats guys like you for breakfast.'

I didn't move a muscle. Neither did Sampson. We continued to stare at the three of them. 'I am curious about one thing, Starkey. How do you know about us? Who told you?'

His answer shook me to the core.

'Foot Soldier,' he said. Then Colonel Thomas Starkey smiled and tipped his ball cap.

Chapter Eighty-Five

S ampson and I rode the Interstate back to Washington late that afternoon. I was really starting to dislike, or at least tire of I-95 and its thundering herd of slip-sliding, exhaust-spewing tractor-trailers.

'The circumstances could be better, but it's good spending all this time with you,' I said as we tooled along in the passing lane. 'You're too quiet, though. What's up? Something's bothering you.'

He looked my way. 'You remember a time – you were about eleven – I came over? Spent a couple of weeks with you and Nana?'

'I remember a lot of times like that,' I told him. 'Nana used to say we were brothers, just not flesh and blood ones. You were always at the house.'

'This time was different, sugar. I even know why you don't remember. Let me tell it.'

'All right.'

'See, I never used to go home after school. Reason being, nobody was there most of the time. That night I got home around nine, nine-thirty. Made myself corned beef hash for dinner. Sat down to watch some tube. I used to like *Mission Impossible* back then, wait for it all week. There was a knock at the door.

'I went to see who was there, and it was Nana. She gave me a big hug, just like she still does when she sees me. Asked me if I had some corned beef hash for her, too. Said she liked hers with eggs on top. Then she cackled her cackle, you know.'

'I don't remember any of this. Why was she at your house so late at night?'

Sampson continued with his story. 'That afternoon my mother was convicted for possession of heroin to sell. She'd been sentenced. Social Services came by, but I was out. Somebody called Nana Mama.

'So Nana came over, and she actually ate a little of the hash I'd cooked. Told me it was pretty good. Maybe I would be a famous chef one day. Then she said I was coming over to your house for a while. She told me why. She had done some of her magic with Child Welfare. That was the first time that Nana saved me. The first of many times.'

I nodded. Listened. Sampson wasn't finished with his story.

'She was the one who helped get me into the Army after high school. Then into the police academy when I got out of the service. She's your grandmother, but she's more a mother to me than my own flesh. And I never had a father, not really. Neither of us did. I always thought that held us together in the beginning.'

It wasn't like Sampson to go on and open up like this. I still didn't speak. I had no idea where he was headed, but I let him go as much as he wanted to.

'I always knew I didn't have it in me to be a father or a good husband. It was just something I felt inside. You?'

'I had some fears before I met Maria,' I said. 'Then they just went away. Most of them anyway. I knew Maria and I would be good together. First time I held Damon the rest of the fears pretty much disappeared for good.'

Sampson began to smile, then he was laughing. 'I met somebody, Alex. It's strange, but she makes me happy and I trust her with my secrets. Look at me, I'm grinnin' like a goddamn Halloween pumpkin.'

Both of us were laughing now. Why not? It was the first time I'd seen Sampson in love, and we'd been friends for a long time.

'I'll mess it up somehow,' he said. But he was still laughing. We joked and laughed most of the rest of the way home. Jesus, John Sampson had a girlfriend.

Billie.

Chapter Eighty-Six

Nana Mama always used to say, *'Laugh before breakfast, cry before dinner.'* If you raise a family, you know there's some truth to that, crazy as it sounds.

When I got back to Fifth Street that night there was a red-and-white EMS truck sitting in front of our house.

I shut down the Porsche and bounded out of it.

It was raining, and the bracing wind and water whipped at my face. Partially blinded by the rain, I hurtled up the front steps and entered the house. My heart was hammering and a voice inside whispered *no, no, no.*

I heard voices coming from the living room and rushed in there expecting the worst.

Nana Mama and the kids were sitting on the old sofa. They were all holding hands.

Across from them sat a woman in a white lab coat. I recognized Dr Kayla Coles from the night with Damon's sick friend, Ramon.

'You missed all the excitement,' Nana said as she saw me enter the room.

'Imagine that, Daddy,' said Jannie. 'You missed the excitement.'

I looked toward the doctor sitting in the easy chair. 'Hello, Doctor.'

She had a good smile. 'Nice to see you again.'

I turned to Nana. 'Exactly what excitement did I miss? For starters, what's the EMS truck doing outside?'

She shrugged. 'I thought I had a heart attack, Alex. Turns out, it was just a fainting spell.'

Dr Coles spoke. 'Nana doesn't remember passing out. I was down the street at the time. I work with a group that brings health care into the neighborhoods of Southeast. Makes it easier for some people to get good care. More personal, and definitely more affordable.'

I interrupted. 'Nana passed out. What happened to her?'

'Damon saw the EMS truck and he came and got me. Nana was already up on her feet. She had an irregular heartbeat. Rapid, threading. The pulse in her wrist wasn't as fast as the actual heart rate, so there could be some diminished circulation. We took her over to St Anthony's for a few tests.'

Nana shrugged the whole thing off. 'I fell down, went boom, in the kitchen. Always hoped it would be there. Damon and Jannie were just great, Alex. About time they started taking care of me for a change.'

She laughed, and so did Dr Coles. I was glad they both saw the humor in the situation.

'You're still here. It's past nine,' I said to the doctor.

She smiled. Good bedside manner, or whatever this

was. 'We were having so much fun I decided to stay for a while. I still have one more stop, but Mr Bryant doesn't get off work until ten.'

'And,' I said, 'you were waiting for me to get home.'

'Yes, I thought that would be the best idea. Nana says you work late a lot of nights. Could we talk for a minute?'

Chapter Eighty-Seven

The two of us stepped out onto the front porch. Heavy rain was pelting down on the overhang and the air was damp and cool. The good doctor pulled a gray car sweater around herself.

'I've already had this chat with your grandmother,' she said. 'Nana asked that I talk to you, answer all your questions. I would never go behind her back, or condescend to her in any way.'

'That's a good idea,' I said. 'I think you'd find that she's awfully hard to condescend to.'

Kayla suddenly laughed. 'Oh, *I know*. I had your nana – sorry, Mrs Regina Hope Cross in eighth grade. She's still probably the most inspirational teacher I've had. That includes undergraduate at Brandeis and medical school at Tufts. Thought I would flash my resume by you.'

'Okay, I'm impressed. So what's the matter with Nana?'

Kayla sighed. 'She's getting *old*, Alex. She admits to eighty-two. The tests we took at St Anthony's won't come back until some time tomorrow or the next day. The lab boys will call me, then I'll call Nana myself. My concern? She's been having palpitations for several weeks. Dizziness, lightheadedness, shortness of breath. She tell you?'

I shook my head. Suddenly I felt more than a little embarrassed. 'I had no idea. She told me she was feeling fine. There was a rough morning a couple of weeks back, but no complaints from her since.'

'She doesn't want you to worry about her. When she was at St Anthony's we did an EKG, an echocardiogram, routine lab work. As I mentioned, her heartbeat is irregular.

'On the positive side of things, there's no sign of edema. Her lungs are clear. No evidence that she's suffered a stroke, even a slight one. Nana has very good general muscle strength for somebody her age, or even younger.'

'So what happened to her? You have any idea?'

'We'll have the test results in a day. Dr Redd in the lab was in Nana's class, too. If I was to hazard a guess, I would say atrial fibrillation. This involves the two small upper chambers of the heart, the atria. They seem to be quivering, rather than beating effectively. There's some risk of clotting.'

'I take it she's okay to be here tonight,' I said. 'I don't want her stubbornness to keep her out of the hospital if she needs to be there. Money isn't a consideration.'

Kayla Coles nodded. 'Alex, my opinion is that it's safe for her to be home right now. She said her sister will be coming from Maryland tomorrow. I think that's a wise precaution. Someone to help with the kids and the house.'

'I'll help with the kids,' I said. 'And the house.'

She raised an eyebrow. 'I believe we've already established that you work too hard.'

I sighed and shut my eyes for a couple of seconds. The news was finally hitting me, sinking in. Now I had to force myself to deal with it. Nana was in her early eighties, and she was sick.

Kayla reached out and lightly patted my arm. 'She's getting up there, but she's strong, and she wants to be around for a long time. That's important. Alex, Nana believes that you and the children need her.'

I finally managed a thin smile. 'Well, she's right about that.'

'Don't let her do too much right now.'

'Hard to keep her down.'

'Well, *tie* her if you have to,' Kayla Coles said, and then she laughed.

I didn't, couldn't right then. I knew a fair amount about heart disease from my days at Johns Hopkins. I would definitely keep a closer watch on Nana. 'What about you, Dr Coles? What about your work schedule? Nearly ten o'clock and you still have more house calls.'

She shrugged, and seemed a little embarrassed by the question. 'I'm young, I'm strong, and I believe the people in these neighborhoods need decent, affordable health care. So that's what I'm providing – trying to. Goodnight, Alex. Take good care of your grandmother.'

'Oh, I will. I promise.'

'The road to hell,' she said.

'Paved with good intentions.'

She nodded and walked off the porch. 'Say goodnight to everybody for me.' Dr Coles headed down Fifth Street to her final appointment of the day.

Chapter Eighty-Eight

I did some more background work on the Three Blind Mice the next day, taped notes to my wall in the attic, but I couldn't get into it, couldn't concentrate worth a damn. Nana's lab tests came back in the afternoon, and as Kayla Coles had promised, she did call the house. The two of us had a talk on the phone after she spoke to Nana.

'I just wanted to thank you for your help,' I said as I got on the line. 'I'm sorry if I was rude the other night.'

'What makes you think you were rude? You were a little frightened is all. I don't think "rude" is part of your makeup. Anyway, let me tell you about your grandmother. She *is* suffering from atrial fibrillation, but given the options, that's not such bad news.'

'Tell me why I should be happy about it,' I said.

'Not happy. But the treatment is non-invasive and has a good success rate. I think we can treat her with a catheter ablation. We'll start there. She'll be able to go home the next day, and hopefully be her old self in a week.'

'When should she go in for the procedure?' I asked.

'That's up to her. I wouldn't wait more than a couple of weeks. She sounded a little stubborn when I brought up a hospital stay. Says she's too busy.'

'I'll talk to her. See if it helps. What do we do until then?'

'Just baby aspirin, believe it or not. One eighty-one milligram tablet a day. She also has to limit her caffeine – coffee and tea. And she should avoid stress-related situations. Good luck on that one.'

'That's it?' I asked.

'For now, yes. Please watch the stress on her. I'll stay involved if she wants me to.'

'I know she does.'

Kayla Coles laughed. 'Good. She's a smart woman, isn't she? We're going to make sure she sees a hundred.'

I laughed. 'I hope *I* get to see her reach a hundred. So, no special precautions until we go in for the procedure?'

'No, not really. Just try not to bring too much excitement into her life.'

'I'll do my best,' I said.

'You do your best and try not to get *shot*,' said Kayla Coles before she hung up.

Chapter Eighty-Nine

No way I was going to get shot staying at home – or so I believed. A couple of mornings after my conversation with Dr Kayla Coles, I came downstairs to make breakfast for the kids. Nana was sitting at her spot at the kitchen table, a large brown mug steaming in front of her.

'Unh, uh.' I wagged a finger at her.

'Decaffeinated,' she said. 'Don't start in on me, Alex.'

'Nope. I won't even say that you're a little touchy this morning. Sleep okay?'

'Nobody my age sleeps okay. I did set up an appointment for the catheter ablation. I go in a week from today. Happy?' she asked.

'Very happy,' I said, then I went and gave her a hug, which Nana returned in kind. Dr Kayla was right – she was strong for her age.

Later that morning I had a pretty good talk with FBI Director Burns. He told me he had someone trying to track the e-mail from the Foot Soldier, but so far no luck on it. He asked if I'd given serious consideration to his offer to work at Quantico. I'd been expecting the question.

'I've thought about it some. My life is suddenly a little complicated. For one thing, I need to get some kind of closure on this case with the Army.'

'They helping or getting in the way? The Army?' Burns asked.

'A little of both. I've met some good people. Army's like everybody else, though. They want to solve their own problems. There's something incredibly nasty going on with this murder case. They know it, and so do I. I feel it in my bones. There will be more murders. That's my fear.'

'If I can help,' Burns said. 'No strings attached, Alex. This is a big case. I think it's important, too.'

'I appreciate that.'

After I got off the phone, I went in search of Nana. She was futzing around in the kitchen as usual. *Her* kitchen. *Her* house.

'I need a rest. So do you,' I said to her. 'Where do you want to go after your procedure?'

'Paris,' Nana said without blinking an eye. 'Then maybe Rome. Venice, of course. Florence would be real nice. Then come home through London. Stop in and see the Queen. What do you think? Sound too rich for your blood? Maybe you were thinking of a train ride to Baltimore?' she asked, and laughed at her own joke. She was a funny lady, always had been.

'I have some money put away,' I told her.

'Me too,' she said. 'Mad money. What about Jamilla? What about your job?'

'If Jamilla could take some time off, that would be great. She likes her job, though.'

'That sounds familiar, doesn't it? How's *your* marble collection? Maybe you should buy a couple of jars for her.'

I laughed. Then I went over and put my arms around Nana. Couldn't help myself lately. 'I love you, old woman,' I said. 'I don't tell you that enough, and when I do, it isn't with the passion I feel.'

'That's nice to hear,' she said. 'You can be so sweet sometimes. I love you too, and I always say it with the passion that I feel.'

'You feeling all right?' I asked.

'Today's good. Tomorrow, who knows?' She shrugged. 'I'm making some lunch. Don't ask if you can help. I'm fine. Still on the right side of the grass.'

After lunch, I went upstairs to my office in the attic to think about what my next steps should be. There was a fax waiting. I wagged my finger at it. '*Unh, uh.*'

It was a copy of a news story in the *Miami Herald*. I read about the execution last night of a man named Tichter at the Florida State Prison in Starke. Abraham Tichter had been in Vietnam. Special Forces.

Scrawled at the bottom of the fax was the following:

Innocent of these murders in Florida. Wrongfully accused, convicted and executed. Abraham Tichter makes six. In case you aren't keeping count.

Foot Soldier

I was keeping count.

Chapter Ninety

E ver since Nana had been under the weather I'd been
doing the grocery shopping and most of the house-
hold chores. Usually I took little Alex with me to the small
Safeway on Fourth Street. That's what I did early in the
afternoon.

I carried him high on my shoulders, out the kitchen
door and down the driveway to my car.

Alex was giggling and yapping as he always does. The
boy never shuts up or sits still. He's a bouncing ball of
pure energy and I can't get enough of him.

I was absently thinking about the last message from
Foot Soldier, so I don't even know why I happened to
notice the black Jeep traveling down Fifth.

It was moving at around thirty, right about the speed
limit.

I don't know why I paid it much attention, but I did. My
eyes never left it as it came toward little Alex and me.

Suddenly, the barrel of a black Tec protruded through
the side window of the Jeep. I pulled down the baby, then

dropped to the ground, whipping my body sideways to avoid landing on Alex.

The shooting started.

Pop-pop-pop-pop-pop.

I bellied across the lawn, shielding my baby under my left arm, and then dragging him behind a shade tree. I needed cover between us and the gunman.

I didn't get a good look inside the Jeep, but I did see that the driver and the shooter were white. Two of them – not three.

I couldn't tell if they were the men from Rocky Mount. Who else could it be, though? The shooters from West Point? Were they the same? What was happening now on Fifth Street? Who had ordered it?

Pop-pop-pop-pop-pop.

Pop-pop-pop-pop-pop.

Bullets cracked into the walls of the house and a front window shattered. I had to stop the attack somehow. *But how?* I crawled to the porch, and made it just before another round of fire.

Pop-pop-pop-pop-pop.

Unbelievable, even for Southeast.

I pushed Alex down behind the porch. He was screaming bloody murder now. Poor frightened little boy. I kept him down on the ground. Then lifted my head and got a quick peek at the Jeep stopped in front of my house.

Pop-pop-pop-pop-pop-pop-pop.

I returned fire. Three carefully aimed shots, so as not to hit someone in the neighborhood. Then two more shots. *Yes!* I knew that I got the shooter. Possibly in the chest, but maybe the throat. I saw him jerk back hard and then slump over the seat. No more shots came.

Suddenly the Jeep took off, tires screeching, backside shimmy-shaking as it skidded around the nearest corner.

I carried Alex inside and herded Nana and the baby into her room. I made them stay down on the floor. Then I called Sampson and he was at the house in minutes. I was just about past being shocked and afraid for my family, when I became as angry as I'd ever been. My body shook with rage and the need for retaliation.

'Lot of broken windows, some bullet holes in the walls. Nobody hurt,' Sampson said after a quick walk around the house.

'It was a warning. Otherwise I think they would have killed me. They came to the house to deliver a message. Just like when we went to Starkey's house in Rocky Mount.'

Chapter Ninety-One

It was just past four in the morning when Thomas Starkey waltzed out the kitchen door of his home. He walked across a dewy patch of lawn, then climbed into his blue Suburban. It started right up. Starkey always kept it in perfect condition, even serviced it himself.

'I'd like to take a few potshots at the fucker right now,' Sampson said at my side. We were parked in deep shadows at the end of the street. 'Blow out a few windows in his house. Spread a little terror his way.'

'Hold that thought,' I said.

A few minutes later, the Suburban stopped and picked up Warren Griffin, who lived nearby in Greystone. It drove on to Knob Hill and picked up Brownley Harris. Then the Suburban sped out of Rocky Mount on US-64, heading in the direction of Raleigh.

'None of them look shot up,' Sampson said. 'That's too bad. So who'd you shoot on Fifth Street?'

'I have no idea. Complicates things though, doesn't it? These three know something. They're in this conspiracy we've been hearing about.'

'The silent gray wall?'

'That's the one. Seems to work pretty well, too.'

I didn't have to follow too closely, didn't even have to keep the Suburban in sight. Earlier that morning, around three o'clock, I'd slapped a radio-direction-finding device under the vehicle. Ron Burns was helping me in any way he could. I'd told him about the shooting at my house.

I kept a good distance behind the killers. The Suburban stayed on US-64 past Zebulon, then I-440 to 85th South. We went by Burlington, Greensboro, Charlotte, Gastonia and then entered South Carolina.

Sampson sat beside me on the front seat, but he fell asleep before we got to South Carolina. He had worked a shift the day before and he was exhausted. He finally woke up in Georgia, yawned, and stretched his big body as best he could in the cramped space.

'Where are we?'

'Lavonia.'

'Oh, that's good news. Where's Lavonia?'

'Near Sandy Cross. We're in Georgia. Still hot on their trail.'

'You think this is another hit coming up?'

'We'll see.'

At Doraville we stopped at a diner and had breakfast. The state-of-the-art device attached to the Suburban was still tracking. It seemed unlikely that they'd check and find it at this point.

The breakfast – cheese omelets, country ham and grits – was a little disappointing. The diner looked just about

FOUR BLIND MICE

perfect, and it sure smelled good when we walked inside, but the generous portions were bland, except for the country ham, which was too salty for me.

'You going to follow up with Burns? Maybe become an FBI man?' Sampson asked after he'd downed his second coffee. I could tell he was finally waking up.

'I don't know for sure. Check with me in a week or so. I'm a little burnt out right now. Like this food.'

Sampson nodded. 'It'll do. I'm sorry I got you involved in all this, Alex. I don't even know if we can bring them down. They're cocky, but they're careful when they need to be.'

I agreed. 'I think they did the hits solely for money. But that doesn't explain enough. What happened to start the killing? Who's behind it? Who's paying the bills?'

Sampson's eyes narrowed. 'The three of them got a taste for killing in the war. Happens sometimes. I've seen it.'

I put down my knife and fork and pushed the plate away. No way could I finish off the omelet and ham. I'd barely touched the grits, which needed something. Maybe cheddar cheese? Onions, sautéed mushrooms?

'I owe you. This is big debt, Alex,' Sampson said.

I shook my head. 'You don't owe me a thing. But I'll probably collect on it anyway.'

We went back out to the car and followed the signal for another two hours. The trip had taken from morning into the early afternoon.

We were on I-75 which we took to US-41, and then *old* 41. Then we were on some narrow, meandering country road in Kennesaw Mountain Park. We were following three killers in northern Georgia, about eight hours from Rocky Mount, close to five hundred miles.

I passed the turn-off the first time and had to go back. A turkey vulture was sitting there watching us. The hills around here were heavily forested and the foliage was thick and ornery-looking.

'We ought to park somewhere along the main road. Hide the car as best we can. Then walk on in through the woods,' I said.

'Sounds like a plan. I hate the fucking woods, though.'

I found a little turn-in that would keep the car hidden. We opened the trunk and took out guns, ammo and night-vision goggles for each of us. Then we walked about half a mile through the thick woods before we could see a small cabin. Smoke was curling out of a fieldstone chimney.

A very cozy spot. For what, though? A meeting of some kind? Who was here?

The cabin was near a small lake that was fed by the headwaters of the Jacks River, at least that was how it was marked. A stand of hemlocks, maples and beech trees enveloped the clearing in deep green. Some of the trees were easily six feet wide.

The blue Suburban was parked in front of the cabin – but so was a silver Mercedes station wagon. It had North Carolina plates.

'They've got company. Who the hell is this?' Sampson asked. 'Maybe we caught a break.'

We saw the front door open and Colonel Thomas

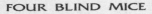

FOUR BLIND MICE

Starkey stepped outside. He had on a green tee-shirt and baggy fatigue pants.

Right behind him was Marc Sherman, Cumberland County's district attorney. *Christ.*

It was the lawyer who had prosecuted and convicted Ellis Cooper for the murders of three women that he didn't commit.

307

Chapter Ninety-Two

'**W**hat the hell is this? You *know* who he is?' Sampson asked. His temperature was rising fast.

'I remember him. Like you said, maybe we caught a little break. But why would Marc Sherman be here?'

Sampson and I were crouched behind a couple of ancient beech trees about a hundred yards from the cabin. The forest was eerily dark and almost seemed primitive. The roots of the huge trees all around us were carpeted by small ferns. On the walk there our legs got a good lashing from the catbrier and blackberry stickers.

'We're in deep shit somewhere around Kennesaw, Georgia. We traveled a lot of hours to get here. Now what?' John asked.

'Now we wait. We *listen*,' I said.

I reached into a cloth duffel bag and pulled out a black box attached to what looked like a silver wand. The apparatus was a long-distance microphone, compliments of my new good buddies at the Bureau in Quantico.

Sampson nodded when he saw what it was. 'FBI wants you *real* bad.'

I nodded back. 'That they do. This is a state-of-the-art unit. But we should get a little closer.'

We made our way up toward the cabin, crawling on our hands and knees between the towering trees. Besides the long-distance mike, Sampson and I had rifles, and 9-millimeter Glocks.

'Take one of these,' I said. 'In case you don't like the NVGs.' I handed him a pocket scope that worked in day or night. Fully extended, it was less than six inches long. Another valuable loan from the FBI.

'Only fair, I guess,' Sampson said. 'The boys probably have a couple of war toys of their own inside that log cabin.'

'That's what I was thinking. It's the argument I used with Burns. That and the fact that they came after me at my house. Burns has three kids of his own. He was sympathetic.'

Sampson glanced over at me. 'I thought you didn't know it was them in Washington?' he whispered.

'I don't. I'm not so sure it was. I had to tell Burns something. I don't know that it *wasn't* them.'

Sampson grinned and shook his head. 'You're gonna get fired before you get hired.'

I stayed close to the ground and trained one end of the mike at the cabin. We were only fifty yards away now. I worked the microphone around until the voices were as clear as if they were just a few feet away from us.

I recognized Starkey's voice. 'Thought we'd party a little

tonight, Counselor. Tomorrow we're going to hunt deer up on the mountain. You in?'

'I have to go back tonight,' said Marc Sherman. 'No hunting for me, I'm afraid.'

There was a brief silence, then a burst of laughter. Three or four men joined in.

Brownley Harris spoke up. 'That's just fine, Sherman. Take your blood money and run, why don't you? You hear this one? The Devil takes a meeting with this lawyer.'

'I heard it,' said Sherman.

'Funny, Marc. Now listen. Devil is slick as shit, you know. I mean, *you know*, right, Counselor? Devil says, "I'll make you a senior partner right now. Today." Young turk lawyer asks, "What do I have to do?" Devil says, "I want your immortal soul. Beat. And also the immortal souls of everyone in your family." The young lawyer stops and thinks, and he eyes the Devil something fierce. Then the lawyer says, "What's the catch?" '

There was raucous laughter from inside the cabin. Even Sherman joined in.

'That's even funny the fourth time. You *do* have the rest of my money?' he asked once the laughter had stopped.

'Of course we do. We've been paid, and you're going to be paid in full. We keep our deals, Mr Sherman. You can trust us. We're men of honor.'

Suddenly, I heard a loud noise off to the left of where we were crouched. Sampson and I swiveled around in a hurry. What the hell was this? A red sports car was coming fast up the dirt road. Too fast.

'Now who the hell is this?' Sampson asked in a whisper.

'More killers? Maybe the shooters from Washington?'

'Whoever it is, they're moving.'

We watched as the red car bounced up the badly rutted dirt road. It pulled in behind the Suburban, screeched to a stop.

The front door of the cabin opened. Starkey, then Harris stepped outside onto the porch.

The doors of the sports car were flung open simultaneously, almost as if the action was choreographed.

Two dark-haired women stepped out. Asian and very pretty. They were wearing skimpy tops and short skirts. Both had on outrageous shoes with high-heels. The driver held up a bottle in silver wrapping paper, smiled, and waved it at Starkey.

'*Chao mung da den voi to am cua chung toi,*' Starkey called from the front porch.

'Vietnamese,' Sampson said. 'Starkey said something like, "Welcome to our hootch."'

Chapter Ninety-Three

We had been observing the rustic cabin for more than two hours, and now we watched the sun dip behind the mountains. It had gotten much colder and my body was feeling stiff and I was tired from the drive. The wind whistled through the forest, whistled and sometimes roared. It felt like it was blowing right through me.

'We're going to get them,' Sampson whispered hoarsely. I think he was trying to cheer me up. 'Maybe tonight, maybe not. They're making mistakes, Alex.'

I agreed with that. 'Yes, they are. They're not invincible. I'm not even sure if they have the whole story themselves. They're just a piece of this.'

We could hear them inside the cabin – every word. Marc Sherman had apparently decided to stay for the party. Rock music echoed from the cabin. Janis Joplin was wailing, and one of the Asian women sang along. It sounded like bad karaoke, but nobody complained. Then the Doors came on. Memories of Vietnam, I suppose. 'This is the end . . .'

Occasionally, someone would pass by a window. The Asian women had both taken off their tops. The taller of the two stepped outside for a few minutes. She smoked a joint, taking greedy puffs.

Harris came out and joined her. They spoke English on the porch.

'I used to know your mama-san,' he said, and giggled.

'You're kidding?' the girl laughed and blew out jets of smoke. 'Of course you're joking. I get it. Sort of.' She looked to be in her late teens, maybe early twenties. Her breasts were large and too round, augmented. She wobbled slightly on the high-heels.

'No, I knew her. She was my hootch mama. I made it with her, and now I'm going to make it with you. See the irony?'

The girl laughed again. 'I see that you're stoned.'

'Well, there's that too, my smart little dink. The thing is, maybe you're my daughter.'

I tuned out on the conversation and stared at the outline of the A-frame cabin. It looked like some family's vacation house. We'd heard that the three of them had been using the place since the mid-eighties. They'd already talked about murders committed in these woods, but it wasn't clear who had been killed, or why. Or where the bodies were buried.

Jim Morrison was still singing 'The End'. The TV was on too, a University of Georgia football game. Georgia versus Auburn. Warren Griffin was rooting loudly and obnoxiously for Auburn. Marc Sherman had apparently gone to Georgia and Griffin was breaking his chops.

Sampson and I stayed in a culvert, a safe distance away. It was getting even colder, the wind screaming through the large hemlocks and beech trees.

'Starkey doesn't seem to be partying,' Sampson finally said. 'You notice that? What's he doing?'

'Starkey likes to watch. He's the cautious one, the leader. I'm going to move a little closer. We haven't seen or heard from the other girl in a while. Makes me nervous.'

Just then, we heard Marc Sherman raise his voice. 'Jesus, don't cut her. Be careful! C'mon, man. Put away the K-Bar!'

'Why the hell not cut her?' Harris yelled at the top of his voice. 'What the hell is she to you? You cut her, then. Try it, you'll like it. You cut her, Counselor. Get your hands dirty for a change!'

'I'm warning you, Harris. Put the goddamn knife down.'

'You're warning *me*? That's pretty rich. Here – take the knife. *Take it!* Here you go!'

The lawyer groaned loudly. I was pretty sure he'd been stabbed.

The girls began to scream. Sherman was moaning in excruciating pain. Chaos had taken over inside the cabin.

'*Cockadau!*' Harris suddenly yelled in Vietnamese. He sounded a little nuts.

'*Cockadau* means kill,' Sampson told me.

Chapter Ninety-Four

Sampson and I were up in a flash and sprinting full-out toward the cabin. We reached the front door together. He went in first with his gun drawn.

'Police!' he yelled over the blaring rock music and TV. 'Police! Hands in the air. Now!'

I was right behind Sampson when Starkey opened up with an MP5. At the same time, Griffin fired a handgun from across the room. The two Asian women were screaming as they scampered out the cabin's rear door. They had enough street smarts to get out of there fast. I saw that the smaller woman had a deep gash across her cheek. Her face was dripping blood.

Marc Sherman lay on the floor, motionless. There were dark splatters of blood on the wall behind the lawyer's body. He was dead.

The big gun erupted again, noise and smoke filling the room. My ears were ringing. I wasn't even sure if I'd been hit or not.

'Move out!' Sharkey yelled to the others.

'*Di di mau!*' Brownley Harris shouted, and actually seemed to be laughing. Was he completely mad? Were they all insane?

The three killers bolted out the back door. Warren Griffin covered the retreat with heavy fire. They didn't want a final shootout inside the cabin. Starkey had other plans for his team.

Sampson and I fired at the retreating men, but they made it out. We approached the back door slowly. Nobody was waiting there, and no more shots were fired at us for the moment.

Suddenly there was the sound of shooting away from the cabin. Half a dozen hollow *pops*. I heard the shrill screams of the two women cut through the trees.

I peeked my head around the corner of the cabin. I didn't like what I saw. The two women hadn't made it to their car. Both lay on the dirt road. They'd been shot in the back. Neither of them moved.

I turned to Sampson. 'They'll come back for us. They're going to take us out here in the woods.'

He shook his head. 'No they're not. We're going to take *them* out. When we see them, we open up. No warnings, Alex. No prisoners. Do you understand what I'm saying?'

I did. This was an all-or-nothing fight. It was war, not police work, and we were playing by the same rules as them.

Chapter Ninety-Five

It was awfully quiet all of a sudden. Almost as if nothing had happened, as if we were alone in the woods. I could hear the distant roar of the Jacks River, and birds twittering in the trees. A squirrel scampered up the trunk of a hemlock.

Otherwise, nothing moved. Nothing that I could see, anyway.

Eerie as hell.

I was getting a really bad feeling – we were in a trap. They knew we would come here after them, didn't they? This was their turf, not ours. And Sampson was right, this was war. We were in a combat zone, behind enemy lines. A fire fight was coming our way. Thomas Starkey was in charge of the opposition and he was good at this. All three of them were pros.

'I think one woman is moving a little,' he said. 'I'm going to check on her, Alex.'

'We both go,' I said, but Sampson was already slipping away from the cover of the trees.

'John?' I called, but he didn't look back.

I watched him run forward in a low crouch. He was down close to the ground, moving fast. He was good at this – combat. He'd been there, too.

He was about halfway to where the women lay when gunfire erupted from the woods to his right.

I still couldn't see anybody, just whispers of gun smoke wafting up into tree branches.

Sampson was hit and he went down hard. I could see his legs and lower torso just over a bramble. One leg twitched. Then nothing.

Sampson didn't move anymore.

I had to get to him somehow. But how? I crawled on my stomach to another tree. I felt weightless and unreal. *Completely* unreal. There was more gunsmoke. Pinging off rocks, thudding into nearby trees. I didn't think I was hit, but they'd come damn close. The fire was heavy.

I could see sheets of smoke from the rifles rising to my right. I could also smell the gunsmoke in the air.

It struck me that we weren't getting out of this one. I could see Sampson where he lay. He wasn't moving. Not even a twitch. I couldn't get to him. They had me pinned down. *My last case.* I had said that right from the start.

'John,' I called. 'John! Can you hear me?'

I waited a few seconds, then I called out again. 'John! Move something. John?'

Please say something. Please move.

Nothing came back to me.

Except another round of heavy fire from the woods.

Chapter Ninety-Six

I hadn't experienced anything like the explosive rage, but also the fear, that I felt. This happened in combat, I realized, and considered the irony. Soldiers lost buddies in the war and went a little mad, or maybe a great deal mad.

Is that what had happened in the An Lao Valley? There was a noisy buzzing inside my head, bright flashes of color in front of my eyes. Everything around me felt completely surreal.

'John,' I called again. 'If you can hear me, move something. Move a leg. John!'

Don't die on me. Not like this. Not now.

He didn't move, didn't respond. There was no sign that he was alive. He didn't shiver or twitch.

Nothing at all.

More rifle fire suddenly erupted from the woods, and I hugged the ground, digging my face into leaves and dirt.

I tried to put Sampson out of my mind. If I didn't, I would wind up dead. I had a terrible thought about John and Billie. Then I let it go. I had to. Otherwise, I'd die out here for sure.

Trouble was, I didn't see how I was going to out-maneuver three Army Rangers in the woods, especially on terrain they were familiar with. These were experienced combat veterans. So they wouldn't risk closing in on me right away. They'd wait until dark.

Not too long from now. Maybe a half-hour. Then I was going to die, wasn't I?

I lay behind a big hemlock, and a lot of disconnected thoughts shunted through my head. I thought about my kids, how unprepared I was to die, and how I would never see them again. I'd had so many warnings, so many close calls, but here I was.

I checked on Sampson again – he still hadn't moved.

I raised my head a couple of times. Just for a second. I turkey-necked a look across the horizon.

There were no moving shadows in the woods. I knew they were there though, waiting me out. Three Army assassins. Led by Colonel Thomas Starkey.

They'd been here before; they were patient as death itself.

They had killed a lot of people. In the Army. And out of it.

I thought of something Sampson had said before he went to help the two women. *When we see them, we open up. No warnings, Alex. No prisoners. Do you understand what I'm saying?*

I understood perfectly.

Chapter Ninety-Seven

Patience.

This was a waiting game, right? I understood that much about tonight. I even knew the military jargon for what I had to do next.

EE. Evade and escape.

I studied the rough terrain behind me and saw that I could slide down into a hollow that would give me some cover but would also allow me to move laterally, east or west. I could change my position without their knowing it.

That would give me a small advantage.

But I'd take anything I could get right now. I felt that I was a dead man. I didn't see any way out of this. So the hollow or gully looked awfully good to me.

I thought about Starkey, Griffin and Harris. How good they were; how badly I wanted to bring them down, Starkey in particular. He was the smart one, the leader, the cruelest of the three. Then I thought of what Sampson had said: *No prisoners.* Only they had to be thinking the same thing.

I started to slide backward. I call it a slide, but I was almost burrowing into the wet leaves and soft ground.

At least I made it down into the hollow without being shot. Catbrier was stuck all over my legs and chest. I wasn't sure, but I didn't think I could be seen from the woods. No one shot me in the head anyway. *That was a good sign, right? A victory in itself.*

I crawled sideways in the hollow – slowly – with my face pressed deep into the cold dirt and leaves. I couldn't breathe very well. I kept moving until I was a good fifteen or twenty yards from my original position. I didn't risk looking up, but I knew my angle to the woods and the house had changed significantly.

Could they be watching me from somewhere close by? I didn't think so. But was I right?

I listened.

I didn't hear a twig break or brush being pushed aside. Just the steady whistle of the wind.

I pressed my ear to the ground, willing to try anything for an advantage. It didn't help.

Then I waited some more.

Patience.

Things Sampson had told me about the Army Rangers surfaced in my head. Odd facts. They had supposedly killed fifty-five VC for every Ranger in the war. That was the story anyway. And they took care of their own. In the Vietnam War only one Ranger was listed MIA. All the others were accounted for, every single one.

Maybe they had gone, fled from the woods, but I doubted it. Why would they leave me here alive? *They wouldn't . . . Starkey wouldn't allow it.*

I felt guilty that I'd left Sampson, but I wouldn't let myself dwell on it. I couldn't think about him. Not now. Later. If there was a later.

When we see them, we open up.

No warnings, Alex.

Do you understand what I'm saying?

I moved again, circling to the northeast, I figured. Were they moving on me, too?

I stopped.

New position.

I waited there some more. Every minute seemed like ten. Then I saw something move. *Jesus! What the hell?* It was a bobcat, eating its own droppings. Maybe twenty, twenty-five yards away. Unconcerned with me. In its own world.

I heard someone coming, and he was very fucking close.

How had he gotten so close without my hearing him before? Shit, he was right on top of me!

Chapter Ninety-Eight

Had he heard me, too?
Did he know I was right there, a few feet away?
I didn't dare breathe. Or even blink my eyes.
He moved again.
Very slow, very careful, a professional soldier. No, a professional killer. There was a big difference. Or was there?
I didn't move an inch.
Patience.
No prisoners.
He was so close – almost to the hollow I was lying in. He was coming for me. He had to know my position.
Which one of them was it? Starkey? Griffin? Harris – who I had avoided crashing into during a softball game? Was he going to kill me now? Or would I kill him?
Somebody was going to die in a minute or less.
Who could it be?
Who was up there over my head?
I shifted my body so I'd see him the instant he came

over the edge. Was that what he would do? What were his instincts? He'd done this kind of tracking before. I hadn't. Not in the woods. And not in a war zone.

He moved again. Inches at a time.

Where the hell was he going? He was just about on top of me.

I watched the uneven ridge of the hollow and I held my breath. Tried not to blink. I felt the sweat streaming through my hair and down the back of my neck, down my back. An incredible cold sweat. The buzzing in my ears returned.

Someone rolled over the edge!

Brownley Harris. His eyes widened when he saw me waiting there for him, my gun aimed at his face.

I fired just one shot. *Boom.* Then there was a dark hole where his nose had been an instant before. Blood spurted from the center of his face. His M-16 dropped from his hands.

'No warnings,' I whispered as I took the rifle. Were the others close behind him? I waited for them. Ready as I'd ever be for a shootout.

Sergeant Warren Griffin.

Colonel Thomas Starkey.

The woods were so eerie. Silent again. I scuttled away under the cover of darkness.

Chapter Ninety-Nine

A three-quarter moon was out and that was both good and bad news. I was sure they would come for me now. It seemed logical, but was my logic the same as theirs?

I was back close to my original position in the woods. I thought so anyway.

Then I was certain.

My eyes teared involuntarily. I saw Sampson, lying still, right where he'd been shot. I could see the body so clearly in the moonlight. And I started to shake. What had happened was finally hitting me with its full force. I swiped at my eyes. A fist seemed to clench my heart and hold it tight, wouldn't let go.

I could see the dead women lying in the dirt road. Flies were buzzing around the bodies. An owl hooted from a nearby tree. I shuddered. In the morning perhaps a hawk or turkey vultures would come to feed on the bodies.

I slipped on the night goggles I'd brought with me. I hoped they would give me an advantage. Maybe not, probably not. Starkey and Griffin would have the best, too. They worked for a company that manufactured high-tech equipment, didn't they?

I kept reminding myself that I'd taken out Brownley Harris. It gave me some confidence. He'd looked so utterly surprised to see me. Now he was dead, his arrogance gone, exploded in an instant by a bullet.

But how could I surprise Starkey and Griffin? They must have heard the shot. Maybe they thought it came from Harris. No, they had to know he was dead.

For a couple of minutes I considered a flat-out run. Maybe I could get to the road. I doubted it, though. More likely I'd be shot down trying.

They were good at this, but Harris had been good, too. He was experienced, and now he was lying dead in a ditch. I had his rifle in my hands.

Patience. Wait on them. They have questions and doubts, too.

I watched Sampson's body for another few seconds, then I had to turn away. I couldn't think about him now. I mustn't, or I would die as well.

I never heard it coming – a sudden blast of deafening gunfire. One or both of them had gotten between me and the cabin. I spun in the direction of the shots. Then a voice pierced the darkness.

Close behind me.

'Put down the gun, Cross. I don't want to kill you. Not just yet.'

Warren Griffin was down in the hollow with me. I saw him now. He had a rifle aimed at my chest. He wore night goggles and looked like an alien.

Then Thomas Starkey appeared, also wearing goggles. He was above the gully, staring down. He had an M-16 aimed right at my face and he was smiling horribly. His victory grin.

'You couldn't leave it alone, asshole. So now Brownley's dead. So's your partner,' said Starkey. 'You satisfied yet?'

'You forgot the two women. And the lawyer,' I said.

It was strange to be looking at Griffin and Starkey through the night vision glasses, knowing that they were seeing me the same way. I wanted to take them down so much it hurt. Unfortunately that wasn't going to happen.

'What the hell happened in Vietnam?' I asked Starkey. 'What started all of this? What the hell was it?'

'Everybody who was over there knows what happened. Nobody wants to talk about it. Things got out of hand.'

'Like what, Starkey? How did it get this bad?'

'At first, there was a rogue platoon on the loose. That's what we were *told* anyway. We were sent to the An Lao Valley to stop them. To clean it up.'

'You mean murder our own soldiers? Those were your orders, Starkey? Who the hell is behind this? Why the murders now?'

I was going to die, but I still wanted answers. I needed to know the truth. Hell of an epitaph. *Alex Cross. Died seeking the truth.*

'I don't even fucking know,' Starkey hissed. 'Not all of it. I'm not going to talk about it anymore either. Maybe what I'm going to do ... is cut you into little pieces. That happened over there. I'll *show* you what was done in the

An Lao Valley. See this knife. It's called a K-Bar. I'm really good with it. I've had some practice recently.'

'I know you have. I've seen some of your butchery.'

Then the strangest thing I could ever imagine happened. It blew my wheels off, completely blew my mind into a thousand pieces.

I was staring past Starkey. But something was different in the background. At first I didn't know what, then I did and my knees became weak.

Sampson was gone!

I didn't see his body anyway. At first I figured I was just disoriented. But then I was sure I wasn't. His body had been over there – near a tall beech tree. Now it wasn't there.

No warnings, Alex.

No prisoners.

Do you understand what I'm saying?

I heard his words echo inside my head. I could hear the exact *sound* of it.

'Put down your guns,' I said to Starkey and Griffin. 'Drop them right now. Now!'

They looked puzzled, but kept their guns aimed at me.

'I'm going to cut you everywhere,' Starkey said. 'This is gonna take hours. We'll be here 'til morning. I promise.'

'*Put down the guns!*' I heard Sampson's voice before I saw him walk out from behind a tree. 'And the knife, Starkey! You're not cutting anybody.'

Warren Griffin spun around. Two shots instantly caught him in the throat and upper chest. His gun went off as he fell over backwards to the ground. Arterial blood pumped from his wounds as he died.

'Starkey, no!' I yelled. 'No!'

Thomas Starkey had raised his gun at me. Then he took one high in the chest. It didn't stop him. A second shot stung him in the side and spun him full around. A third blasted through his forehead and he went down for good in a bloody heap. His gun and K-Bar fell into the gully near my feet. His blank eyes stared into the night sky.

No prisoners.

Sampson was weaving toward me. As he came forward he rasped, 'I'm okay, I'm okay.'

Just before he collapsed into my arms.

PART FIVE

FOUR BLIND MICE

Chapter One Hundred

As it turned out, Jamilla was a life-send after the shootings in Georgia.

She called every day, often two or three times, and we talked until she could tell I was healing some. Sampson was the one who'd been physically wounded, and he was healing now too, but I was the one who seemed hurt the most. There had been too much killing, for too long, in my life.

Early one morning Dr Kayla Coles arrived at the house on Fifth Street. She marched right into the kitchen where Nana and I were eating breakfast.

'What's that?' she pointed an accusatory finger and asked with an arched eyebrow.

'It's decaf. Just terrible. A memory of real coffee, and a bad one at that,' Nana told her with a straight face.

'No, I'm talking about *Alex's* plate. What are you eating?'

I pointed out the ingredients for her. 'These are two eggs, over-easy. What's left of two hot sausage patties.

Home fries, slightly burned. The remains of a homemade sticky bun. Mmm mmm good.'

'You made this for him?' She looked at Nana in horror.

'No, Alex made it for himself. He's been cooking most of the breakfasts since my fainting spell. He's treating himself this morning because his big murder case is finally over. And he's feeling better.'

'Then I take it you don't always eat like this?'

I smiled at her. 'No, Doctor. I don't usually eat eggs, sausage, sticky buns and greasy potatoes. I was almost killed down in Georgia, and I'm celebrating that I wasn't. I guess that I prefer death by breakfast. Care to join us?'

She laughed out loud. 'I thought you'd never ask. I smelled something heavenly when I opened the car door. I followed it all the way to the kitchen.'

Kayla Coles asked a few questions about the case while she ate – a single egg, orange juice, just a bite of a sticky bun. I glossed over most of the details of the case, but I gave her a feel for the three killers and what they had done, and what I knew about *why*, which wasn't enough, but that's the way it goes sometimes.

'Where's John Sampson now?' she wanted to know.

'Mantoloking, New Jersey,' I said. 'He's recovering from his wounds, among other things. He has a nurse. A live-in, I hear.'

'She's his girlfriend,' said Nana. 'That's what he really needed anyway.'

After breakfast Dr Coles gave Nana a physical right there in the house. She took her temperature, pulse, blood pressure, listened to her chest with a stethoscope, then did a P and A. She checked for fluid buildup in Nana's ankles, the tops of her feet and hands, under her eyes. She looked into Nana's eyes and ears, tested her reflexes, looked at the color of her lips and nail beds. I knew all the elements of the test and possibly could have done the exam myself, but Nana liked getting visits from Kayla Coles.

I couldn't take my eyes off Nana during the checkup. She just sat there, and she seemed like a little girl to me. She never said a word, never complained.

When Kayla was finished, Nana finally spoke up. 'Am I still alive? I haven't passed, have I? Like that scary movie with what'shisname Willis.'

'Bruce Willis . . . Yes, you're still with us, Nana. You're doing beautifully.'

Nana took a deep breath and sighed out loud. 'Then I guess tomorrow's the big day. Go in for my catheter ablation, my radio-frequency ablation, whatever it is.'

Dr Coles nodded. 'You'll be in and out of the hospital in a snap. I promise you that.'

Nana narrowed her eyes. 'You keep your promises?'

'Always,' said Kayla Coles.

Chapter One Hundred and One

In the early evening, Nana and I took a ride out to Virginia in the old Porsche. She'd asked if we could take the drive, just the two of us. Aunt Tia was home with the kids.

'Remember when you first got this car? We used to take a ride just about every Sunday. I looked forward to it all week,' she said once we were out of Washington and on the highway.

'Car's almost fifteen years old now,' I said.

'Still runs pretty good, though,' Nana said. She patted the dash. 'I like old things that work. Long, long time ago, I used to go for a car ride every Sunday with Charles. This was before you came to live with me, Alex. You remember your grandfather?'

I shook my head. 'Not as much as I'd like to. Just from the photographs around the house. I know the two of you came to visit in North Carolina when I was little. He was bald and used to wear red suspenders.'

'Oh, those awful, awful suspenders of his. He had a couple dozen pairs. All red.'

She nodded, then Nana seemed to go inside herself for a moment or two. She didn't talk about my grandfather very often. He had died when he was just forty-four. He'd been a teacher, just like Nana, though he taught Math, and she was English. They had met while working at the same school in Southeast.

'Your grandfather was an excellent man, Alex. Loved to dress up and wear a nice hat. I still have most of his hats. You go through the Depression, things we saw, you like to dress up sometimes. Gives you a nice feeling about yourself.'

She looked over at me. 'I made a mistake, though, Alex.'

I glanced over at her. '*You* made a mistake? This is a great shock. I'd better pull over to the side of the road.'

She cackled. 'Just one that I can recall. See, I knew how good it could be to fall in love. I really loved Charles. After he died, though, I never tried to find love again. I think I was afraid of failing. Isn't that pathetic, Alex? I was too afraid to go after the best thing I ever found in this life.'

I reached over and patted her shoulder. 'Don't talk like you're leaving us.'

'Oh, I'm not. I have a lot of confidence in Doc Kayla. She would tell me if it was time for me to start collecting on all my old debts. Which I plan to do, by the way.'

'So, this is a parable, a lesson?'

Nana shook her head. 'Not really. Just an anecdote while we're taking this nice ride in your car. Drive on, young man. Drive on. I'm enjoying this immensely. We should do it more often. How about every Sunday?'

The whole ride out to Virginia and back, we never once

talked about Nana's procedure in the hospital the next morning. She obviously didn't want to, and I respected that. But the operation, at her age, scared me as much as any murder case could. No, actually it scared me more.

When we got back to the house I went upstairs and called Jamilla. She was at work but we talked for nearly an hour anyway.

Then I sat down at my computer. For the first time in over a week I pulled up my notes on the Three Blind Mice. There was still one big question I needed to answer if I could. Big *if*.

Who was behind the three of them?

Who was the real killer?

Chapter One Hundred and Two

I fell asleep at my work desk, woke up around three in the morning. I went down to my bedroom for a couple of hours. The alarm sounded at five.

Nana was scheduled to be at St Anthony's Hospital at six-thirty. Dr Coles wanted her to be one of the first operations of the day, while everybody on the staff was fresh and alert. Aunt Tia stayed at the house with little Alex, but I brought Damon and Jannie with me to the hospital.

We sat in the typically antiseptic-looking waiting room, which really started to fill up with people around seven-thirty. Everybody in there looked nervous and concerned and fidgety, but I think we were probably right up there with the worst of the lot.

'How long does the operation take?' Damon wanted to know.

'Not long. Nana might not have gone in first, though. It all depends. It's a simple procedure, Damon. Electrical energy is delivered to the AV node. The electricity is a little like the heat in a microwave. It disconnects the pathway between the atria and the ventricles and will stop the extra impulses causing Nana's irregular heartbeat. Got all that? Don't hold me to it, but that's fairly close to what's happening.'

'Is Nana wide awake while it's happening?' Jannie wanted to know.

'Probably. You know your Nana. They gave her a mild sedative and then local anesthesia.'

'Won't touch her,' Jannie said.

So we talked and waited, and fretted and worried, and it took longer than I thought it should take. I tried not to let my mind wander to bad places. I wanted to stay in touch with the moment.

I conjured up good memories of Nana, and they were a little like prayers. I thought about how much she meant to me, and also to the kids. None of us would be where we were without Nana's unconditional love, her confidence in us, and even her needling – irritating as it could be sometimes.

'When is she coming out?' Jannie looked at me. Her beautiful brown eyes were full of uncertainty and fear. It struck me that Nana had really been a mother to all of us. Nana Mama was more mama than nana.

'Is she all right?' Damon asked. 'Something's wrong, isn't it? Don't you think this is taking too long?'

Unfortunately, I did. 'She's just fine,' I said to the children.

More time passed. Slowly. Finally, I looked up and saw Dr Coles coming into the waiting room. I took a quick breath and tried not to let the kids see how anxious and nervous I really was.

Then Kayla Coles smiled. What a beautiful, glorious smile that was, the very best I've seen in a long while.

'She's all right?' I asked.

'Aces,' she said. 'Your nana is a tough lady. She's asking for you already.'

Chapter One Hundred and Three

W e visited with Nana in the recovery room for an hour, then we were asked to leave. She needed to rest up.

I dropped the kids off at school around eleven that morning. Then I went home to do a little more scud work in my office.

I was looking into something for Ron Burns, a strange but intriguing case involving convicted sex-offenders. In return he'd gotten me some US Army records that I wanted to check out. Some of it had come off ACIRS and RISS, but most had come straight from the Pentagon. One of the subjects was the Three Blind Mice.

Who was the real killer? Who gave orders to Thomas Starkey? Who sanctioned the murders?

I kept thinking about Nana, and how tough she was, and how much I would have missed her if something had gone wrong that morning. The terrible, guilt-ridden fantasy kept running through my head that I was going to get a call from Kayla Coles and she would say, *I'm sorry, Nana passed away. We don't know what went wrong. I'm so sorry.*

The call didn't come, and I threw myself into the work. Nana would be home tomorrow. I needed to stop worrying about her and put my mind to better use.

The Army records were interesting, but also about as depressing as an IRS audit. Obviously there had been rogue activity in Vietnam, Laos and Cambodia. The Army, at least officially, seemed to turn away and not look too closely at what had happened. There weren't civilian review boards, of course, like the police departments had to investigate misconduct. The press had no way to judge what was going on either. They rarely interviewed victims' families in the small villages. Plus, few of the American reporters spoke much Vietnamese. The good and the bad of it was that the Army had sometimes fought fire with fire. Maybe it was the only way to effectively fight a guerrilla war. But I still didn't know what had happened over there to inspire the murders stateside during the past few years.

I spent several grueling hours looking through more records of Colonel Thomas Starkey, Captain Brownley Harris and Sergeant Warren Griffin. I saw that their Army careers were exemplary, at least in written form. I went back as far as Vietnam and the pattern continued. Starkey was a highly decorated officer; Harris and Griffin were good soldiers. There was nothing in the records about assassinations in Vietnam committed by the trio. Not a single word.

I wanted to know when they had met and where they had served together. I kept leafing through records, hoping, but not finding the connect point. I knew they'd fought together in Vietnam and Cambodia. I went through every page a second time.

But there was nothing in any of the records to indicate they'd worked together in Southeast Asia. Not a goddamn word.

I sat back and stared out onto Fifth Street, letting my eyes glaze over. There was only one conclusion I could come up with, and I didn't like it.

The Army records had been doctored.

But why? And by whom?

Chapter One Hundred and Four

It wasn't over yet.

I could feel it in the pit of my stomach, and I hated the queasy feeling, the uncertainty, the lack of closure. Or maybe I just couldn't let go. All those unsolved murders. *Who was the real killer? Who was behind the strange murders?*

A week after the shootings in Georgia, I sat in Ronald Burns's office on the fifth floor of FBI headquarters in Washington. Burns's assistant, a crew-cut male in his mid-twenties, had just brought us coffee in beautiful china cups. There were also fresh mini-pastries on a silver tray.

'Pulling out all the stops?' I asked the director. 'Hot coffee and Danish.'

'You got it,' he said, 'shameless manipulation. Go with it.'

I'd known him for years, but it was only during the past few months that I'd worked closely with Burns. What I'd seen so far, I liked, but I'd been fooled before.

'How's Kyle Craig doing?' I asked him.

'We're trying to make it as uncomfortable as possible for him out in Colorado,' Burns said. He allowed himself a smile. 'We have to keep him in solitary most of the day. For his own protection, of course. He hates being by himself. Drives him crazier. No one to show off to.'

'No psychiatrists in there trying to figure him out?'

Burns shook his head. 'No, no. Not a good idea. That would be too dangerous for them.'

'Besides, Kyle would like the attention. He craves it. He's a junkie for it.'

'Exactly.'

We smiled at the image of Kyle locked away in seclusion, hopefully for the rest of his life. Unfortunately, I knew he had made contact with others in the max security unit – particularly Tran Van Luu.

'You don't think Kyle had anything to do with these killings?' Burns finally asked.

'I checked that out as much as I could. There's no evidence he knew Luu before he was assigned to Florence.'

'I know he visited out there, Alex, when he was still with the Bureau. He was definitely on the max security unit as well as death row. He could have met Luu. It's possible. I'm afraid you never know with Kyle.'

I almost didn't want to think about the possibility that Kyle might be behind the diabolical murder scheme somehow. But it *was* possible. Still, it seemed so unlikely that I didn't give it much credence.

'You had any time to think about my offer?' Burns asked.

'I still don't have an answer for you. I'm sorry. This is a big decision for me and my family. If it's any consolation, once I land I don't jump around.'

'Okay, that's fine with me. You understand I can't leave the offer on the table indefinitely?'

I nodded. 'I appreciate the way you're handling this. You always this patient?'

'Whenever I can be,' Burns said, and left it at that. He picked up a couple of manila folders from the coffee table between our chairs and slid them my way.

'I have something for you, Alex. Take a look.'

Chapter One Hundred and Five

'**M**ore of the Bureau's resources that you want me to see?' I said, and smiled at Burns.

'You'll like this. It's real good stuff. I hope it's helpful. I want to see you get some closure on this Army case. We're interested in this one, too.'

I reached into one of the folders and pulled out what looked like a faded patch off of a jacket. I held it up to examine the cloth more closely. The patch was green khaki with what looked like a crossbow sewn into the fabric. *There was also a straw doll on the patch. An eerie, awful straw doll. The same kind I'd first seen in Ellis Cooper's house.*

'The patch came from the jacket of a sixteen-year-old gang member in New York City. The gang he belonged to is named Ghost Shadows. They use different coffee shops on Canal Street in New York as headquarters. It's called roving turf,' Burns said.

'A task force we ran with the NYPD brought the gangbanger in. He decided to trade some information he thought might be valuable to them. It wasn't. But it could be valuable to you.'

'How so?' I asked.

'He says he's sent you several e-mails during the past month, Alex. He used computers at a technical high school in New York.'

'He's Foot Soldier?' I asked, and shook my head in amazement.

'No. But he may be a messenger for Foot Soldier. He's Vietnamese. The symbol of the crossbow is from a popular folktale. In the story, the crossbow could kill ten thousand men every time it was fired. The Ghost Shadows think of themselves as very powerful. They're big into symbols, myth, magic.

'As I said, this kid and his fellow gangbangers spend most of their time in the coffee shops. Playing ding lung, drinking Café Su Da. The gang moved to New York from Orange County in California. Over one hundred fifty thousand Viet refugees have settled in Orange County since the seventies. The gang in New York favored Vietnamese-style criminal activities. Smuggling illegal aliens – called snakeheads – credit card fraud, software and computer parts heists. That help you?'

I nodded. 'Of course it does.'

Burns handed me another folder. 'This might help too. It's information about the former leader of the Viet gang.'

'Tran Van Luu.'

Burns nodded. 'I did a tour in sixty-nine and seventy. I was in the Marines. We had our own re-con people. They'd get dropped into hostile territory, just like Starkey and company. Vietnam was a guerrilla war, Alex. Some of our people acted like guerrillas. Their job was to wreak havoc behind enemy lines. They were tough, brave, but more than a few of them got incredibly desensitized. Sometimes they practiced situational ethics.'

'Wreak havoc?' I said. 'You're talking about terrorism, aren't you?'

'Yeah,' Burns nodded. 'That's what I just said.'

Chapter One Hundred and Six

The FBI flew me out to Colorado this time. Ron Burns had made this his case now. He wanted the person or persons behind the long string of murders.

The isolation unit at Florence seemed as oppressive as it had been on my first visit there. As I entered the Security Housing Unit, guards in khaki uniforms watched me through bulletproof-glass observation posts. The doors were either bright orange or mint green – odd. There were cameras every ten feet along the bland, sand-colored walls.

The cell where Tran Van Luu and I met had a table and two chairs, which were dead-bolted to the floor. Three guards in body armor and thick gloves brought him to me this time around. I wondered if there had been trouble recently. Violence?

Luu's hands and ankles were cuffed for our meeting. The gray hairs hanging from his chin seemed even longer than at our last visit.

I took the jacket patch Burns had given me out of the

pocket of my coat. 'What does this mean? No more bullshit.'

'Ghost Shadows. You know that already. The crossbow is just folklore. Just a design.'

'And the straw doll?'

He was silent for a moment. I noticed that his hands were curled into fists. 'I believe I told you that I was a scout for the American Army. Sometimes, we left calling cards in villages. One, I remember, was a skull and crossbones with the words *"When you care enough to send the very best"*. The Americans thought that was very funny.'

'What does the straw doll mean? Is it your calling card? Was it left at all the murder scenes? Or afterwards at the soldiers' homes?'

He shrugged. 'Perhaps. You tell me, Detective. I wasn't at the murder scenes.'

'What would this particular calling card mean? The straw doll?'

'Many things, Detective. Life is not so simple. Life is not merely sound bites and easy solutions. In my country, popular religion is flexible. Buddhism from both China and India. Taoism. Confucianism. Ancestor worship is the oldest and most indigenous belief throughout Vietnam.'

I tapped my finger on the jacket patch.

'Straw dolls are sometimes burnt or floated away on a river as part of rituals honoring the dead. Evil spirits are the ghosts of those who were murdered or who died without proper burial. The straw doll is a threatening message reminding the offending person it is *they* who should rightfully be in the doll's place.'

I nodded. 'Tell me what I need to know. I don't want to have to come back here.'

'Nor should you. I don't have any need for confession. That's more of a Western concept.'

'You don't feel any guilt about what's happened? Innocent people have died.'

'And will continue to. What is it that you really want to know? Do you believe I owe you something because of your crackerjack detective work?'

'You admit that you used me?'

Luu shrugged. 'I don't admit anything. Why should I? I was a guerrilla fighter. I survived in the jungles of An Lao for nearly six years. Then I survived in the jungles of California and New York. I use whatever is provided to me. I try to make the most of the situation. You do the same, I'm sure.'

'Like at this prison?'

'Oh, especially in prison. Otherwise, even a reasonably bright man could go mad. You've heard the phrase "cruel and unusual". A cell that is seven by twelve feet. Twenty-three hours a day in it. Communication only through a cell slot in the door.'

I leaned across the table, my face close to Luu's. Blood was pounding inside my head. Tran Van Luu was the Foot Soldier. He had to be. And he had the answers that I wanted. Was he also responsible for all these murders?

'So why did you kill Sergeant Ellis Cooper? The others? Why did they have to die? Is it all just revenge? Tell me what the hell happened in the An Lao Valley. Tell me and I'll go away.'

He shook his head. 'I've told you enough. Go home, Detective. You don't need to hear anymore. Yes, I am Foot Soldier. The other answers you seek are too much for the people in your country to hear. Let these murder cases go. Just this once, Detective, *let them go.*'

Chapter One Hundred and Seven

I made no move to get up and leave.

Tran Van Luu stared at me impassively, then he smiled. Had he expected this? Stubbornness? Obtuseness? Was that why he'd involved me in the first place? Had he talked to Kyle Craig about me? How much did he know? Everything, or just more pieces of the puzzle?

'Your continuing journey is interesting to me. I don't understand men like you. You want to know why terrible things happen. You want to make things right, if only occasionally.

'You've dealt with vicious killers before. Gary Soneji, Geoffrey Shafer, Kyle Craig, of course. Your country has produced so many killers, Bundy, Dahmer, all the others. I don't know why this happens in such a civilized country. A place with so many blessings.'

I shook my head. I really didn't know either. But Luu wanted to hear what I had to say on the subject. Had he asked Kyle the same questions?

'I've always felt it has something to do with high

expectations. Many Americans expect to be happy, expect to be loved. When we aren't, some of us go into a rage. Especially if it happens to us as children. If instead of love, we experience hatred and abuse. What I don't understand is why so many Americans abuse their children.'

Luu stared at me, and I could sense his eyes probing into mine. Was he a strange new kind of killer – a lord executioner? He seemed to have a conscience. He was philosophical. A philosopher-warrior? *How much did he know? Did the case end here?*

'Why did someone orchestrate the murder of Ellis Cooper?' I finally asked. 'Simple question. Will you answer it for me?'

He frowned. 'All right. I will do that much. Cooper lied to you and your friend Sampson. He had no choice but to lie. Sergeant Cooper was in the An Lao Valley, although his records don't say so. I saw him execute a girl of twelve. Slender, beautiful, innocent. He killed the girl after he had raped her. I have no reason to lie about that. Sergeant Cooper was a murderer and rapist.

'They all committed atrocities; they were all murderers. Cooper, Tate, Houston, Etra, Bennett and Tichter. Harris, Griffin and Starkey, too. The Blind Mice. They were among the worst, the most bloodthirsty. That's why I chose them to hunt down the others. Yes, *I was the one*, Detective. But I'm already condemned to death here. There's nothing more you can do to me.

'Colonel Starkey was never told why the murders were taking place in the US. He didn't know my identity. He was an assassin; he never asked. He just wanted his money.

'I believe in rituals and symbolism, and I believe in revenge. The guilty have been punished and their punishments fit the crimes. Our unburied dead have been revenged and their souls can finally rest. Your soldiers left their calling cards, and so did I. I had plenty of time to think about it in here, plenty of time to make my plans. I hungered for revenge, and I didn't want it to be simple or easy. As you Americans say, I wanted payback. I got it, Detective. Now I am at peace.'

Nothing was as it seemed. Ellis Cooper hadn't been entirely straight with us from the start. He'd proclaimed his innocence to Sampson and me. But I believed Tran Van Luu. The way he told the story was entirely convincing. He had witnessed atrocities in his country, and maybe even committed them himself. What was the phrase Burns had used – wreak havoc?

'There was a saying the Army had in the An Lao Valley. Do you want to hear it?' he asked.

'Yes. I need to understand as much as I can. It's what drives me.'

'The phrase was, *If it moves, it's VC.*'

'Not all our soldiers did that.'

'Not many actually, but some. They came into villages in the out country. They would kill everyone they found. *If it moves* . . . They wanted to frighten the Viet Cong, and they did. They left calling cards – like the straw dolls, Detective. In village after village. They destroyed an entire country, a culture.'

Luu paused for a moment, possibly to let me think about what I had heard so far. 'They liked to paint the faces and bodies of the dead. The favorite colors were red, white and blue. They thought this was so humorous. They never buried the bodies, just left them for their loved ones to find.

'I found my family with their faces painted blue. Their *ghost shadows* have been haunting me since that day.'

I had to stop him for a moment. 'Why didn't you tell anyone? Why didn't you go to the Army when this was happening?'

He looked straight into my eyes. 'I did, Detective. I went to Owen Handler, my first CO. I told him what was happening in An Lao. He already knew. His CO knew. They all knew. Several teams had gotten out of control. So had the assassins sent in to clear up the mess.'

'One more question,' I said to Luu while everything he'd told me was boiling inside my head.

'Ask. Then I want you to leave me alone. I don't want you to come back.'

'You didn't kill Colonel Handler, did you?'

'No. Why should I put him out of his misery? I wanted Colonel Handler to live with his cowardice and shame. Now go. We are finished.'

'Who killed Handler?'

'Who knows? Perhaps there is a fourth blind mouse.'

I got up to leave and the guards came into the cell. I could see they were afraid of Luu, and I wondered what he had done in his time here. He was a scary and complicated man, a Ghost Shadow. He had plotted several murders of revenge.

'There's something else,' he finally said. Then he smiled. The smile was horrible – a grimace – no joy or mirth in it. 'Kyle Craig says hello. The two of us talk. We even talk about you sometimes. Kyle says that you should stop us while you can. He says that you should put us both down.' Luu laughed as he was led from the cell. 'You *should* stop us, Detective.'

'Be careful of Kyle,' I offered some advice. 'He isn't anybody's friend.'

'Nor am I,' said Tran Van Luu.

Chapter One Hundred and Eight

As soon as Luu was taken away, Kyle Craig was brought into the interview room in the isolation unit on death row. I was waiting for him. *With bells on.*

'I expected you'd stop by and visit, Alex,' he said as he was escorted inside by three armed guards. 'You don't disappoint. Never, ever.'

'Always one step ahead, isn't that right, Kyle?' I asked.

He laughed, but without a trace of mirth as he looked around at the cell, the guards. 'Apparently not. Not anymore.'

Kyle sat across from me. He was so incredibly gaunt and seemed to have lost even more weight since I'd seen him last. I sensed that his mind was going a mile a minute inside that bony skull.

'You were caught because you wanted to be caught,' I said. 'That's obvious.'

'Oh Christ, spare me the psycho-babble. If you've come as Dr Cross, the psychologist, you can turn around and leave right now. You'll bore me to tears.'

'I was talking as a homicide detective,' I said.

'That's a little better, I suppose. I can stomach you as a sanctimonious cop. You're not much of a shrink, but then again it's not much of a profession. Never did anything for me. I have my own philosophy: *Kill them all, let God sort'm out.* Analyze that.'

I didn't say anything. Kyle had always liked to hear himself talk. If he asked questions, he often wanted to ridicule whatever you said in response. He lived to bait and taunt. I doubted that anything had changed with him.

Finally, he smiled. 'Oh, Alex, you are the clever one, aren't you? Sometimes I have the terrifying thought that you're the one who's always a step ahead.'

I didn't take my eyes away from his.

'I don't think so, Kyle.'

'But you're persistent as an attack dog from hell. Relentless. Isn't that right?'

'I don't think about it much. If you say so, I probably am.'

His eyes narrowed. 'Now you're being condescending. I don't like that.'

'Who cares what you like anymore?'

'Hmmm. Point taken. I must remember that.'

'I asked before if you could help me with Tran Van Luu, the murders he's involved in. Have you changed your mind? I suspect there's still one murderer out there.'

Kyle shook his head. His eyes narrowed. 'I'm not the Foot Soldier. I'm not the one trying to help you. Some mysteries just never get solved. Don't you know that yet?'

I shook my head. 'You're right,' I said. 'I am relentless. I'm going to try to solve this one, too.'

Then Kyle slowly clapped his hands, making a hollow popping sound. 'That's our boy. You're just perfect, Alex. What a fool you are. Go find your murderer.'

Chapter One Hundred and Nine

Sampson was recuperating on the Jersey shore with Billie Houston, his own private nurse. I called him just about every day, but I didn't tell John what I'd heard about Sergeant Ellis Cooper and the others.

I also called Jamilla every day, sometimes a couple of times a day, or she'd call or e-mail me. The distance separating us was becoming more and more of an issue. Neither of us had a good solution for now. Could I ever move the family to California? Could Jamilla move to Washington? We needed to talk about it face to face, and pretty soon.

After I returned from Colorado I spent a couple of days working in Washington. I knew that I had one more important trip to make, but I needed some more preparation first. *Measure twice, cut once.* Nana had always preached that to me.

I spent countless hours on Lexis, but also the military databases, ACIRS and RISS. I made a visit to the Pentagon and talked to a Colonel Peyser about violence against civilians committed by American soldiers in Southeast Asia. When I brought up the An Lao Valley, Peyser abruptly cut off the interview, and then he refused to see me again.

In a strange way, that was a very good sign. *I was close to something, wasn't I?*

I talked to a few friends who had served in Vietnam. The phrase, *'If it moves, it's VC'* was familiar to most of them. Those who knew about it justified it, since violent outrages were constantly being committed by the North Vietnamese. One Army vet told this story: He'd over-heard other soldiers talk about a Vietnamese man, in his mid-eighties, who'd been shot down. 'Got to hand it to him,' a gunnery sergeant had joked, 'man his age and he volunteers for the Viet Cong.'

And one name kept coming up whenever I talked about the An Lao Valley.

In the records.

Everywhere I looked.

One name that was a link to so much that had hap-pened – there, and here.

The fourth of the blind mice?

I had to find that out now.

Early on Thursday morning I left for West Point. It would be about a five-hour drive. I was in no particular hurry. The person I wanted to see there wasn't going anywhere. He didn't think he had any reason to run and hide.

I loaded up the CD player with the blues mostly, but also the new Bob Dylan which I wanted to hear at least once. I brought along a thermos of coffee as well as sandwiches for the road. I told Nana that I would try to be home tonight, to which she curtly replied, 'Try harder. Try more often.'

The drive gave me time to think. I needed to be sure that I was doing the right thing by going to West Point again. I asked myself a lot of tough but necessary questions. When I was satisfied with the answers, I gave some more thought to taking a job with the FBI. Director Ron Burns had done a good job showing me the kind of resources I'd have at Quantico. The message was clear, and it was also clever: *I would be better at what I did working with the FBI.*

Hell, I didn't know what I wanted to do, though.

I knew that I could make it in private practice as a psychologist, if that was what I really wanted. Maybe I could do a better job with the kids if I had a regular job instead of *the Job*. Use those marbles wisely, savor those precious Saturdays. Make a go of it with Jamilla, who was constantly in my thoughts, and should be.

Eventually, I found myself on Route 9W, following road signs for Highland Falls and West Point.

As I got close to the Point, I checked my Glock and put a clip in. I wasn't sure if I'd need a gun. Then again, I hadn't thought I'd need one the night Owen Handler was murdered near here.

I entered West Point through the Thayer gates at the north end of Highland Falls.

Cadets were all over the Plains, practicing for parade, still looking beyond reproach. Smoke curled lazily from a couple of chimneys on top of Washington Hall. I liked West Point a lot. I also admired most of the men and women I'd met in the Army. But not all of them, and everybody knows what a few bad apples can do.

I pulled up in front of a redbrick building. I had come here for answers.

One name was left on my shopping list. A big name. A man beyond reproach.

General Mark Hutchinson.

The commandant of West Point.

He had avoided me the night Owen Handler had been murdered, but that wasn't going to happen again.

Chapter One Hundred and Ten

I climbed steep stone steps and let myself into the well-kept, redbrick building that housed the offices of the commandant of West Point. A soldier with a 'high and tight' haircut was sitting behind a dark wood desk that held a highly polished brass lamp and orderly stacks of papers and portfolios.

He looked up, cocking his head like a curious and alert grade-school student. 'Yes, sir. Can I help you, sir?'

'My name is Detective Alex Cross. I believe General Hutchinson will see me. Please tell him that I'm here.'

The soldier's head remained tilted at the curious angle. 'Yes, sir, Detective. Could you tell me something about your business with the general, sir?'

'I'm afraid that I can't. I believe the general *will* see me, though. He already knows who I am.' I went and sat on a stuffed chair across the room. 'I'll be right here waiting for him.'

The soldier at the desk was clearly frustrated; he wasn't used to civil disobedience, especially not in General

Hutchinson's office. He thought about it, then he finally picked up the plain black phone on his desk and called someone farther up the chain of command. I figured that was a good thing, a necessary next step.

A few minutes passed before a heavy wood door behind his heavy wood desk opened. An officer in uniform appeared and walked straight over to me.

'I'm Colonel Walker, the general's adjudicator. You can leave now, Detective Cross,' he said. 'General Hutchinson won't be seeing you today. You have no jurisdiction here.'

I nodded. 'But I do have some important information General Hutchinson should listen to. It's about events that took place during his command in the An Lao Valley. This was in sixty-seven through seventy-one, but in particular sixty-nine.'

'I assure you, the general has no interest in meeting with you or hearing any old war stories you have to tell.'

'I have a meeting set up with the *Washington Post* about this particular information,' I said. 'I thought the general should hear the allegations first.'

Colonel Walker nodded his head once, but he didn't seem impressed or worried. 'If you have someone in Washington who wants to listen to your story, you should go there with it. Now please leave the building or I'll have you escorted out.'

'No need to waste the manpower,' I said, and got up from the cushy armchair. 'I'm good at escorting myself.'

I went outside on my own steam and walked to my car. I got in and slowly drove up the pretty main drag that cuts through West Point. I was thinking hard about what to do next. Eventually I parked on a side street lined with tall maples and oaks that had a majestic view of the Hudson.

I waited there.

The general will see me.

Chapter One Hundred and Eleven

I t was past dark when a black Ford Bronco turned into the driveway of a large Colonial-style house that was flanked by elm trees and ringed by fort-style fencing.

General Mark Hutchinson stepped out of his vehicle. The interior lights illuminated his face for a few seconds. He didn't look one bit worried. Why should he? He had been to war several times, and he'd always survived.

I waited about ten minutes for him to put the houselights on, then get settled in. I knew that Hutchinson was divorced and lived alone. Actually, I knew a lot about the general by now.

I walked up the front steps, much as I'd gone up the steps to the general's office earlier that afternoon. The same deliberate pace. Relentless, unstoppable, stubborn as hell. I was going to talk to Hutchinson today, one way or the other. I had business to finish. This was my 'last case', after all.

I banged the front door's iron knocker a couple of

times, a tarnished winged goddess that I found to be more imposing than inviting.

Hutchinson finally came to the door in a blue-checked sport shirt and pressed khaki slacks. He looked like a corporate executive caught at home by a pesky door-to-door salesman, and none too happy about the interruption at this time of night.

'I'm going to have you arrested for trespassing,' he said when he saw me. As I'd told the soldier in his reception area, the general knew who I was.

'That being the case—' I pushed my way in the front door. Hutchinson was a broad-shouldered man, but in his sixties. He didn't try to stop me, didn't touch me at all.

'Haven't you caused enough trouble?' he asked. 'I believe you have.'

'Not really. I'm just getting started.'

I walked into a spacious living room and sat down. The room had deep couches, brass floor lamps, curtains in warm blues and reds. His ex-wife's taste, I assumed.

'This won't take too long, General. Let me tell you what I know about An Lao.'

Hutchinson tried to cut me off. 'I'll tell you what you *don't* know, mister. You don't know how the Army works, and you don't seem to know much about life in power circles either. You're out of your depth here. Leave. Now. Take your goddamn stories to the *Washington Post*.'

'Starkey, Griffin and Brownley Harris were military assassins assigned to you in Vietnam,' I began.

The general frowned and shook his head, but finally seemed resigned to hearing me out. He sat down. 'I don't know what the hell you're talking about. I've never heard of any of those men.'

'You sent ten-person teams into the An Lao Valley specifically to intimidate the Vietnamese. It was a guerrilla war, and your teams were instructed to act like guerrillas. They committed murders, mutilations. They slaughtered non-combatants. They had a calling card – they painted their victims red, white or blue. It got out of control, didn't it, General?'

Hutchinson actually smiled. 'Where did you dig up this ridiculous shit? You have some fucking imagination. Now get the hell out of here.'

I continued. 'You destroyed the records showing that these men were even in the An Lao Valley. The same was true of the three assassins, Starkey, Griffin and Harris, the ones you sent to clean up the mess. That's how I first found out about the deception. They *told* me they were there. But their Army records said otherwise.'

The general looked disinterested in what I had to say. It was all an act, of course. I wanted to get up and punch him until he told me the truth.

'The records *weren't* destroyed, General,' I went on.

Finally, I had his attention. 'What the hell are you talking about?'

'Just what I said. The records weren't destroyed. A Kit Carson scout named Tran Van Luu brought the atrocities to the attention of his CO. None other than Colonel Owen Handler. No one would listen, of course, so Luu stole copies of the records – and took them to the North Vietnamese.

'Those records were held in Hanoi until nineteen ninety-seven. Then the CIA happened to obtain copies. I got my copies from the FBI, as well as the Vietnamese Embassy. So maybe I do know a little about life in Washington's power circles. I even know that you're being considered for the Joint Chiefs. But not if any of this started to come out.'

'You're crazy,' Hutchinson huffed. 'You're out of your mind.'

'Am I? Two teams of ten men each committed a hundred or more civilian murders in villages during nineteen sixty-eight and sixty-nine. You were the commanding officer. You gave the orders. When the teams got out of control, you sent in Starkey and his men to tidy up. Unfortunately, they killed a few civilians themselves. More recently, you gave the order to have Colonel Handler killed. Handler knew about your role in the An Lao Valley. Your career would have been ruined and you might have even gone to jail.

'You went up country with Starkey, Harris and Warren Griffin yourself. You were there, Hutchinson, in the An Lao Valley. You're responsible for everything that went wrong. You were there – the *fourth* Blind Mouse.'

Hutchinson suddenly turned around in his chair. 'Walker, Taravela,' he said, 'you can come in now. We've heard more than enough from this bastard.'

Two men entered through a side door. They both had guns drawn, pointed at me.

'Now you don't get to leave, Dr Cross,' said Colonel Walker. 'You don't get to go home.'

Chapter One Hundred and Twelve

My hands were cuffed tightly behind my back. Then I was pushed outside and shoved down into the trunk of a dark sedan by the two armed men.

I lay curled up like a blanket in there. For a man my size, it was a tight squeeze.

I could feel the car back out of Hutchinson's driveway, bump over the gutter, then turn onto the street.

The sedan rode inside West Point at a reasonable speed. No more than twenty. I was sure we were leaving the grounds as the car finally sped up.

I didn't know who was up front. Whether General Hutchinson had come along with his men. It seemed likely that I was going to be killed soon. I couldn't imagine how I could get out of this one. I thought about the kids and Nana, and Jamilla, and I wondered why I'd risked my life again. Was it a sign of good character, or a serious character flaw? And did it really matter anymore?

Eventually, the car turned off the smooth highway surface onto a seriously bumpy road that was probably unpaved. I estimated we were about forty minutes from West Point. So how much longer did I have to live?

The car rolled to a stop and I heard the doors open and slam shut. Then the trunk was sprung.

The first face I saw was Hutchinson's. There was no emotion in his eyes. Nothing human looked back at me.

The two others were behind him. They had handguns pointed my way. Their stares were blank as well.

'What are you going to do?' I asked a question that I already knew the answer to.

'What we should have done the night you were with Owen Handler. Kill you,' said Colonel Walker.

'With extreme prejudice,' added the general.

Chapter One Hundred and Thirteen

I was lifted out of the car trunk and unceremoniously dropped on the ground. I landed hard on my hip. Pain lanced my body. Just the beginning, I knew. These bastards were out to hurt me before they killed me. I was handcuffed and there was nothing I could do to stop them.

Colonel Walker reached toward me and ripped my shirt open. The other man was pulling off my shoes, then my pants.

Suddenly, I was naked and shivering in the woods somewhere in upstate New York. The air was cold, probably in the low forties.

'Do you know what my real crime is? Do you know what I did that was so wrong in Vietnam?' Hutchinson asked. 'I gave the fucking order to fight back. They killed and maimed our men. They practiced terrorism and sadism. They tried to intimidate us in every way they could. I wouldn't be intimidated. I fought back, Cross. Just like I'm fighting back now.'

'You also murdered non-combatants, disgraced your command,' I spat the words at him.

The general leaned in close. 'You weren't there, so don't tell me what I did or didn't do. We *won* in the An Lao Valley. Back then, we used to say there were only two kinds in the world, the motherfuckers and the mother-fucked. I'm a motherfucker, Cross. Guess what that makes you?'

Colonel Walker and the other man had paint and brushes. They began to swab cold paint onto my body. 'Thought you would appreciate this touch,' Walker said. 'I was in the An Lao Valley, too. You going to tell the *Washington Post* on me?'

There was nothing I could do to stop this. No one could help me either. I was naked in the world, and all alone, and now I was being painted. Their calling card before they killed me.

I shivered in the cold. I could see in their eyes that killing me meant nothing to them. They'd murdered before. Owen Handler for one.

So how much longer did I have? A few minutes? Maybe a couple of hours of torture? No more than that.

A gunshot rang out in the blackness. It seemed to come from beyond the headlights of the sedan we'd driven there in. *What the hell?*

A dark hole opened in Colonel Walker's face, just below his left eye. Blood spurted. He flopped over backwards, landing with a heavy thud on the forest floor. The back of his head was gone, just blown away.

The second soldier tried to duck, and a bullet drilled his

lower spine. He screamed, then fell and rolled right over me.

I saw men come swarming out of the woods – at least half a dozen. I counted nine, ten of them. I couldn't see who they were in the darkness. Who in hell was rescuing me?

Then, as they came closer, moonlight illuminated some of the features. My God! I didn't know them, but I knew where they had come from and who had sent them – either to follow me, or to kill Hutchinson.

The Ghost Shadows were here.

Tran Van Luu's people had been tracking me. Or Hutchinson.

They were speaking in Vietnamese. I didn't understand a word they were saying. Two of them grabbed the general and threw him to the ground. They began to kick him in the head, the chest, stomach, and the genitals. He cried out in pain, but the beating continued, almost as if they couldn't hear him.

They left me alone. But I had no illusions – I was a witness to this. I lay with my face pressed against the ground. I watched the attack from the lowest vantage point. The beating of General Hutchinson seemed unreal and almost inhuman. They were kicking Colonel Walker and the other soldier now as well. *Beating the dead!*

One of them took out a serrated knife and cut Hutchinson. His scream pierced the night. It was obvious they wanted to hurt the general, but not kill him. They meant to torture and terrorize, to wreak havoc.

One of Luu's men pulled out a straw doll. He threw the

doll at Hutchinson. He then stabbed the general in the lower stomach. Hutchinson screamed again. The stomach wound wouldn't be fatal. The torture was going to continue. And sooner or later they would paint all of our bodies.

I believe in rituals and symbolism, and I believe in revenge. Tran Van Luu had told me that in prison.

One of his men finally came for me. I curled into a protective ball. No one could save me now. I knew the Ghost Shadows' plan – wreak havoc, get revenge for ancestors who had been murdered but never buried.

'You want watch? Or go?' the man asked. His voice was surprisingly calm. 'You free to go, Detective.'

I looked into his eyes. 'Go,' I said.

The Ghost Shadow helped me to my feet, took off my cuffs, then he led me away. He threw me rags to clean up with. A second man brought my clothes and shoes. They were both respectful.

Then I was brought to the gates of West Point, near 9W, where I was released unharmed. I had no doubt that those were Tran Van Luu's explicit orders.

I ran to get help for General Hutchinson and his men, but I knew I was already too late.

The Foot Soldier had killed them.

Chapter One Hundred and Fourteen

R on Burns finally reached me at home the following afternoon. I was up in my office, standing at the bay window looking down on Fifth Street and the rest of the neighborhood.

Jannie was on the front lawn teaching little Alex how to play tag. She was even letting her brother win, but that wouldn't last long.

Burns was saying, 'Alex, I just got off the phone with a special agent named Mel Goodes. He called me from a small town in upstate New York called Ellenville. You ever hear of Ellenville?'

'Actually, no. But I think I've been there recently,' I said. 'Have I?'

'Yeah, you have,' Burns said. 'That's where they took you from West Point.'

'What was Agent Goodes doing in Ellenville?' I asked.

'We were called in by the local police from up that way. They were puzzled and, frankly, shocked, by a mess some local deer hunters found in the mountains this morning.'

'I'll bet they were. Three murder victims. A grotesque death scene. Ritualistic.'

'Three unidentified males. It really shook up the locals. They blocked off half the mountain. The victims had severe cuts and electrical burns all over their bodies. The initial police report said they'd been "sodomized slash cauterized." The faces had been painted.'

'Red, white and blue.'

I was only half listening now. Jannie was teaching little Alex how to *lose* at tag. He started to cry, and she picked him up and hugged him. She looked up at my window and waved. She had it all under control. That was Jannie. Meanwhile, I was thinking about torture, terrorism, things that happen in the name of war. Jihad. Whatever. When would it stop? Probably never, or not until somebody blew up our beloved planet. How totally insane of us.

'I was wondering if you could shed any more light on the three murders?' Burns asked. 'Can you, Alex?'

I waved back to the kids, then I walked over to my desk and sat down. There was a picture of Maria with Jannie and Damon when they were little. I wondered what she would have thought of all this. The kids? Me? Jamilla? Murder victims painted the colors of the American flag?

'Two of the victims are probably General Mark Hutchinson and a Colonel named Walker. The third man is a PFC at West Point. I didn't catch his name. Hutchinson was responsible for some atrocities over thirty years ago in Vietnam. It finally caught up with him.'

I told Burns almost everything I knew about the night

before. As always, he was a good listener. I appreciated that more and more. And I was beginning to think that I trusted him.

'You know who killed the three West Pointers?' he finally asked.

I thought about that for a moment, then I said that I didn't. Technically, that was true. Burns asked a few more questions, but he accepted what I'd told him. I liked that. It meant that he accepted my judgment. I made another judgment then and there about the FBI director.

'I'll come and work for you,' I told him. 'I'll join the FBI. Like you said, it'll be fun.'

'Who says the offer is still open?' Burns said, and laughed. I liked that, too.

EPILOGUE

THE GARTER

Chapter One Hundred and Fifteen

The last thing I expected this year was a big, joyful wedding. I stood holding Jamilla's hand and looking out over the beautiful grounds in Church Falls, Virginia.

The setting was a sprawling meadow behind a small restaurant-inn. Yellow and white lights had been strung in the elm trees and along the patio rails. Everywhere I looked there were roses, and marigolds, and simple but quite beautiful English daisies.

The bride was absolutely gorgeous in a simple white satin gown, with no fussy train or veils. The dress was in the Empire style and draped elegantly on Billie's small frame. She wore a necklace and earrings made from brightly colored courie shells to celebrate her African-American heritage. Her hair was swept back in a chignon with sprigs of baby breath tucked in just so. Billie couldn't have looked happier. Her smile was radiant all through the day.

Sampson never stopped smiling either. He was dressed in a dove gray suit, and I swear he looked like a prince. A friend of ours, Reverend Jeffrey Campbell, had agreed to perform the ceremony in front of nearly a hundred of us who loved John and Billie with all our hearts.

Reverend Campbell asked if we would do everything in our power to support this new family in the community? '*We will!*' everyone answered with great enthusiasm and warmth.

The reception followed and I got to say a few words in a champagne toast.

'I have known this large man since we were both small boys. At least *I* was a boy. He has always been a part of our family, and always will be. John is loyal to his friends, his word is the truth, he's honorable, kind, generous, sweet – believe it or not – which is why he is my best friend in all the world. I have not known Billie quite as long. But I already like her a lot better than John.

'To a long, happy life together. I love you, John and Billie. Now let's hear some music. Let's dance until tomorrow.'

John and his wife danced to 'Let's Stay Together'. Then Jamilla and I joined in with several other couples. 'Nice wedding,' she said. 'I like John and Billie as a couple. They're great.' Folks started to stack their plates with food – coconut chicken, and cornbread stuffing, dumplings, dirty rice, greens. Everybody was snapping pictures with the single-use cameras left on each table. Billie's best friend from nursing school sang 'Our Love Is Here to Stay' and it was good. John and I got together on 'Sexual Healing' and it was pretty bad, which was why it was so good. The children were underfoot at all times. And

Sampson still hadn't stopped smiling.

Late in the afternoon, Damon and Jannie each grabbed one of my arms and escorted me out into the yard. 'I'll be right back,' I said to Jamilla. 'I hope.'

Billie was seated on a wooden chair with her back to half a dozen woeful-looking, even terrorized single males.

'You don't have to actually catch the garter,' she said turning and winking. 'The first one who *touches* it is the lucky winner.'

I stood on one side of the rag-tag boys club, winking and making ridiculous faces at Damon and Jannie, and, of course, Jamilla. Suddenly, they all pointed toward the sky.

I looked up – and the purple garter was spinning and spiraling down toward me. I couldn't get out of the way if I wanted to.

So I caught it and I twirled it around my outstretched finger. 'Doesn't scare me,' I said.

I looked to my left – and there was Jamilla with Nana. Jam was laughing and clapping her hands, and her smile said, doesn't scare me either.

I looked away – and by God, there was Dr Kayla Coles. And she wasn't clapping, just smiling coyly. Then she winked at me. Now what did that mean?

I shook my head, still laughing, but then I saw one more face. Director Ron Burns of the FBI.

My new boss was motioning for me to come over and see him. He had some kind of thick folder under his arm, which I had absolutely no plans of reading that Saturday.

But I did.

Turn the page for a preview of the next compelling thriller featuring Alex Cross . . .

JAMES PATTERSON

THE BIG BAD WOLF

Prologue

The Godfathers

Chapter One

There was an improbable murder story told about the Wolf that had made its way into police lore, and then spread quickly from Washington to New York to London and to Moscow. No one knew if it was true, but it was never officially disproved, and it was consistent with other outrageous incidents in the Russian gangster's life.

According to the story, the Wolf had gone to the high-security supermax prison in Florence, Colorado, on a Sunday night in early summer. He had bought his way inside to meet with the Italian mobster and don, Augustino 'Little Gus' Palumbo. Prior to this visit, the Wolf had a reputation for being impulsive and sometimes lacking patience. Even so, he had been steadily planning this meeting with 'Little Gus' Palumbo for nearly two years.

He and Palumbo met in the Security Housing Unit of the prison where the New York gangster had been incarcerated for seven years. The purpose of the meeting was to reach an arrangement to unite the East Coast's Palumbo family with the Red Mafiya, thereby forming one of the most powerful and ruthless crime syndicates in the world.

Nothing like it had ever been attempted. Palumbo was said to be skeptical, but agreed to the meeting just to see if the Russian could get inside Florence Prison – and then manage to get out again.

From the moment that they met, the Russian was respectful of the sixty-six-year-old don. He bowed his head slightly as they shook hands and appeared almost shy, contrary to his reputation.

'There's to be no physical contact,' the captain of the guards spoke from the intercom into the room. His name was Larry Ladove and he was the one who had been paid $75,000 to arrange the meeting. The Wolf ignored Captain Ladove's order. 'Under the circumstances, you look well,' he said to Little Gus. 'Very well indeed.'

The Italian smiled thinly. He had a small body, but it was tight and hard. 'I exercise three times a day, every day. I almost never have liquor, though not by choice. I eat well, and not by choice, either.'

The Wolf smiled, then said, 'It sounds like you don't expect to be here for your full sentence.'

Palumbo coughed out a laugh. 'That's a good bet. Three life sentences served concurrently? The discipline's in my nature, though. The future? Who can know for sure about these things?'

'Who can know? One time I escaped from a gulag on the Arctic Circle. I told a cop in Moscow, "I spent time in a gulag, you think *you* can scare me?" What else do you do in here? Besides exercise and eat Healthy Choice?'

'I try to take care of my business back in New York.

Sometimes, I play chess with a sick madman down the hall. He used to be in the FBI.'

'Kyle Craig,' said the Wolf. 'You think he's crazy like they say?'

'Yeah, totally. So tell me, boss, *pakhan*, how can this alliance you suggest work? I am a man of discipline and careful planning, in spite of these humbling circumstances. From what I'm told, you're reckless. Hands-on. You involve yourself with even the smallest operations. Extortion, prostitution, stolen cars. How can this work between us?'

The Wolf finally smiled, then shook his head. 'I am hands-on, as you say. But I'm not reckless, not at all. It's all about the money, no? The bling-bling? Let me tell you a secret that no one else knows. This will surprise you, and maybe prove my point.'

The Wolf leaned forward. He whispered his secret, and the Italian's eyes suddenly widened with fear. With stunning quickness, the Wolf grabbed Little Gus's head. He twisted it powerfully, and the gangster's neck broke with a loud, clear snap.

'Maybe I am a little reckless,' said the Wolf. Then he turned to the camera in the room. He spoke to Captain Ladove of the guards. 'Oh, I forgot, no touching. Now let me out of here.'

The next morning, Augustino Palumbo was found dead in his cell. Nearly every bone in his body had been broken. In the Moscow underworld, this symbolic kind of murder was known as *zamochit*. It signified complete and total dominance by the attacker. The Wolf was boldly stating that he was now the Godfather.

Part One

The 'White Girl' Case

Chapter Two

The Phipps Plaza shopping mall in Atlanta was a showy montage of pink granite floors, sweeping bronze staircases, gilded Napoleonic design and lighting that sparkled like halogen spotlights. A man and a woman watched the target – 'Mom' – as she left Nike Town with sneakers and whatnot, for her three daughters, packed under one arm.

'She *is* very pretty. I see why the Wolf likes her. She reminds me of Claudia Schiffer,' said the male observer. 'You see the resemblance?'

'Everybody reminds you of Claudia Schiffer, Slava. Don't lose her. Don't lose your pretty little Claudia, or the Wolf will have you for breakfast.'

The abduction team, 'the Couple', was dressed expensively, and that made it easy for them to blend in at Phipps Plaza, in the Buckhead section of Atlanta. At eleven in the morning, Phipps wasn't very crowded, and that could be a problem.

It helped that their target was rushing about in a world of her own, a tight little cocoon of mindless activity, buzzing in and out of Gucci, Caswell-Massey, Nike Town, then Gapkids and Parisian (to see her personal shopper, Gina), without paying the slightest attention to who was around her in any of the stores. She worked from an at-a-glance leather diary and made her appointed rounds in a quick, efficient, practiced manner, buying faded jeans for Gwynne, a leather dopkit for Brendan, Nike diving watches for Meredith and Brigid, a Halloween wreath at Williams-Sonoma. She even made an appointment at Carter-Barnes to get her hair done.

The target had style, and also a pleasant smile for the salespeople who waited on her in the toney stores. She held doors for those coming up behind her, even men, who bent over backward to thank the attractive blonde. 'Mom' was sexy in the wholesome, clean-cut way of many upscale American suburban women. And she did resemble the supermodel Claudia Schiffer. That was her undoing.

According to the job's specs, Mrs Elizabeth Connelly was the mother of three girls; she was a graduate of Vassar, class of '87, with what she called, 'a degree in art history that is practically worthless in the real world – whatever that is – but invaluable to me'. She'd been a reporter for the *Washington Post* and the *Atlanta-Constitution* before she was married. She was thirty-seven, though she didn't look much more than thirty. She had her hair in a velvet barrette that morning, wore a short-sleeved turtleneck crocheted top, slim-fitting slacks. She was bright, religious – but sane about it – tough when she needed to be, at least according to the specs.

Well, she would need to be tough soon. Mrs Elizabeth Connelly was about to be abducted. She had been 'purchased', and she was probably the most expensive item for sale that morning at Phipps Plaza.

The price – $150,000.

London Bridges

James Patterson

Alex Cross, FBI agent, is back in his most explosive adventure yet. And so is the Wolf. And so is the Weasel.

Alex Cross is on vacation when he gets the call. A town in Nevada has been annihilated and the Russian super-criminal known as the Wolf is claiming responsibility. Major cities around the globe are threatened with total destruction and the thought of such dark genius at work makes Alex's blood run cold.

Cross is catapulted into an international chase of astonishing danger. Arriving in London, he fights his way through a torrent of false leads, impersonators and foreign agents. Then, in the most unforgettable finale, Alex Cross confronts the truth of the Wolf's identity – a revelation that even Cross himself may be unable to survive.

Full of the high-voltage action and enthralling intrigue for which James Patterson is best known, LONDON BRIDGES is an unforgettable thriller that will grip you from cover to cover.

'A good time is had by all' *Telegraph*

'Patterson's simple but effective style and short, punchy chapters keep the action moving nicely' *Mirror*

'Ticks like a time bomb – full of threat and terror' *Los Angeles Times*

978 0 7553 4938 8

headline

Judge and Jury

James Patterson and Andrew Gross

IT'S THE TRIAL OF THE DECADE

Andie DeGrasse, aspiring actress and single mother, does not want to do jury service. But despite her attempts to get dismissed, she still ends up as Juror No. 11 in a landmark trial against notorious Mafia Don Dominic Cavello.

THE JUDGE IS TERRIFIED OF THE DEFENDANT

Cavello, aka the Electrician, is linked to hundreds of unspeakable crimes and his power knows no bounds. But Senior FBI agent Nick Pellisante has been tracking him for years and conviction is a sure thing.

SO IS THE JURY

As the jury reaches its verdict, the Electrician makes a devastating move. The entire nation is reeling, and Andie's world is shattered. The hunt for Cavello just got personal, and she and Pellisante join together, determined to exact justice – at any cost.

THE VERDICT: RUN FOR YOUR LIFE

James Patterson spins a heart-pounding legal thriller that pits two people against the most vicious and powerful mobster since John Gotti.

Praise for James Patterson's bestselling novels:

'James Patterson's books might as well come with movie tickets as a bonus feature' *New York Times*

'A novel which makes for sleepless nights' *Daily Express*

978 0 7553 3049 2

headline

Now you can buy any of these bestselling books by
James Patterson from your bookshop or *direct from his publisher.*

FREE P&P AND UK DELIVERY
(Overseas and Ireland £3.50 per book)

Miracle on the 17th Green *(and Peter de Jonge)*	£8.99
Suzanne's Diary for Nicholas	£8.99
The Beach House *(and Peter de Jonge)*	£7.99
The Jester *(and Andrew Gross)*	£8.99
The Lake House	£7.99
Sam's Letters to Jennifer	£8.99
Honeymoon *(and Howard Roughan)*	£7.99
Lifeguard *(and Andrew Gross)*	£7.99
Beach Road *(and Peter de Jonge)*	£7.99
Judge and Jury *(and Andrew Gross)*	£8.99
Step on a Crack *(and Michael Ledwidge)*	£8.99
The Quickie *(and Michael Ledwidge)*	£7.99
You've Been Warned *(and Howard Roughan)*	£8.99

Alex Cross series

Cat and Mouse	£8.99
Pop Goes the Weasel	£8.99
Roses are Red	£8.99
Violets are Blue	£8.99
Four Blind Mice	£8.99
The Big Bad Wolf	£8.99
London Bridges	£8.99
Mary, Mary	£8.99
Cross	£8.99
Double Cross	£8.99

Women's Murder Club series

1st to Die	£8.99
2nd Chance *(and Andrew Gross)*	£8.99
3rd Degree *(and Andrew Gross)*	£8.99
4th of July *(and Maxine Paetro)*	£8.99
The 5th Horseman *(and Maxine Paetro)*	£8.99
The 6th Target *(and Maxine Paetro)*	£8.99

Maximum Ride series

Maximum Ride: The Angel Experiment	£7.99
Maximum Ride: School's Out Forever	£7.99
Maximum Ride: Saving the World and Other Extreme Sports	£7.99

TO ORDER SIMPLY CALL THIS NUMBER

01235 400 414

or visit our website: www.headline.co.uk
Prices and availability subject to change without notice.